Three Wishes in Bardo

Feng Chi-shun

Proverse Hong Kong

November 2018

I0615930

Bardo: A Tibetan word referring to the intermediate state of the soul after death and before rebirth. – *The Merriam-Webster Dictionary*

According to Tibetan tradition, when one's consciousness is not connected with a physical body, karma governs one's mental condition – ranging from hallucination to liberation. Karma also determines one's rebirth.

An asexual is a person who lacks sexual interests of any kind.

Supported by

Hong Kong Arts Development Council

Hong Kong Arts Development Council fully supports freedom of artistic expression. The views and opinions expressed in this project do not represent the stand of the Council.

THREE WISHES IN BARDO draws an intimate picture of twentieth century Hong Kong while telling the story of a typical Hong Kong bright boy and his devoted mother. It is also a story of scientific labour and discovery, where single-mindedness, integrity, talent and skill rise from the mire of academic sharp-practice and envy. Different strands of the plot weave together to form a climactic ending where all characters' lives resolve into fulfillment with a touch of humour and true catharsis created from genuine surprise.

FENG CHI-SHUN was born in Wuhan, China, and grew up in Hong Kong. After graduating from the University of Hong Kong's medical school, he went to the US for specialist training. He enrolled in the pathology training program at the Albert Einstein College of Medicine in the Bronx, New York. After obtaining his specialist qualification, he stayed on in the US to work. For thirteen years, he lived through a tumultuous period of culture shock, experiencing unforgettable encounters with colourful characters. His last job was with the Charity Hospital in New Orleans. Upon returning to Hong Kong, he worked for the Department of Health as a consultant, and later as a private pathologist at St. Paul's Hospital, until his retirement in 2010. He plays golf, tennis and ping-pong. Late in life, he developed an interest in writing. He contributes to local English newspapers as a columnist and has published three books to date: *Diamond Hill* (2008), *Hong Kong Noir* (2010), and *Kitchen Tiles* (2015).

Three Wishes in Bardo

Feng Chi-shun

Winner of the Proverse Prize 2017

Proverse Hong Kong

Three Wishes in Bardo
by Feng Chi-shun.
1st edition published in paperback in Hong Kong
by Proverse Hong Kong under sole and exclusive licence,
November 2018.
Copyright © Feng Chi-shun, November 2018.
Alternate edition, ISBN: 978-988-8491-49-0

Distribution and other enquiries to:
Proverse Hong Kong, P.O. Box 259, Tung Chung Post Office,
Lantau, NT, Hong Kong SAR, China.
Email: proverse@netvigator.com;
Web: www.proversepublishing.com

The right of Feng Chi-shun to be identified
as the author of this work
has been asserted by him in accordance with
the Copyright, Designs and Patents Act 1988.
Cover design by Artist Hong Kong.
Colour image edited by Janine Claase.

All rights reserved. No part of this publication may be reproduced, stored in a retrieval
system, or transmitted, in any form or by any means, electronic, mechanical,
photocopying, recording or otherwise, without the prior written permission of the
publisher or publisher and author. The book is sold subject to the condition that it shall
not, by way of trade or otherwise, be lent, re-sold, hired out or otherwise circulated
without the author's prior written consent in any form of binding or cover other than that
in which it is published and without a similar condition including this condition being
imposed on the subsequent owner or purchaser. Please contact Proverse Hong Kong
(acting as agent for the author) in writing, to request any and all permissions (including
but not restricted to republishing, inclusion in anthologies, translation, reading,
performance and use as set pieces in examinations and festivals).

British Library Cataloguing in Publication Data
A catalogue record is available
from the British Library

PREFACE

What sort of fiction is this? I scratch my head to find the specific genre and come up with Science In Fiction, or even Fictional Science! It is not Science Fiction, though there is a lot of scientific vocabulary in the novel. Genres are not necessarily important in assessing a book, though any writer will tell you that if they ignore genre fiction, they risk being ignored by readers despite whatever merits their writing has. People like to know what they are getting. They expect things. Well, in this case, expect the unexpected. Expect...Karmic Fiction!

Bardo, the Buddhist inbetween state of being present in some form after death, but not reincarnated, pervades the narrative in many ways. Jason, the main character is inbetween everything. He is asexual, so somehow a perpetual boy. He is a eurasian Hong Konger—so, like a whole subclass of Hong Kong born and bred, he is of the place, and uniquely formed by its society, and yet ignored and marginalised. His mother was brought up in an orphanage, and so all his "family" are members of that orphanage, people whose provenance has been lost or is illegitimate...which is, once again, a not uncommon Hong Kong subclass. And he moves to America, where he finds himself in some kind of career and social limbo, also a not uncommon Hong Kong belonger experience!

All of this is told by an all-knowing narrator, who is not afraid of showing that knowledge. The lofty matter-of-fact tone builds a story much like a fairground ride where one is slowly cranked up the slope, getting higher and higher, seeing the ground moving further and further away, waiting for the sudden drop. And of course, all is destined and preordained...sort of. One might have wishes, but they only come true if they conform to Mother Nature's rules. But do you know what those rules are? Is free will, merely ignorance? And is intention the sole criterion of one's moral worth? Despite the raising of such issues, the characters never reflect upon their lives. They do not have the time as they have to make a living, have to pursue their goals, and in Jason's case, he pursues ways of digitally reading people's minds. But there is a moral subtext concerning crime, punishment, and justice; and how circumstance, ignorance and willfulness can lead us into bad situations.

Jason's nature is to pursue ruthlessly knowledge of the mysteries of memory, to the exclusion of all frivolous pursuits like sex and love, and in some way epitomises the perfect Hong Kong son: studious, polite, filial, and not without martial arts skills. But despite his dullness, his goodness wins others over to him. And it also creates enemies. Karma eventually has its way in this story, but I do not want to spoil the surprises by going any further into details. But expect details, grand narrative sweeps, and a menagerie of varied characters! This is how Mother Nature sees us all.

Lawrence Gray
Founding President, Hong Kong Writers' Circle
Author of the novels, *Cop Show Heaven*
      and A*dam's Franchise*
and the short story collection, *Odds and Sods*.

Dedicated to the orphans of the world

Author's note and disclaimer

None of the characters and names in this novel are based on real life. Any resemblances to actual names or actual persons, living or dead, are entirely coincidental.

Many of the organizations and places are well-known and real. These include (in Hong Kong) Queen Elizabeth and Queen Mary Hospitals, the Po Leung Kuk, King George's Secondary School, The Old China Hand Bar, The Spring Deer Restaurant, Lockhart Road; and (in the USA) the City College of San Francisco, Stern's, Yeshiva, the Albert Einstein College of Medicine, Rikers Island, and the Waldorf Astoria hotel. The medical journals named are also real (*The Lancet, The New England Journal of Medicine*, the *British Medical Journal*, and the *Texas Medical Journal*). These and any and all other references to other organizations, places, journals are used fictionally. All events are a product of the author's imagination and are used fictionally. Any resemblance to actual events is entirely coincidental.

JUICI, Genepharma and the Hot Pistol are fictional.

All the medical details are accurate, except those involving Jason's invention.

1

Jason Lee had sex twice in his life.

The first time was when he was fifteen.

The sex happened as an indirect result of him having a bust-up with some soldiers to rescue a young girl in a bar. Like the narrative arc of a Hollywood oater – cowboy sees damsel in distress, cowboy intervenes, cowboy fights valiantly despite being outnumbered by villains, villains back off, but cowboy is hurt, girl kisses cowboy to make it better, then they make love; later, cowboy rides into the sunset, alone.

Not exactly like that for Jason, but close enough.

Jason rode off into the sunset all by himself a lot; he was a loner – like another oater character the lone ranger, but without the sidekick, mask, élan, coolness, and looks. Jason was bespectacled, lanky, nerdy, and had bad hair days all year round.

He was eccentric, but not inhuman. He still liked being around people sometimes, even emotionally close to some, though never physically close with any, except his mother. He would never stand out in a crowd, or try to attract attention.

That would become his social modus operandi throughout his life.

The year he had his first sexual encounter was 1974, when he was attending St. George's, a secondary school that catered specially for children of British military personnel based in Hong Kong.

Hong Kong in the 70s was a British colony with a long history of being a fishing village, an administrative outpost at the southern tip of China for the Qing Dynasty, a territory ceded to the British Empire after the Opium War, and for a few years, another part of Asia occupied by the brutal Imperial Japanese

11

military; a dynamic city which quickly morphed into a bustling industrial and trading centre after the second world war, powered by Chinese denizens with a short memory of the past, and the work ethics of a people living on edge in a borrowed place on borrowed time.

Jason was a Eurasian, his mother was a local Chinese, father a Scottish taipan with a British hong. Jason was the result of an illicit liaison, not so uncommon in an era when the Western men ruled the world, many of whom residing in underdeveloped countries would want a native woman on the side apart from the Western wife more acceptable for most social and official functions.

Life for Eurasians in Hong Kong was full of mixed blessings. They were regarded as Chinese by expatriates, and Westerners by locals, not usually to their advantage in either situation. Jason was always considered an outsider, an oddity, a maverick. All his classmates were Westerners, so he was considered a local Chinese even though he did look more occidental than oriental. He could easily have become a pariah, class clown or town idiot. Luckily, he was blessed with a superior intellect and an insatiable appetite for knowledge and hard work. Smart people are somehow always looked up to in any community under any circumstance.

He stayed home after school and studied in his room all the time, but every Saturday, his mother made him go out with his classmates. They usually hung out in Kowloon, the peninsula across Hong Kong's Victoria Harbor.

His classmate Colin McBride was the most precocious among them. Colin was loud and obnoxious, and always wanted to be the centre of attention. He had developed a taste for beer from the age of 12, when he started to help himself to his father's stash. Instead of going to a playground or a bowling centre, he led all his classmates bar-hopping in Kowloon's Tsim Sha Tsui area.

Colin was a good drinker, and could go on drinking all night until he ran out of money. Jason could not handle alcohol. He tried it; but didn't like its taste or aftertaste. He disliked the feeling when alcohol went to his head and even more the hangover the morning after. Instead, he sipped soft drinks all night long, and out of loyalty to his friends stayed behind to look after whoever became too drunk to find their way home. He was also the one who always had some spare cash in his pocket to pay for the taxi fare, since he didn't spend any on alcohol.

Rachel O'Reilly was a regular. She was pretty, and at 15, already had a body with more curves than the TWISK highway, a two-lane thoroughfare in Hong Kong's New Territories – notorious for its hilly ups and downs and zigzag curves – a motorists' nightmare, but illegal road racers' dream. Rachel was prone to drink until she dropped. She lived in Jason's neighbourhood. Jason routinely shared a taxi home with her after a long night of drinking.

Colin teased them often, thinking for sure Jason got his taxi money's worth by groping her in the taxi.

"Are those boobs real?" he asked Jason. "You ought to know. You squeezed them enough times."

As usual, when Jason was confronted with embarrassing questions, especially those concerning sex, he clammed up. His face turned crimson; his lips pursed.

Rachel was used to such crude teasing, and always had a ready retort.

"Colin will always wonder, won't he?"

"They are too big to be real," Colin said loudly.

"You mean they are too good to be true, you asshole," Rachel yelled back.

Jason was uncomfortable with what they were bantering about, and tried changing the subject quickly.

The truth was that he was polite to Rachel at all times, even though Rachel, in her drunken state, was usually quite amorous with her trusted friend. She liked to rest her head on his shoulder and put her arms round his waist in the back of the taxi on their way home. Jason tolerated her, knowing she was too drunk to respond to any request to put some space between them. She also routinely planted a wet kiss on Jason's lips before she reeled out of the cab. Jason always made sure she had entered her building safely before he allowed the cab driver to drive away.

All the while, he kept his hands to himself.

A pretty young thing built like Rachel and who drank as much as she did was surefire jail bait for men, especially in a bar. Hong Kong was then more a seaport than today, and seafarers from all over the world drank in bars in Tsim Sha Tsui on their shore leaves.

Quite a few of Jason's classmates were in a bar on Hankow Road that Saturday evening. The bar was owned by Jane Chan, a close friend of Mary Lee, Jason's mother. They had been drinking there since the early afternoon.

All the bars in the British colony in that era followed the decor and style of a typical British pub. Wood panels were everywhere. Booths and bar stools were all made from dark hard wood. There was a darts area and a corner with a coin-operated jukebox playing loud music. Jason and his classmates' favourite spot was at the bar area close to the jukebox.

Business in Jane's bar was hopping because a few US navy ships were docked in Victoria Harbor, taking a short break before they reached their destination somewhere in Vietnam.

It was getting late and everyone except Jason was getting drunk. Rachel was quite inebriated and she began to entertain herself by dancing solo in front of the jukebox. When Rachel the pretty girl with the roller-coaster body rocked and rolled, it was like an indoor fireworks spectacle.

A few soldiers got excited watching her and joined her in dancing to the music. They were getting more and more aggressive towards her. One grabbed her from the back, trying to drag her out to another bar that offered live music. She declined repeatedly, but they wouldn't take no for an answer.

Rachel was soon in tears. While Colin and the other boys were too drunk or too scared to get involved, Jason stepped in and told them to stop. The soldiers told him to mind his own business. Jason told them it was his business to take care of the young lady, who was his friend and classmate. They pushed and they shoved, and they started to get real hostile.

They threw the first punch. Jason defended himself by putting up his arms to block. Jason was trained in martial arts but had no actual fighting experience. He used Kungfu moves to fend them off, and broke the nose of one of them. It was not in his nature to hurt anyone, but people trained in martial arts could inflict injury from sheer reflex. He was about to apologize to them when one soldier cleverly got behind him and bear-hugged him from behind while the other two used him as a punching bag for a couple of minutes before they fled into the darkness.

Jane the owner was on the verge of calling the police, but changed her mind in the last minute, realizing that her bar was full of underage schoolchildren. It was Hong Kong in the 70s; bar owners could get away with things like that as long as they didn't taunt the police by flaunting the law in front of them and also paid them their monthly bribe.

Instead, she patched Jason up and called his mom. Jane knew what Mary was like with her precious child, so she downplayed it a few notches when she called.

"Hi Mary, Jason got into a fight and was slapped around a bit. Just so you know."

"My son never causes trouble; it was Colin, wasn't it?"

"It wasn't any of the kids' fault. Just some roughnecks who got drunk. They ran away before I came out of the kitchen. I think you should come over and decide for yourself whether he needs to go to the emergency room or not."

"It is serious, isn't it? That's why you called. I am taking a taxi."

Mary was frugal. She only splurged on taxi service for big hurries.

Mary took one look at Jason's face, and repeated "Oh my God" a dozen times. She hailed a taxi again and took Jason to the Accident & Emergency Department at the nearby Queen Elizabeth Hospital for medical evaluation and some X-rays.

She badgered the medical staff to see her son first because according to her, the beating he suffered in the hands of the three big Western men was too treacherous for words. And it lasted for hours. She was spilling tears and making a scene. Mary was usually cool, calm, and collected, but when Jason was in any kind of danger, real or imagined, she became so worked up she was quite overbearing.

Jason was a little embarrassed by her antics; he said, "Mom, I'm all right."

"You be quiet. Let me handle this," she said under her breath.

The doctor quickly came over to see Jason. He and his staff wanted to get Mary out of there as quickly as possible.

Apart from scratches and cuts, lumps and bumps, Jason had no serious internal injury.

For days, Jason walked around the schoolyard with two shiners and bruises all over his face.

It was a painful experience, but everyone in school knew what happened in the Tsim Sha Tsui bar, and Jason reached a new level of respectability in the schoolyard.

Rachel told everyone she owed Jason one.

And she meant it.

One day during lunch hour, she quietly asked Jason to go with her to the music room, where a surprise would be waiting for him. Jason had no idea what that was about, but politely went along. After they entered the room and found themselves alone, Rachel locked the door behind her. Then she wrapped her arms around Jason's neck.

"Touch me all you want, sweetie, anywhere, for as long as you want."

Jason was stunned and did not know how to respond. He stammered something about their being too young and they shouldn't be doing that.

"Oh, Jason. Don't be such a..... It isn't my first time, you know," Rachel cooed. "Do you know how many guys in the school, including some of the teachers, are willing to die for this moment?"

She then pulled off her top, revealing her breasts, and guided Jason's hands to cup them, while she unzipped Jason's pants. Jason backed up until he was against the wall.

Jason was in shock. He stood there, paralyzed. Among many things running through his mind, one thing he knew for certain – Rachel was doing him a favour, and it would be rude to forcibly push her away.

He continued trying to talk her out of it, bringing up the risk of pregnancy, hoping that it would be a deterrent.

"Oh, Jason, you fool. It's only going to be a blow job," she whispered in his ear.

That said, she went down and expertly worked on Jason's phallus.

The human male can have an erection and an ejaculation, as long as his phallus receives the right kind of sustained physical stimulation, even in the extremely rare occasion when he isn't in the mood. Jason wasn't in the mood. When it was all over, Jason was more embarrassed than ecstatic. It was like having answered the call of nature in full view of a stranger. With her mission accomplished, Rachel zipped Jason back up, wiped her mouth, gave him a peck on the cheek, and took off.

Most boys Jason's age would have had some experience with orgasm, from masturbation and wet dreams. But Jason never had those. Instead of experiencing exhilaration and a buzz, Jason felt sick and light-headed. He had to sit on the floor leaning against the wall to rest a while before he could get up and walk again. All he could think about was how to find ways to avoid similar unbecoming and unwelcome situations in the future.

When Jason came home that day, Mary took one look at him and knew something was wrong. She asked him what had happened to him; he mumbled something incoherent. She persisted in questioning him. She knew something was wrong and there was no use hiding it. He reluctantly and awkwardly told her it was Rachel. Jason was incapable of lying, but he did not elaborate on what Rachel did. Instead, he retreated to his room and locked the door. Mary knocked at his door; he ignored her.

Mary called Rachel and asked her what had happened to her son. Rachel said: nothing really.

"Rachel, there is no use lying. Jason already told me it was you."

"It's nothing," said Rachel.

"Since it's nothing, I'll go to the headmaster tomorrow and let him ask all the questions. Jason is incapable of lying, you know."

Rachel kept quiet for a while. Then she sighed.

"I'll tell you; but please please keep it to yourself. I don't want anyone else to know."

Before Rachel confessed, she made it clear she was only trying to do Jason a favour, to compensate him for getting beaten up in the Tsim Sha Tsui bar because of her.

She then proceeded to tell Mary the whole incident, in detail. Mary wished Rachel had spared her some of the details; but Rachel didn't care, she didn't leave anything out.

Mary couldn't believe a young girl like Rachel was capable of doing something like that. How could she possibly have forced it on Jason even though her intention was to reward him?

Jason shunned Rachel like the Ebola virus since that "romantic" encounter in the music room, when she took away his virginity. Unlike Bill Clinton, most people consider oral sex real sex, and Jason was a virgin boy no more, thanks to Rachel.

Rachel acted as if nothing had happened. But for months after, Jason felt awkward in her presence. He stopped going out with his classmates on Saturdays just to avoid her. He needed some time with other people, not only his mother. Mary was worried, and forced him out of the house every Saturday afternoon. He went to the theatre, all by himself.

Naughty Rachel didn't make life easy for him, either. She continued to flirt with him openly in school. She did not have to do much to bend Jason out of shape. All she had to do was to wink at him from across the room, and he would be totally flustered and immediately scrambled for cover. It took almost six months before he thought it safe to talk to her again. They remained friends, but Jason would never want to be alone in a room with her ever again.

Mary thought long and hard over that incident. Why did Jason feel so repugnant over his first sexual encounter? All the men she knew would have loved to take Jason's place in that Music Room.

Would they not have gone back for a second helping?

Jason at 15 years old had been through all the secondary sexual developments, and had all the male sexual characteristics in place, but it seemed odd that his attitude towards sex was so different from other boys and men, that Mary knew of.

It bothered her enough for her to consult a psychologist.

In his office, the specialist told Mary it was too early to draw any conclusion. The possibilities included Jason's sexual immaturity, his proclivity to homosexuality, and last of all, he might be suffering from an extremely rare sexual condition called asexuality – an anomaly in which the person was uninterested in sex of any kind.

Mary was holding her breath then, hoping in time Jason would become more and more interested in girls. Had she lived long enough to watch him over the years in his adult life, she would have resigned herself to the fact that he was never going to be sexually interested in women. Or men.

He was a diehard asexual.

It bothered only Mary. Jason didn't care. He had always thought having "fun" of any kind was a waste of time anyway. To him, life's greatest pleasure could be found inside the covers of a book, as in the Chinese saying: houses made of gold, and women as pretty as jade can be discovered from reading. That the saying is metaphorical was not lost on Jason, who loved books but had only limited interest in gold and wouldn't know what to do with a beautiful woman.

Being asexual meant even a girl like Rachel didn't do anything for him. He was there with all the rogue characters just to be seen to have some semblance of a normal teenager's lifestyle.

After Rachel, he was able to avoid having sex again for more than thirty years.

2

Mary Lee was an orphan.

She led a life full of miseries; then she died, at the age of forty.

Before she died, she and her son Jason, as the Chinese put it, had struggled through life together inter-dependently and closely, like lips and teeth.

Everyone has a karmic number. For Mary, it was eight. Something significant happened every eight years or so in her life, most of them disastrous.

At eight years old, she contracted rheumatic fever, which left her with the life-long debilitating rheumatic heart disease. At sixteen, she was deflowered by an older married man. She started an affair with another married man a few years later. She became pregnant and gave birth to Jason at twenty-four. Jason's father died eight years later. She died eight years after that, age only forty, at the end of her fifth eight-year cycle.

Right after Jason graduated from secondary school, Mary took a trip to San Francisco to prepare for Jason's American tertiary education. It was her first overseas trip. And her last. She became sick on the plane, and died in the emergency room of Queen Elizabeth Hospital shortly after landing in Hong Kong.

She died before she had a chance to talk to Jason one last time. She was dying to hold him and tell him that he needed to go for an interview at the City College of San Francisco soon. She needed also to tell him to stand up to all the bullies, and be careful with money. There were just too many evil people in this world. Jason was too trusting of people.

When she was on her way to the next world, she made a solemn pledge with the gods, whoever they might be, that she was willing to give up anything in the afterlife to be able to continue to care for her son. She was willing to forgo heaven if there ever was one, in exchange for her son's happiness on earth.

She never believed in any gods when she was alive, and she didn't find any in her afterlife.

She found only Almighty Mother Nature.

Mary was new to the afterlife, and she was confused and scared. But the thought of not being able to be with her son emboldened her. She came right out and asked Mother Nature why her life had been full of heartaches? Why had she been born an orphan? Why had she had to live with a defective heart? Why had she never for long had a man who loved her, and most of all, why had he died young, leaving an adolescent son fending for himself?

Mother Nature told her it was in her life's blueprint – certain hardships and sufferings were pre-destined for her time on earth, and nothing could change that.

Nevertheless, Mother Nature took pity on her; that was why they were talking.

"I shall grant you three wishes in your afterlife, which you can use to enhance the well-being of your son's life on earth," said Mother Nature.

"Thank you thank you thank you," said Mary.

There were terms and conditions, though. The wishes must be specific and not all-encompassing. They must apply directly to Jason's well-being, and not do harm to others. And they must not contravene the law of nature.

"Abide by the rules and apply the wishes judiciously," Mother Nature advised. "If you misuse one of them, you may have to waste another one just to correct your mistake."

Mary had heard enough of the genie-and-three-wishes jokes to know that if she was too impetuous in realising the wishes, she could end up back to square one, or worse. But even with these limitations, having such wishes was more than any mother could hope for.

If karma is to be believed, Mary's sufferings in life, and her heartfelt plea with the gods at her deathbed succeeded in trading for a few breaks in Jason's life. A mother's sacrifice in exchange for her son's happiness – what else is new?

Armed with the priceless three wishes from Mother Nature, Mary later followed Jason to the United States of America where he had emigrated, to closely watch his life unfold. Mary planned to use the three wishes fully, each and every one of them, in the most timely fashion and for exactly the right reason, to make sure they would each have the maximum positive impact on Jason's life.

How many mothers would be willing to forgo heaven in exchange for their children's well-being on earth?

Is it possible that an orphan's love for her children is the greatest love of all?

Psychologists believe someone abandoned as a child often feels as though his or her life is misaligned with destiny; hence, he or she must answer to a higher calling, such as, in Mary's case, to become the best mother in the world.

Christina Baker Kline, an American novelist, thought so, too. She said: "Many people, for many reasons, feel rootless – but orphans, and abandoned or abused children have particular cause."

3

Mary never knew her mother. It turned out her life also had been a tragedy.

Mary's mother began her life in the worst of times. It was in the late Qing Dynasty at the beginning of the twentieth century, when China had just lost two opium wars, the Sino-French war, and the first Sino-Japan war. The foreign forces were armed with modern weapons based on gunpowder, and the Chinese military still depended mainly on spears and swords, and martial arts.

Her mother was born not long after the Boxer Rebellion, which was violently quelled by the Eight-Nation Alliance, and the Qing Government had to sign a humiliating treaty which ceded control of Peking the capital, and had to offer numerous concessions including an astronomical amount of compensation money to the Alliance.

In those tumultuous years, people's lives were worth close to nothing, and the life of Mary's mother was no exception. She was sold to a wealthy merchant in Canton when she was still a young girl for a mere five taels of silver.

She worked as a mui chai (girl slave) for the rich man's fourth concubine. The concubine was a difficult person to please. Despite her mui chai's obsequiousness and diligence attending to her every need day and night, she frequently punished her slave with rattan cane beatings for minor offenses. She was too feeble to lift a finger to do housework, but she knew how to crack the rattan cane forcefully like a whip, landing sharply on her mui chai's buttock with pants pulled down, leaving red and raw lash marks on the tender skin. Whenever the power struggle between her and the man's other concubines didn't go her way, she would take it out on her slave. The girl slave's only comfort came from her friendship with the gardener's son. She got some time off about once every fortnight when her mistress told her to prepare for her husband's night visit by burning some incense and placing his slippers outside her private quarters. She would also be told to make herself scarce for the night. Mary's parents would spend the night holding hands and cuddling in the kiosk at the far end of the garden, and it didn't take long for the two young lovers to do what young lovers do when no one is there to stop them. Soon, the two of them would lunge for each other whenever the rich man's slippers appeared anywhere near his fourth concubine's bedroom.

Mary's mother became pregnant with her when she was barely sixteen. The two young lovers eloped with the help of his parents and fled to Hong Kong. Mary's young father found work as a coolie in the Sheung Wan district where boats carrying merchandise were docked at piers in the harbor front and young men with muscles were always needed to haul goods from boats to shops nearby. Even though the money paid to the coolies was minuscule, competition for jobs was keen because it was the livelihood for many refugee families. The coolies formed gangs for self-protection, and fights among the gangs were frequent.

During a melee between rival coolie gangs, her father was knifed in the stomach and later died unattended when he tried to hide from the rival gang in a dark alley.

The year was 1935. Social services did not exist, and, being illiterate, the only legal job her mother could possibly find was working as an amah for wealthy families. She knew absolutely nobody in the city who could help her. With baby Mary in tow, she knocked on doors from street to street in search of employment. All the families shooed her away when they saw the baby, and chided her for wasting their time. Even though some of them could use the help of an amah, hiring a woman with a newborn baby meant not having a full-time devoted servant and having an extra mouth to feed as well.   She knocked on hundreds of doors by walking the streets by day, and sleeping in them by night. One day, she was so hungry she passed out near a Catholic Church in Causeway Bay. The nuns found her, and gave her food and temporary shelter. For the first time in her life, she experienced kindness from fellow human beings.

She saw no future in taking care of the baby on her own. So she came back to the Catholic Church with a bundle in her arms at the break of dawn. She carefully placed the bundle on the top doorstep in the church's front. She opened up the bundle a little and a small face appeared. She tugged on the cloth wrapping the baby until she was sure the baby was warm and could breathe easily. She then took one last look at the baby, wiped away tears with the dirty sleeve of her cheongsam, and turned away briskly without looking back.

She had no choice. She had no husband, no money, and no job. Both of them would have starved to death if she didn't take that chance.

After working as an amah for a few years, Mary's mother married a shopkeeper. He owned a small stall in the wet market selling seafood, and needed a wife and a pair of helping hands around the shop. It was a marriage arranged by another amah who worked in the same neighbourhood.

She did go back to the church to look for Mary when the Japanese war was over, but the church had been ruined by bombings and was torn down, replaced by a school, and no one could tell her about a child left there a few years before.

The Catholic nuns didn't keep the baby orphan for long. They relinquished Mary to the Po Leung Kuk orphanage in Causeway Bay, close to the horse racing grounds of Happy Valley.

Had Mary known about the circumstances of her abandonment, that is, had some kind of closure to explain her orphanage, she would have been a much happier person throughout her life.

She used to make up stories in her mind why her parents were not around.

Her favourite fantasy was that her parents were actually alive and well, and were living in nearby Happy Valley, where they owned and trained thoroughbred racehorses. They had a busy schedule and that was why they couldn't take care of their only daughter. But as soon as Mary was able to take care of herself, they would be a family again. After the family reunion, they would teach her how to train horses for a living.

Early every morning, she would be awaken by the commotion and clatter when the horses were led out of the stable, followed by the horse-shoes hitting the concrete paths leading to the large oval shaped tracks where they had their morning workout. Then she heard the horses' hoofs galloping across the turf and their occasional neighs. She would imagine her parents on horseback, looking smart in their riding gear while barking orders for the horses to follow.

Mary tried her hardest to act grown up throughout childhood, just in case her parents dropped by to check on her progress.

They never did. But she dreamed on until she became a teenager when she was finally resigned to the fact that dreams never came true for orphans.

She spent the first 18 years of her life in Po Leung Kuk.

Po Leung Kuk translated into English is "An Organization for the Protection of the Innocent". A group of Hong Kong philanthropists started it in the nineteenth century and its mission was to rescue abducted women and to protect girl slaves from their cruel masters. In more recent years, it evolved into a charity organization mainly dedicated to providing welfare for the orphans living under its roof.

Mary started life there when Hong Kong was in the midst of an era under British rule, with the expected tribulation of a colonial seaport – anti-British sentiment, hardship, injustice, widespread corruption, crime, people dying young of tuberculosis and other infectious diseases, starvation, turmoil and unrest. Life went on, and new lives procreated, usually unintentionally. Any unwanted pregnancy was dealt with by giving birth to the baby and then abandoning it, especially if it was a girl. One more mouth to feed was too much to bear for most couples.

Mary was too young then to know all that, but the governess of Po Leung Kuk reminded them enough times how lucky they were compared to orphans living in the street and those sold as slaves. Other options for orphans were limited and many others had it so much worse, especially for girls. Many of them ended up working in brothels.

They were especially lucky during the Japanese occupation from 1941 to 1945, when they were at least sheltered in a secure building and shielded from military brutality, even though like everyone else then, they were starving to death.

Life in the orphanage was monotonous, regimental, and austere. It was run like the military. There were innumerable rules and regulations, and disciplinarian actions to go with rules broken and regulations breached, something the orphans got used to as a way of life as early as five or six years old.

For primary education, all attended a special grade school for orphans located inside the Po Leung Kuk compound. It made life easier for the school children, since everyone was in the same boat; envy or name-calling was seldom an issue.

At eight years of age, Mary contracted a Streptococcal throat infection that led to rheumatic fever, complicated later by rheumatic heart disease. She was hospitalized in Queen Mary Hospital for more than eight weeks. Hong Kong was in the middle of the Japanese occupation, and she did not receive the best of medical care. The hospital was converted into a military hospital for Japanese soldiers, who had priority of treatment of all kinds. Throughout her hospital stay, the doctors there visited her perhaps only once a week and her prescribed medicines were not always filled. The antibiotics all went to the Japanese soldiers first.

Upon discharge, she was told she required long-term clinic follow-up and prophylactic penicillin injections once a month for the rest of her life. The reason for the penicillin injections was to protect her heart from further damage, but she didn't get them until after the war in 1945, more than two years after discharge from the hospital. By then, there was already irreversible damage to her heart. Her rheumatic heart problem worsened gradually over the years.

Rheumatic fever leads to rheumatic heart disease in which the valves of the heart, particularly the mitral, are disfigured by chronic inflammation and fibrosis. Over time, the valves invariably become rigid and leaky, and the heart has to pump extra hard to maintain adequate circulation. Her whole life was punctuated by hospitalizations and doctors' visits related to treatment of its complications.

At age thirteen, Mary entered a catholic all-girls secondary school outside Po Leung Kuk, run by the Maryknoll Sisters. On the first day of school, the nuns there demanded a Christian name from all the new students. She changed her name from Lee Lai Chun, the name on a piece of paper attached to the baby clothes on her when she was found, to Mary Lee Lai-Chun or Mary Lee for short. She just knew she should be called Mary.

Hardships cultivated great friendships. Her best friends were fellow orphanage dwellers Jane Chan and Judy Fung, having known each other since they were toddlers. Their bunk beds were in the same corner of the large dormitory. Whenever there was a thunderstorm at night, Mary and Jane would creep into Judy's bed, against the rules of the institution, to hug each other to sleep until the storm blew over.

They had dreams for the future and talked about them often. Mary stopped fantasizing having horse trainers as parents when older, and started to dream about being a parent herself. She was the biggest dreamer of all. She frequently dreamed of being a busy mother taking good care of all her children. They all wanted to get out of the orphanage as soon as possible. They wanted independence, wealth, and most of all, men who loved them. Jane and Judy didn't want children, but Mary did, the more the merrier. Having dreams was the tonic that made life bearable in the orphanage, and kept them going.

There was a boy named Andrew Chu who was the crybaby in the Kuk. Jane teased him and bullied him. Judy took pity on him and befriended him. He hung around and ran errands for them.

Judy was the strong one, emotionally. She was the one everyone turned to for help with his or her problems.

Jane was the wild one, and the one who got into trouble the most. She was caught smoking at the age of fourteen, and her punishment was to clean the toilet for a month. Mary and Judy stayed behind to help her. When Jane snuck out during curfew hours to meet up with her boyfriend in her early teens, she was grounded for long periods. Mary delivered love letters for her. Jane also couldn't put together a sentence without the help of a four-letter word or two, and was often punished for her foul mouth.

Mary was the pretty one. She might have had a few secret admirers among the boys in the Kuk ever since she had become a young adult. But she wasn't interested in any of them; she was in love with someone else.

She was in love with an older married man – always a tragedy in the making.

4

Mary first met Kyle Sanders when she was twelve years old, a couple of years after the end of the Japanese occupation. Po Leung Kuk started a foster parenthood program, and Kyle and his wife Elizabeth applied successfully to become Mary's part-time foster parents.

They were Americans who worked as reporters for the South China Morning Post, the leading local English language newspaper. Both husband and wife were affectionate with Mary and they were touchy feely. For the first time in young Mary's life, she could enjoy the kind of human contact she had never experienced but had longed for.

She was a socially awkward pre-teen when they first welcomed her to their home.

Elizabeth was a serious but polite woman. Mary learnt good manners and social graces from her.

Kyle was Harvard educated and spoke with colourful Americanisms. Mary learned colloquial English from him. She even tried to emulate his accent and his clichés. She enjoyed spending time with him because in her eyes he was incredibly handsome, looking a lot like the teen idol of her time – Ricky Nelson, with his big blue eyes and luxuriant brown hair. And he was fun to be with. She developed a huge crush on him.

She used to sit on his lap, smelling his eau de cologne mixed with his pheromones, while he read to her and taught her the finer points of the English grammar. It was innocent enough in the beginning, when she was a scrawny pre-teen.

The Chinese compare the transformation of a girl into a woman to the blossoming of a flower. It is imperceptible and slow when you are staring at it. But if you take your eyes off, even briefly, the transformation seems to hasten and the blossoming is already quite advanced before you know it.

Kyle must have looked away too long when he continued to put Mary on his lap when she was almost fifteen.

By then, she had grown a few inches in all the right places. Her narrow waist accentuated her widening hip and enlarging cup size. And when physically close to Kyle, her cheeks turned rosy, her eyes wide and watery.

She had no experience with men at all then, but when she felt a rise of his hard manhood against her bottom while sitting on his lap, she blushed like a bride in a blind marriage unveiled on her wedding night. He gently pushed her away, and it took him quite a while to be able to stand up straight to get himself a cold drink. After that incident, no more sitting on his lap but hugs and kisses from him seemed more sensuous, especially when they were alone.

During one weekend when Elizabeth was out of town to attend a seminar, Kyle brought Mary home for dinner. He opened a bottle of Cabernet Sauvignon, and encouraged Mary to have some wine for the first time.

One thing led to another, Mary lost her innocence that night. She was a few months shy of her sixteenth birthday.

She was a willing participant. When he held her and kissed her on the mouth, she offered him her tongue. When he was taking off her clothes, she shifted her body to make it easier for him to pull off her bra and underwear. Her mind went blank and her body became nearly paralyzed when he pressed his naked body against hers and spread her legs apart. He caressed her body over and over until he went wild and abruptly entered her. She let out a loud scream. He covered her mouth with his to muffle the scream while moving frantically on top of her until he too let out a scream.

She was not completely ignorant of sex education but the amount of blood staining the bed sheets startled her. She assisted him in changing the bed sheets and pillow cases; but when he took the linens to the laundry shop down the street, she didn't want to be around.

They met again the next day and she told him she was still bleeding. He said he had cured her of the "medical condition" known as virginity, and that the bleeding would stop if she let him continue with the long-term healing process. They had sex again later that day, and the bleeding stopped.

For months afterwards, Mary traveled all the way from Causeway Bay to the Central Business Area on Hong Kong Island to meet up with Kyle, ostensibly for English tutorship. Somehow, they always ended up in nearby Wan Chai, a district full of bars and love motels. Instead of receiving an education in the English language, Mary was schooled in sex in a motel room. He even taught her how to put a condom on the target with her mouth in one smooth motion. It didn't seem odd to her that he should know the technique so well. She presumed he knew everything because he was so well educated and so much older than she was.

During that period, Mary could hardly function. She adored Kyle. All she wanted was to be with him; and all he wanted was sex. He loved her smooth and hairless body and never seemed to have enough of it.

The affair lasted until Mary was almost seventeen. As with all teenagers in love, Mary didn't do a good job hiding her feelings, and Elizabeth sensed it. She came to Po Leung Kuk one day to see Mary and was able to coerce a confession out of her.

Elizabeth was one classy woman. She simply turned her back and walked away without saying a word.

Kyle Sanders, Mary's first love, abandoned her after his wife found out about the affair. They met one last time before he packed up and left Hong Kong for good with his wife the next day. He told Mary he didn't have a choice but leave because his wife had a very powerful weapon against him. He never told Mary what that weapon was, but when Mary became older and more worldly, she figured out it must have been his wife's threat to report him to the police for statutory rape, because the affair started when Mary was under sixteen.

However, the threat from his wife did not stop him from having sex with Mary one last time, before he loved her and left her.

During the tearful farewell, he promised her they would always be friends. And he promised to write.

*

31

Mary turned into an emotional wreck after Kyle left her. She overreacted to his disloyalty, even though it was expected of an affair with a married man.

The lyrics of Bonny Tyler's classic song – Married Men – were spot on: The song says married men just wanted to have sex, and at the earliest sign of trouble, they ran back to their wives. They said they wanted to remain friends, sure."

In later years, Mary often self-analyzed and she blamed her exaggerated despair when Kyle ended the affair on her being an orphan. She felt the pangs of abandonment all over again. As any psychologist will attest to – "Abandonment is the most powerful precipitant of psychosis."

She considered killing herself. That was stupid, but stupidity was a part of growing up. She wanted to shorten her life at that age, but when she became older, she made a pledge with the gods to give up everything to prolong it, so that she could spend more time with her son Jason.

She thought of hanging herself, but she was too vain to have her tongue sticking out while lying in the coffin for everyone to see. Same with jumping from a height; she didn't want people to see her messed-up face. At that young age, she was not even resourceful enough to commit a proper suicide. But still, she might have succeeded if Judy and Jane were not there for her. They took away all the sharp objects in the dorm, and organized a round-the-clock vigil over her during that difficult period.

It was during that time that Mary fell in love again, not with a person, but a country.

Kyle used to tell her wonderful stories of his childhood in Mississippi. He was also very knowledgeable about American culture and history, and his speech was littered with American folksy sayings and colloquialisms. After he left, Mary read books about America, and watched as many Hollywood movies as she could afford. Her radio was permanently tuned to The Voice of America.

Jane tried to cheer her up by playing American pop songs in their dorm. They owned a second-hand record player and a small collection of 45s and 78s. They sang along with Nat King Cole and Frank Sinatra. They especially liked those cute songs by Patti Page and Doris Day. Also the soulful voices of jazz legends Ella Fitzgerald, Dinah Washington and Lena Horne. When Elvis the Pelvis crashed onto the world stage, they listened to him and didn't have time for anyone else. Jane could do an impeccable impersonation of The King and never failed to make them bend over with hysterical laughter when she did it.

Mary adored everything American, and she dreamed of visiting the country one day.

Her depression slowly dissipated over that period, thanks to loyal friends and American pop culture. She finally snapped out of it when high school ended and they all turned eighteen around then. They all found jobs and moved out of the Po Leung Kuk.

5

One good thing that came out of Mary's tragic affair with the American was that she became proficient in the English language. She had no difficulty finding a job in the British colony. She found one working as a clerk in a British hong.

She lived alone. She had associates at work who were local Chinese and they wanted to go out with her, but she was not interested in them at all. She had always found older Western men attractive, and it was difficult for her to find camaraderie with local Chinese men, or women, unless they too were from Po Leung Kuk.

She enrolled in an evening school, to study shorthand, typing, and other secretarial skills. After she obtained the diploma, she was promoted to the rank of "Personal Secretary", and was assigned to one of the hong's taipans, John Macfadzean.

She took one look at the tall and debonair Scotsman, and thought: What an attractive man. Too bad he was very much married with children, judging from all the family photos decorating his office.

With the lessons learned from getting involved with Kyle still fresh in mind, she vowed not to fall for another married man ever again. For the first few months being John's secretary, she went out of her way to avoid any intimacy with her new boss, not even looking him in the eye. But when it comes to matters of the heart, a vow to refrain from having feelings for someone is as futile as an alcoholic's promise to stop at one drink.

Every time she was near him, be it in his grand office taking dictation or him standing next to her desk giving instructions, she blushed and her heart started to race. At the end of the working day, she went into John's office and demurely asked for permission to leave, secretly hoping that he would ask her to stay longer, or god forbid, invite her out for a date.

The date she was longing for did not come until almost nine months later. It was around Christmas, and John invited her out for a Christmas drink at his beloved bar the Old China Hand in Wan Chai.

By then, John had been spending far more time with Mary than with his family in his waking hours. He later told Mary he liked her companionship because she was attractive, respectful and competent – qualities in short supply at home. A wretched life at home made him vulnerable to an extra-marital relationship. Mary was barely 22 years old, but she instinctively felt John's unhappiness and disarray in his life at home, in spite of his impeccable manners, perfect grooming, and calm demeanor. She was all too willing to be a good listener.

By rationalizing that it should be part of her job as a personal secretary to listen to the boss's personal problems, she made the same mistake of getting involved with a married man again.

Going to the Old China Hand for a drink after work became a routine for them.

She asked John why he loved drinking in Wan Chai so much when he could afford drinking at the Hilton Hotel or the Hong Kong Club in Central. He said he was sick and tired of swanky places and hoity toity people. He preferred relaxing and drinking in blue-collar environs, just like Wan Chai and the small town in Scotland where he grew up.

Wan Chai in that era was actually not only a blue-collar neighbourhood, it was also a red light district. Wan Chai was The World of Susie Wong, and the people there were like William Holden and Nancy Kwan in that movie. The people in Wan Chai were no doubt more down-to-earth and real than those in the Hong Kong Club. Jane used to work there as a bartender before she moved to Tsim Sha Tsui, and no one was more real and down-to-earth than Jane.

Mary and John were discreet about their dating. They never walked out of the office together. She left first and took a bus to Lockhart Road, a two-lane thoroughfare lined by pubs, girlie bars, and restaurants. Many downstairs establishments owned upstairs hourly motels. Old China Hand, a British-styled pub was in the midst of them.

Lockhart Road was a narrow street, made narrower still by bargirls spilling out from joints with bright neon signs and jukeboxes pushed half-way out into the street, blasting the latest hits. During that period, Black is Black by The Los Bravos and The House of the Rising Sun by The Animals were the two songs most popular in Wan Chai bars and they were played loudly over and over again. Mary usually hung around the jukeboxes listening to the music to kill time, while pretending to be somewhat confused and lost, so that the girls with miniskirts, stilettos and long glue-on eyelashes crowding the entrances of the bars, who ogled her suspiciously, didn't think she was competing with them for business.

She checked her watch often and when she thought the time was right, she ducked into the Old China Hand and took a corner table, praying John would show up before some drunk came over to chat her up.

It was such a hassle but being able to be with John was worth all of it. He was so drop dead gorgeous; William Holden had nothing on him. She was drawn to him like a tiny iron needle close to a powerful magnet. They became more and more intimate.

One evening, John told her of his unhappiness at home. He was married to a woman whose father owned a large shipping company in Europe, and she was a spoilt rich kid. After the birth of their second child, they couldn't see eye to eye on anything. There were frequent screaming altercations. Life was unpleasant for both of them but divorce was not an option. It was simply not done in their circle. Big hongs in Hong Kong did not seem to tolerate such scandals, either. Protocol required a high-ranking taipan like John to show up at social functions accompanied by a white wife with a posh accent and upper-class social etiquette.

John evaded life at home by spending long hours at work and drinking after work at seedy watering holes in either Wan Chai or Tsim Sha Tsui where he could stay until 2 o'clock in the morning without risking being spotted by friends or colleagues.

Mary listened quietly. When he reached for her hands, she let him hold them. When he leaned over to kiss her, she closed her eyes and responded.

Later that evening, they ended up in a love motel called the Ming Court on Lockhart Road half a block away; incidentally, the same one Kyle regularly took Mary to a few years before.

The Ming Court hadn't changed much over the years. The décor was still gaudy. The main colour was hot pink, down to the wallpaper and the bed cover; and the obligatory mirror on the ceiling. The TV in the room had blue movies on, as if people who went there needed the inspiration or the instruction for what they had come to do.

The room brought back memories of Kyle as Mary sat on the edge of the bed lost in thought. John thought he had somehow offended Mary by taking her to a joint with a hot pink bedspread. He put his arm around her and explained that had they gone to the Hilton, at least half a dozen people would have come over to shake his hand before he could even try to reach the elevator. Mary told him she understood. She thought the room was clean and the bed was comfortable enough. She was not about to let him know she used to be a regular customer there.

She leaned over to kiss him, unbuttoning his shirt at the same time.

John was a tender and affectionate lover, and Mary fell very much in love with a married man once again, in the same hourly motel no less.

Such was her fate with men.

Before long, John's routine was to go home to his peak mansion for dinner and spend time with his two children until they were tucked in at nine. Then he took off to Mary's apartment on Observatory Road in Tsim Sha Tsui and stayed there until 6 o'clock the next morning, before taking the earliest ferry across the harbor and returning to his peak home to shower and change clothes. He then began a new day at work, with Mary by his side again.

John's wife put up with all that in exchange for the prestige associated with life as the tai tai of a taipan, and lots of money in her own account to spend and invest. They put up a good front at company functions and among their circle of friends.

6

A few months into their affair, Mary became pregnant.

The question of contraception never came up. She had not had a boyfriend since Kyle. She'd heard of various methods of contraception, but the only one she was familiar with was the condom, thanks to Kyle; but she was not about to use it with her new lover, showing off her well-honed oral technique.

The real reason, of course, was that subconsciously she wanted to become a mother.

She did not know what kind of reaction to expect from the rich Scotsman with a powerful British hong in a British colony. Would he think it was a trap to make him provide monetary support – for a money baby? Would he dump her like the proverbial hot potato?

Bonny Tyler's waxing lyrical about married men couldn't be more apt in this situation.

It was an era when pregnancy out of wedlock was a disgrace, and when it was interracial, a double dose of ignominy. Sexual relationships between Western men and local Chinese women were not uncommon, though, and the children that resulted from the liaisons were referred to as "mongrels" by the Westerners or "harm har tsan" by the Cantonese – a code name for mixed-blood freaks.

She knew the social implications, but was willing and ready to face the music from living the taboo and tough it all out. She adored John; and there was no other man she would rather have a child with. She had desperately wanted a child, ever since she was a child herself. She decided to keep the baby, and keep it to herself.

When the pregnancy was becoming impossible to hide, she tried to pick fights with John to give him a reason to fire her, or an excuse for her to resign from the company. But every time she bitched about her job to John, he took her seriously. He tried his best to pacify her by listening patiently to her purported grievances and he was accommodating to her demands, no matter how outrageous they could be. She also tried being snarky with him, but when she saw the way he looked at her, she felt so bad she apologized to him right away. She just didn't have the heart to hurt his feelings, so she took the easy way out instead.

John always took a vacation around Christmas to visit his folks back in Scotland, so Mary planned her resignation from the company in that month, without prior notice, forfeiting a severance pay.

She told everyone in the company she was quitting her job to go back to school.

She did enroll in a diploma course in education, specializing in teaching Chinese as a second language to expatriate children. She was able to obtain the diploma a few weeks before her due date.

The gestation period for an unwed mother with no family support could be the longest and loneliest few months, having to go through morning sickness, and to waddle her way with a huge belly to the obstetrician's clinic all by herself.

At least Jane was there for her.

Jane found employment in bars after leaving Po Leung Kuk and was working and living in Tsim Sha Tsui at that time. Her waking hours were the exact opposite of those of most other people, including Mary's. That came in handy when there was a baby to take care of.

When John returned from vacation, he was surprised, disappointed, and perplexed that Mary had resigned from the company without letting him know in advance. He tried contacting her, but she did not leave any contact details with the company. None of her co-workers knew where to find her.

John went to her old abode to look for her, but she had vacated her flat and moved in with Jane. Her neighbours could not tell him anything, either.

Mary thought of John's possible predicament and anxiety and was tempted to call him up. The isolation was killing her. It took great resolve from her to dismiss the thought.

It was too expensive to go to a private hospital, so she chose Kwong Wah Hospital on Waterloo Road in Yau Ma Tei, Kowloon for prenatal care and the delivery.

She went into labour on the third of July and gave birth to a baby boy on the fourth, the Independence Day of the US of A, and Mary thought it was a sign from heavens that she and her son should eventually emigrate to the US.

The childbirth was uneventful. The midwife who took care of Mary told her it was the easiest delivery for a woman's first pregnancy in her twenty years of experience delivering babies. As could be seen later, not only giving birth to her son was easy, raising him was also the easiest thing in the world.

Mary named him Jason, and used the father's first name as his middle name. In those days, if the entry under "father" on the birth certificate application form was left blank, the hospital would use the mother's last name for the newborn. So, Jason John Lee came into this world, and Mary's dream of motherhood came true.

When the nurse brought in the baby for her to breastfeed for the first time, she was so ecstatic she couldn't stop her tears from falling on Jason's tiny face. The pleasure derived from her baby sucking on her nipples was like heaven on earth. She could not wait for feeding time. She told the nurse she fell asleep during the last feeding session and she forgot to put her nipple in Jason's mouth. Could she do it earlier than scheduled? The nurse smiled and let her have Jason before everyone else. Jason had her nipple but fell asleep mid-feed, and she told the nurse the baby didn't have enough to eat because he fell asleep, could he stay a little longer?

Oh, motherhood! Could she have it 24 hours a day, please?

Mary was ordinarily quite laid back, even shy. Now, when it came to her new baby, she became aggressive.

She couldn't wait to be discharged, so that her son wouldn't be sequestered to another room most of the day. They sent her home after three days, and she almost wanted to jump up and down to celebrate, forgetting her postpartum wounds.   They put the baby crib between Mary's bed and Jane's in the bedroom, so that either of them could easily reach for him when he cried.

Money was running out, and Mary soon had to look for a job. Jane suggested contacting John for child support, but Mary had reservations about it. Even though she did miss John, she wanted to be with her newborn son more. In colonial days, the Western man usually got what he wanted. There were cases of Western men taking babies away from local women, to be raised "properly" back in the United Kingdom. Dumping the woman but taking the baby away was not unheard of.

Mary found out later that she was paranoid about the situation. Orphans did not think straight. John was not that kind of person, and he truly loved Mary. But she did not know that.

For months, he tried desperately to contact her but she seemed to have vanished into thin air. He spent a lot of after-hours walking the streets of Tsim Sha Tsui in the neighbourhood where her old apartment was, and ended up drinking in bars in the same neighbourhood until wee hours of the morning. One of the bars he regularly went to was the one Jane working in.

Jane knew who John was, but she had been sworn to secrecy regarding the baby and Mary's whereabouts. Seeing John slowly getting wasted every night, she decided to do something about it.

Jane and Mary talked at length about the situation, and they agreed that John was definitely unhappy. The fact that he was in Tsim Sha Tsui all the time must be because he was hoping to find Mary; but he was turning into a hopeless alcoholic dying of liver disease, and Jason would never get to know his father.

Mary did miss John. They had been apart for almost a year. It was driving her crazy. She would love to reunite with John, but would he still be interested in her when he learned of the child? And most of all, would he take Jason away?

"Trust me, it won't happen," Jane said.

Jane could be trusted. She could be quite convincing.

Jane had at one time a triad 426 red pole (an enforcer) as a boyfriend; she had seen him in action and had learned a thing or two from him about "negotiation". And she was by nature melodramatic. She could assume the persona of a triad member, or a drama queen.

Mary finally agreed to re-connect with John, with Jane's help. Jane would talk to John.

She didn't tell Mary what she said to John, but when she came to see Mary the next day, there was smugness in the way she pranced around the room.

Mary imagined it could have gone like this:

"John, you bastard, you got my good friend Mary pregnant, and what the fuck are you gonna do about it?" To achieve the greatest effect, at some point, she would have slammed her fist on the table and looked fierce.

Alternatively, the talk could have gone like this:

"John, you remember Mary Lee, don't you? Mary, like me, is an orphan. We are used to people treating us like doormats. She cries and cries every day. That is why I am talking to you." She would then have sighed and paused. "I'm sorry; you mean you don't know? She was pregnant with your child.

"Mary said it was her fault, and she is not asking for anything. She doesn't want to cause you any trouble and she especially doesn't want anyone to take the baby from her."

Either way, it worked.

"What happened?" Mary asked.

"I fucking told you so," Jane said. "John is begging to see you."

"What did you tell him?"

"I told John what he needed to know, and we are going to play hard to get."

"Jane, don't toy with me."

"Trust me," said Jane.

John promised Jane he would not take the baby away from Mary, and he wouldn't allow anyone else to do so either, not his wife, not even the Governor of Hong Kong.

Jane was not about to make it too easy for him. She said she would think about it and would discuss the situation further with Mary, who, she lied, lived very far away in the New Territories. She told John to come back the next day and she might have some news for him.

The following evening, Mary took the baby to a back room at Jane's bar. John arrived at eight o'clock as instructed. Jane, toying with him, told him Mary could not decide what to do. After making him wait for half an hour, she pushed him into the back room.

When he went in and saw Mary with a baby in her arms, it was like the last scene in An Affair To Remember, when Cary Grant finally discovered Deborah Kerr's condition, and what had caused it. There was a smorgasbord of emotions on display —

anger, pity, sadness, forgiveness, joy, love, and understanding. The scene concluded with tears and kisses.

They embraced. She passed on the baby for him to cradle in his arms, followed by more tears and kisses.

He expressed great gratitude to Mary for her discretion, and promised to support the baby. She declined any monetary support from John. She did not want John to think that Jason was intended to be a meal ticket.

She had just started a teaching job at King George's, a special secondary school for children of the British military personnel based in the colony. Her job was to teach Chinese as a second language to the English-speaking students. The salary was more than enough for a household of two. She had moved out of Jane's place, was renting an apartment in Kowloon Tong close to the school, and had hired a part-time amah to help out.

*

After the reunion, John resumed his late night visits to Mary's apartment a few nights a week, making his early morning trips across the harbor on the Star Ferry. He stopped his frequent alcohol binges and was healthier, happier and more efficient at work.

Mary was also happy. She had a man who loved her, and a son for her to love. She accepted the fact that she didn't have a husband and her son didn't have a full-time father, but what she had was good enough for her. She was especially thankful for having a child of her own. Apart from going to work, she and Jason were inseparable. His bed was next to hers, and she breastfed him until he was more than one and a half years old. She read somewhere that breastfeeding could enhance the bonding of mother and child. It was recommended for six months. She tripled the recommended period, just to be sure.

When John was with his Chinese family, he took off his tie and jacket, even when they went out to movies and restaurants. He said he was happiest that way, relaxed and with someone he was comfortable with. They went to Jane's bar often, and the three always had a good time together drinking and listening to music from the jukebox.

Those were the happiest days of Mary's life.

*

When Jason turned eight, John had another promotion and became the vice president of the company.

The following Christmas, he bade farewell to Jason and Mary before he took off with his other family to Scotland to see his folks. Mary received one postcard from him dated two days before Christmas but never again, contrary to his customary habit of sending at least one every other day.

John was scheduled to return three days after New Year's Day, but there were no calls from him that day. A week went by without any news. Mary repeatedly called his office, and was told he was not available. She still had a few old colleagues she could call on the phone to gossip, but none had heard anything about what happened to Mr MacFadzean whose office was on the executive floor. The huge company occupied seven floors of a swanky building in the Central Business Area, and it was difficult to get personal information concerning a high-ranking executive.

*

Jane broke the devastating news to Mary.

In the *South China Morning Post*, the local English newspaper, Jane saw John's obituary.

He had died in a car accident in Scotland on Christmas Day.

*

Mary was distraught beyond words. She had looked for love her whole life, and it seemed that every time she found it, it would be taken away from her. She was fortunate to have a good friend like Jane close by, to lend sympathy and support, and to offer timely help to raise young Jason so that she didn't have to do it alone. Jane visited Mary's house as often as she could, to cook and to take care of little Jason while Mary was busy mourning and struggling to fulfill her duties as a teacher, and getting back on her feet.

The obituary stated that John left a widow and their two children.

A month later, a team of men in dark pinstriped suits paid Mary a visit at King George's. They had already talked with the headmaster of the school, a retired admiral who was very much one of the old boys. The men were lawyers hired by John's widow. John had included Mary and Jason in his will, and his widow was fighting with a scorned woman's fury to deny them their share of the inheritance.

In the Headmaster's office, they tried to coerce Mary into signing some legal papers to agree to abjuration of the inheritance from Mr John MacFadzean, threatening a lengthy lawsuit and possible dismissal from her post at King George's.

Mary was thirty-two years old and a local woman surrounded by a band of authoritative older Western men. She was outnumbered, outranked and utterly intimidated. She was on the verge of signing the papers until Jane's face came into her mind. What would Jane have done under this circumstance? Jane was the same age but much more worldly. No one could push her around even though she was all but 100 lb. in weight and 5 feet tall; not even an inebriated 200 lb. gorilla in her bar.

Mary asked to go to the restroom and instead went outside the school to call Jane at home from a payphone. Jane was still in bed, but she woke up real quick when Mary told her what was happening.

"Stop everything. Don't talk to those motherfuckers. I'm on my way." She would come with a lawyer, a regular customer in her bar, who happened to have spent the night with her and was in the shower at that very moment and they could show up in King George's within minutes.

"I don't have time to put make-up on. My face alone will scare the crap out of them, even without the lawyer beside me," Jane added before hanging up.

Meanwhile, Mary hid in the lady's restroom.

Jane's lawyer friend Malcolm confronted the pinstriped brigade and demanded to see the papers, and after glancing through them, tore them into pieces. He threatened to sue the law firm for malpractice, and to call journalists of the local newspapers to do some investigative reporting. He handed them his business card, and told them to contact him and not Mary in all matters relating to John's will, effective immediately. In parting, he also threatened to haul the headmaster in front of the Labour Tribunal to answer a few questions.

The lawyers hired by John's widow left Mary alone after that. She carried on teaching at King George's and caring for young Jason.

Malcolm told her John's will was made in a lawyer's office in front of credible witnesses, while he was of sound mind and health. It was indisputable. But the widow's lawyers were contesting the will based on some archaic legal technicalities. But he was confident the judgment would be in Mary's favour.

His advice to her was that a legal dispute of this nature could go on for years and it would be in her interest to strike a deal.

She consented.

Six months later, Malcolm called her into his office.

In return for a few signatures, Mary received an inheritance check for two hundred thousand British pounds.

The year was 1967, and that was a lot of money.

7

For the first few months after John's sudden death, Mary asked Jason to come to bed with her every night so that she could hug him while crying herself to sleep. Jason was only eight years old and even at that young age preferred sleeping alone, but he was a sweet boy and he understood his mother's needs; so he stayed in her bed until she fell asleep before he returned to his own bed.

Jason was not distressed by his father's death. He remembered the man he called father, who showed up in their apartment late at night when young Jason was about to be tucked in. By the time Jason woke up the next morning, the man had already left for work. The man never showed up during weekends and holidays, and he went away for long vacations twice a year. Jason didn't know what a father was supposed to do, and he asked no questions. He seemed to be happy having only Mary around, who kept telling him she was happy and contented having him as a son and a companion.

Mary bought an apartment on Broadcast Drive in Kowloon Tong, so that her life had at least some kind of stability.

Broadcast Drive was so named because it was home to radio and TV stations such as the privately owned Rediffusion and TVB, and the Government owned Radio & Television Hong Kong.

It was a one-way street; so if a car missed an entrance or a ramp, it had to go around once again. Only low rises lined the roads in that area because it was close to the landing paths of the nearby Kai Tak Airport.

They were at the foot of The Lion Rock, the most prominent peak in the Kowloon peninsula. From their rear windows, a rock shaped like a lion atop a tall peak loomed large and mighty over the backyard, and a giant golf-ball-shaped radio transmission station perched on a neighbouring peak. The modest homes at the foot of the Lion Rock were built for grassroots citizens of Hong Kong.

The regal looking leonine rock sculpture turned its face towards the west, as if it were in disdain of the power centres of Hong Kong towards the south – the Victoria Harbor and Hong Kong Island.

Directly across the harbor stood its counterpart, the Victoria Peak, where stand-alone mansions were built for the very elite of society.

Mary had no doubt where she belonged – an orphan residing in the Lion Rock area; nonetheless, a millionaire, thanks to a lover whose home used to be in one of the mansions on the Victoria Peak.

She resided on Broadcast Drive and lived for the radio. She did not go out much, and Jason preferred reading in his room after school. Radio was her major form of entertainment. It was tuned either to The Voice of America, or one of the music stations.

A disc jockey named Ray Cordeiro on Rediffusion loved golden oldies as much as Mary did, and he played them non-stop. Mary sometimes called in and requested songs by Patti Page and Doris Day to cheer herself up.

He played Elvis during his whole show on The King's birthday. Jane always took that day off and came over with a bottle of whiskey and a case of beer. She still could do a good impersonation of Elvis the Pelvis, and Mary laughed her heart out watching Jane, the foul-mouthed Elvis impersonator. The two drank until drunk; then they invariably began to feel sorry for themselves and cried their hearts out in each other's arms.

Ray Cordero also liked to introduce new singing artists to Hong Kong. Matt Monroe was one of them, with his signature song Walk Away. Jane and Mary first listened to The Jarmels' one-hit wonder 'A Little Bit Of Soap' on Ray's show and they both went crazy over it. It was a song stereotypically popular with people who felt sorry for themselves.

Jane had her own version of its lyrics. She replaced every adjective in it with "Fucking".

Jane could never have children because she had too many abortions and ectopic pregnancies. Mary offered to share Jason with her, and she took Mary's offer too literally. She was so over-the-top with disciplining Jason that Mary often had to pull her aside to tell her to lighten up. Something as trivial as accidentally breaking a rice bowl would prompt her to punish Jason by making him write "I'm sorry" in Chinese 100 times on a book she bought for the purpose, a book she called "Atonement Record."

Then she would feel bad about it the next day and buy Jason loads of gifts.

Mary asked why she was so strict with Jason, when she knew he was a good boy. She said that was because she didn't want Jason to grow up like them.

"Jane, who smokes like a fucking chimney and drinks like a fucking Kennedy. And Mary, who specializes in fucking married men," she sang those lines to the tune of the Righteous Brothers' The Unchained Melody, followed by rolling her eyes and contorting her face as if she was in the middle of a grand mal seizure.

Jane, the drama queen.

*

Jason did not really need any disciplining; he was such a good boy, a perfect child even. He was so different from other boys. He preferred books to toys and sports. He didn't care about new clothes or designer sneakers. He was a young Einstein; his hair was always a mess. He was constantly asking questions about new words he stumbled upon, and was able to read on his own at a young age. He was always polite and respectful.

Mary stayed on to teach at King George's despite her newfound wealth, because she liked her teaching job, and she had hopes that Jason would attend the elite school one day. One of the fringe benefits of being a teacher there was that their children had priority of admission into the school. It would be a few years yet since Jason was only eight years old when John passed away.

She sent him to a local Chinese school for his primary education, and planned his secondary education at King

George's so that he would be proficient in both Chinese and English.

Jason was one of the top students at Pui Ching Primary School. The teachers said he seemed to daydream all day and he got bored easily, but still, he scored well in exams. His best subjects were science and mathematics. He could tackle all the mathematical problems instinctively.

Mary was over-protective of him but soon found out that he preferred independence, not so much by his telling his mother so but by his body language. He proved that he could take care of himself even at a young age by being careful when crossing the street, for example. His room was disorderly, but he could always find things because he had a system in arranging things only he could fathom.

Mary spent all her free time with him, doing things he liked to do, such as visiting libraries, bookstores, and museums, and hiking in the country parks in the Lion Rock region.

*

Mary continued to live modestly. As with most people who had lived through the Japanese war, she was exceedingly frugal, as if another world war might be visited upon her anytime. She was also saving her money for missions dear to her heart.

She had never had closure with her orphan status. She was hoping to meet her parents someday. She supposed they must have been dirt poor; otherwise, they would not have given up their child. If she found them, she wanted to give them money, lots of it.

She wanted to give everything else to Jason when he grew up so that he would be a rich man like his late father. Like most Chinese, giving money would be the ultimate gesture of love for someone.

She also used her money to help friends. Jane borrowed and bought the bar she used to work in on Hankow Road in Tsim Sha Tsui. Under her shrewd management and marketing, the bar made loads of money and she opened branches in Central and Wan Chai within three years. She paid back the loan with interest to Mary, interest that Mary did not demand but Jane insisted on giving.

50

Po Leung Kuk veterans Judy Fung and Andrew Chu borrowed from her when they emigrated to San Francisco to go into the restaurant business there. They, too, prospered. Mary refused to charge them any interest. After they paid back the loan, they promised Mary and Jason a lifetime of free food at their restaurant.

Meanwhile, what to do with all the money? She followed the advice of an old banker, another one of Jane's regular customers and occasional lover, and bought up properties in Kowloon and Hong Kong Island, especially in up and coming new residential developments. She also invested in blue chips in the emerging Hong Kong Stock Market.

*

Money was not what Mary worried about those days; Jason was, in a strange way. It was not because Jason was naughty or lazy or anything of that sort. On the contrary, Jason was the perfect child. He was always polite. He liked books. He never fought with other children, but became bored playing and talking with them. Mary tried her best to interest Jason in what other children found amusing, such as kicking a ball or playing balls with a racket or paddle, or reading comics and playing with toys that made noises, or boys' favourite – toy weapons. None of those seemed to engage Jason long before he returned to his books. After a while, Mary went with the flow and let him be: a loner and a bookworm, a nerd and the next Einstein.

They regularly took long hikes in the country parks on weekends. Jason's questions about nature became harder and harder for her to answer, so she brought along a notebook and jotted down all the unanswered questions so they could find the answers the best they could from the library later.

When Jason was in high school, the subjects became too difficult for Mary and he went to his teachers and the library by himself to get answers. With his intellect and diligence, he would later become the top boy in King George's Secondary School, which he attended after graduating from Pui Ching Primary.

8

Jason's first day attending King George's was a disaster.

Everyone at King George's spoke only English and it was intimidating for young Jason who normally spoke only Cantonese at home and in school.

Jason's proficiency in the English language was typical of someone who learned it in a classroom. He was actually better than most locals because of his early exposure to the language talking with his late father, but he forgot most of it after John died and he didn't use it much with Mary and Jane.

The class mistress, Mrs Stewart, spoke in a Scottish drawl that was hard on Jason's ear, and Jason's faltering conversational English was difficult for Mrs Stewart to understand. There were few non-British students in the school, and none would have Jason's problem because they were all native English speakers, regardless of nationality.

After a few failed attempts at understanding each other, Mrs Stewart announced to the class something to the effect that a Chinaman should really go to a local school; otherwise, he would drag the whole class down with his slow learning.

That much Jason understood. With his head bowed, he said almost inaudibly: "I'll try my best." The "try" came out more like "tie".

"Tongue-tie won't do you any good," said Mrs Stewart.

The whole class erupted in a prolonged hysterical laughing outbreak.

Facing such humiliation, Jason's head bowed and face reddened, for the rest of the lesson.

Mary got wind of what happened, and asked Jason if he wanted to quit King George's and return to a local school. Jason looked at her intensely, and said a curt no, as if the decision was final and non-negotiable. Mary could tell from his expression he was angry and he was determined to prove Mrs Stewart wrong.

During his whole life, he became that way whenever he was challenged, and he was formidable in that regard.

In spite of Jason's good nature, he could be the most stubborn person in the world.

Mary went to Mrs Cunningham, an English teacher in the school, for advice. She told Mary there was no shortcut – practice, practice, and practice some more. By the way, if Mary wanted Jason to sound smart and educated, one way was to listen to BBC news on the radio and learn from the presenters.

That became Jason's passion in the ensuing few years. Every night before falling asleep and every morning on waking up, he had the radio tuned to the BBC. Such was Jason's determination, perseverance, and intellect that he could learn anything as quickly as any human being possibly could.

In a matter of weeks, Jason was able to manage simple conversation in English. In another six months, not only he could speak the language flawlessly, he could easily audition for a job with the BBC as a broadcaster.

His progress didn't impress Mrs Stewart, though. She continued to ignore him or pretend she didn't understand him. One time, she punished Jason by ordering him to stand outside the classroom, because Jason was talking to a neighbouring student, even though it was the other student asking him a question.

When Jason tried to answer a question she asked the class, she always found fault with Jason's pronunciation. But there are always more good people than bad in this world, especially among children. After a while, some students actually stood up for Jason, and said under their breath, but loud enough for Mrs Stewart to hear: "We understand him perfectly; he speaks better than you do."

Many students laughed, but Mrs Stewart wasn't amused. She disliked Jason even more.

It was not in Jason's nature to gloat or be vindictive. In spite of Mrs Stewart's prejudice, Jason stayed quiet mostly. He told his classmates he was still in the process of learning the English language, and that meanwhile, he needed to practice his Cantonese lest he forget it.

Gradually, Jason was starting to get respect from all the other teachers. He scored well in all the subjects not taught by Mrs Stewart.

*

His time in the schoolyard was not getting easier, however.

Thanks to Mrs Stewart, many fellow students called him Ching Chong, and asked him if he had eaten any dogs lately.

When Jason told Mary what they said, she laughed so hard she almost had a heart attack. Jason asked why she was laughing. She told him maybe she should serve dog meat for dinner so he could tell his classmates what it tasted like. Jason said no way he would eat dog meat, and he did not think it was funny at all. Joking with Jason was always a challenge.

A large boy with flaming red hair named Colin McBride was particularly brutal with Jason. That was years before they became pals and gallivanted together in Tsim Sha Tsui.

Colin liked to slap Jason around for no particular reason. Jason would run away from his tormentor who was overweight and slow on his feet. Jason had no interest in sports of any kind, while his classmates were all crazy about cricket, field hockey, or soccer. He picked up distance running instead, more for self-preservation than to attain jock status.

Academically, though, Jason excelled in every subject. He kept his vow to himself to prove Mrs Stewart wrong and demonstrate that he was intellectually equal to other students. He was in fact intellectually superior to all the other students in his class. He could tackle math and science subjects effortlessly. He even put extra effort into subjects that required rote learning, and aced them all.

Colin was not good at math. He made Jason hand over his math assignments in the mornings so that he could copy them, and the two of them always led the class in scores.

Colin, ever the mischievous one, one day altered some of Jason's answers after copying the correct version and handed in the homework for Jason, and Jason ended up having a goose egg while Colin himself earned top score.

When Jason confronted Colin, he feigned innocence. "I didn't do anything," he said.

Jason would never bring his troubles up with Mary. He knew what his mom was like. She would go to the math teacher or even the principal and make a big deal of it. She was gentle and laid back generally, but morphed into a tiger mom whenever her son was at any disadvantage or in danger. Jason would rather deal with it his own way.

On the next assignment, Jason deliberately put in all the wrong answers, and both Colin and he ended up scoring zero that day.

Colin was furious. He glared at Jason during the whole class and whenever Jason looked his way, he mouthed: "See you at recess."

He cornered Jason during recess and hollered: "Ching Chong, you are dead meat."

He put Jason in a headlock with his right arm and tried to punch Jason's stomach with his left fist. Jason struggled and fought back and the two of them ended up wrestling on the floor. While Colin was trying to pound on Jason with his fist, Jason defended himself by tickling Colin's underarm. Colin tickled him back.

Soon they started to roll on the ground laughing uncontrollably.

When Colin regained his breath, his hostility had dissipated. Jason firmly told Colin he would not let him copy his homework anymore, pursing his lips and staring at Colin until Colin averted his gaze.

"I need to get good grades," Colin told him. "Otherwise my dad will beat me. That means I would have to bloody beat you."

"No. That's cheating. I can't do that anymore."

"Do you want to die?"

"No. Can we try something different?"

Colin promised he would simply copy Jason's answers without messing with them. Jason suggested he give Colin tutorials on mathematics after school instead.

Colin said they could try; but if it didn't work, Ching Chong Chinaman had better be prepared for some serious punishment.

Colin was more attentive after school with Jason than during regular math classes, and Jason proved to be a better teacher than the regular math teacher. He was able to explain the mathematical principles in a simpler and clearer way for Colin to comprehend and apply. Not only did Colin score decently in all the math subjects from then on, he began to develop a sense of self-worth and confidence he had never had before. He stopped bullying Jason and calling him names.

At the end of the school year when the results of the final examination came out, Jason was not only the top boy, his test scores exceeded those who came in second by a wide margin, even with Mrs Stewart dragging down his average a notch or two.

The following years Jason had an easier time. His class mistress was Mrs Cunningham, and she was not biased towards any student. She actually liked Jason's new-found BBC tongue. In the school yard, Colin had changed from being his tormentor to his protector. Jason had a reputation for being always willing to help fellow students with their schoolwork. He had a way of explaining things to young people like no grown-up could.

He continued to run long distance and hike, and his mother thought it would be a good idea for her son to learn Kung Fu, since he was vulnerable to bullying. They went to Lau sifu who specialized in the Wing Chun style at a studio owned by the legendary master Ip Man.

Mary went with him to the Tsim Sha Tsui studio on Nathan Road occasionally to see what it was like. Jason's sifu was one of Ip Man's chief disciples. He took Jason in only after Mary agreed to pay him two hundred dollars a month, a hefty sum, considering most blue collared workers' monthly salary was around three hundred dollars. Lau sifu was actually a head shorter than Jason and did not look like a fierce fighter, but became a legend after he single-handedly floored six young thugs who tried to take over his mother's newspaper stand at the entrance of a teahouse. It was reported in the newspaper and that was how Mary knew where to find him. He devoted quite a bit of time to teaching Jason himself, most definitely because of the two hundred dollars. Other students often practiced by themselves.

They had this contraption in there, which they called the wooden man zhuang. It had numerous wooden logs sticking out at different angles from a central shaft. Students sparred with the logs to build strength and stamina. Lau sifu made Jason practice with the wooden man zhuang for a whole hour followed by sparring with him using a technique called Chi Sau (sticky hands). At the end of each session, Jason's fists and arms would be all red and raw. Mary asked if that was necessary. Sifu told her over time, Jason's arms would be so tough and strong he could dip them in burning oil without getting hurt. Once, while Mary was preparing Koo Lo pork and had the frying pan filled with oil, she called Jason over, and asked him if he was ready to dip his arms into the boiling oil. Jason recoiled and chided her for playing with fire.

If Jason had a character flaw, it would be his enduring seriousness and lack of a sense of fun or humor.

Lau sifu gave Mary a medicinal wine to rub on Jason's arms after each session. He grimaced in pain when the wine stung his raw flesh. She asked if he wanted to continue training, and he vowed he would not quit until he obtained the certificate given to all disciples who passed the grade of sheung zhuang (mount the zhuang).

The most advanced level would be har zhuang (dismount the Zhuang), which, unlike Chi Sau and Sheung Zhuang, was intended for severely maiming your opponents and not just for self-defense. Sifu said if Mary gave him five hundred dollars a month, he could teach Jason to reach that level.

Jason declined. Maiming people was not one of his ambitions.

He never had to come close to using any of his Kung Fu moves, because he was always polite and forgiving; and Colin had stopped hitting him. Despite all the effort put in to obtaining his sheung zhuang certificate, he used his fighting skills just once – not in school, but in Jane's bar in Tsim Sha Tsui, when he tried to rescued Rachel from three soldiers' harassment. His Kung Fu skills didn't do him any good, either. He was badly beaten. And that fight was indirectly responsible for his loss of virginity in the hands (and mouth) of Rachel O' Reilly.

After he graduated in sheung zhuang and obtained his certificate, he stopped going to sifu's studio, but paid for a wooden man zhuang so that he could spar with it at home. Such exercise had allowed him some serious workouts and helped him maintain his sanity during times of frustration, when he was jobless and being sued, during the many years later in his life.

*

After Mary died, Jason moved around quite a bit. The only personal belongings he held fast to were his wooden man zhuang and the vanity that Mary had sat at while she applied make-up, with him at her side when he was a small child.

9

Mary never dated after John died. She was content being with Jason in her spare time, doing housework quietly when he was studying, fussing over him when he was not studying, and accompanying him to all his extra-curricular activities. She was fascinated watching her son grow from a baby into a young man a couple of inches taller than herself. Jason never changed. He loved reading and his hair was always a mess.

Jason socialized with his schoolmates after school, but not too much. Saturday afternoon was his scheduled time with them. The rest of the time was reserved for reading and studying, martial arts practice, and hiking with Mary.

Mary was touchy-feely with him, and he tolerated it; he recoiled from intimacy offered by other people, though. Even with Jane, whose feelings were hurt, and she chided him for being ungrateful, since she was like a second mother to him, and had even changed his diapers numerous times.

After she heard from Mary Jason's unusual reaction to sex, she just couldn't comprehend it. Jane avoided hugging and kissing him, but held a grudge. Whenever she got drunk, she teased Jason and called him a weirdo. Jason responded by bowing his head and pursing his lips.

His classmates were all Westerners, and were inclined to be physical. Jason stood out, always maintaining a certain physical distance from other human beings.

Rachel, of course, when drunk, was impossible to push away. After the oral sex encounter, Jason avoided her whenever she started drinking.

*

In year five, every student in the British secondary education system had to take a city-wide examination to determine their eligibility for matriculation class, which led to entry into universities in U.K. and other countries that had been part of the British Empire. Even Colin and Rachel cut down on their drinking, to cram for the exam. Mary invited them to her flat so that Jason could help them while having a little social life.

Jane came over sometimes to cook for everyone. Jane being Jane, she brought over a bottle of whiskey for herself and Mary, and a six-pack of beer to reward Rachel and Colin when they were done with the study. Everyone was happy.

The results of the School Certificate Examination were satisfactory for Rachel and Colin, good enough for them to continue into form six, and admittance into universities.

The results for Jason were outstanding; he was in a league of his own; he aced every subject.

Jane said that called for some kind of celebration. She took them to the famous Spring Deer Peking restaurant on Mody Road in Tsim Sha Tsui, and had a Peking duck dinner. After, they continued the celebration at Jane's bar on Hankow Road. Rachel got drunk, Colin ran out of beer money, Jane took Rachel home so Jason didn't have to. It was a blast.

For high school graduation, his classmates elected Jason the valedictorian.

The speech was just like Jason – modest, forgiving, and boring. He thanked everyone, including the bully turned good friend Colin. Without him, Jason said, he would not have been such a good runner. Thanks to Rachel, referring to the incident at the Tsim Sha Tsui bar, he wouldn't have had his face reshaped to its current striking form. He even thanked Mrs Stewart – without her words of encouragement, he would never be able to try to find a job with the BBC, even as a janitor. It was typical Jason, not holding any grudges and always self-effacing. The audience appreciated Jason's good nature, and gave him a standing ovation. The applause lasted for a full minute. Everyone there had no doubt that Jason would never become a politician or a movie star, but likely a great scholar.

Mary cried at his valediction address, tears of joy and pride, and also tears of sorrow and despondence, because she was worried sick about not being around when her son became somebody someday, given her worsening heart condition.

Her worry became a reality a few days later when she took her fatalistic journey to San Francisco and died on her way back.

10

When Mary was in her early thirties, she began to have problems doing any strenuous exercise. When they hiked in the Lion Rock country parks she had to take numerous breaks while Jason waited. The doctors started her on Digoxin and Lasix to combat the ever worsening heart failure. Her heart became double the size of a normal one, and was getting bigger still by the day. Eventually, it would break down, like an overworked motor. A heart transplant would be the only definitive treatment but it wasn't widely available in her day.

Jason told her then he was very much interested in studying Medicine and he would take up cardiology as his specialty so that he could find a cure for her. And he meant it. That gave Mary an excuse to kiss him, hug him, and thank him, but she wondered aloud whether she could wait that long.

Visits to hospitals and doctors became more frequent and a few months before Jason's high school graduation, she resigned from King George's so that she could rest at home.

Always the planner, she immediately worked on her bucket list.

First, she needed to set up a trust so that Jason would never have to worry about money. Secondly, she would prepare Jason to study medicine. She asked around and was told medical schools in the United States were the most advanced in science and technology.

That was fortuitous because she wanted to emigrate with him so that she could fulfill her lifelong dream of living the American way of life.

She decided to make a trip to San Francisco where Judy and Andrew had moved to a few years earlier. She planned to buy a home there, and enroll Jason to study in a junior college in the city. That turned out to be last thing she did for him during her time on Earth.

*

The Chinese nickname for San Francisco was Old Gold Mountain, no doubt owing its origin to history when it was the point of entry for Chinese laborers imported for the Gold Rush dating back to the nineteenth century.

Judy Fung and Andrew Chu found their pot of gold when they went there to open a restaurant. They were the reason Mary picked that city for Jason's schooling.

Jason couldn't go with her because he still had a few things to wrap up before high school finally came to an end for him. He accompanied her to Kai Tak airport, and for the first time they would be apart for more than a few hours in all of his life.

At the departure gate, Mary used her hand to tidy Jason's hair, and seeing tears welling up in her eyes, he let her do it for as long as she wanted without protesting. All the time, she was giving him detailed instructions for his daily activities while holding his hand.

Jason was patient with her, as always, and promised to follow the routine she prescribed for him, including what he'd eat for his three meals, his exercise regimen, and vitamin supplements. He knew where to find his pocket money, and he must not go to Tsim Sha Tsui when she wasn't around. He was beaten up there once, and she did not want to have one more thing to worry about while she traveled so far away.

Air travel was only beginning to become popular in Hong Kong, and it was Mary's first overseas trip. An old colleague from King George happened to be on the same flight. She was well aware of Mary's heart problem. She was a frequent traveler and she helped Mary with getting more comfortable on the plane by asking the flight attendant to put Mary in a row with empty seats and close to the lavatory. After arriving at San Francisco International Airport, she also helped Mary with the many forms which she had to fill out. Mary was able to get through immigration almost hassle-free.

Judy and Andrew, now married, collected her from the airport and they went straight to Chinatown, where their restaurant Dragon Inn was located. They had prepared a ten-

63

course meal for Mary. They grew up together, so they knew exactly what Mary's favourite dishes were. They were easy with the salt and soy sauce, knowing her heart condition.

Mary discussed with them her plans for Jason. He was to study two years in the City College of San Francisco, in preparation for getting into an Ivy League university followed by a prestigious medical school, if things were to go according to plan.

He planned to live in the hostel but Mary had to look for an apartment in the city for Jason to live in during school breaks and also for herself to stay during her visits. She wanted him to live close to Dragon Inn so that Judy and Andrew could take care of him. Judy told Mary they should make him come to their restaurant every weekend – that way, he could at least enjoy some "home cooking" once a week.

Mary purchased a modest apartment on Bush Street in San Francisco's Chinatown two blocks from Dragon Inn, and left it with Judy to furnish. She then went to the City College to see the dean.

Mrs Cunningham, the English teacher from King George's Secondary School, knew him well and had highly recommended Jason to him. The school had already agreed to take Jason, after looking at his test scores and birth certificate sent to them a while ago, and it was mere formality for Mary to fill in all the necessary papers. It was agreed that Jason should attend an interview whenever he arrived at San Francisco, preferably no later than a week before the start of the school year.

Mary was not worried about Jason not doing well in school, she was more concerned about him not getting used to living on his own. Andrew and Judy volunteered to be his surrogate parents in her absence.

She opened a bank account with the Wells Fargo Bank in Jason's name, and the trust in Hong Kong would direct more than enough money into the account each year.

All that taken care of, there was only one thing left for Mary to do. She wanted to look up the man who took her virginity and ran off to California.

She had been heartbroken for a long time after Kyle left her, and had vowed to meet him again one day. While she was in Old Gold Mountain preparing for Jason's schooling, she figured it could be her "it's now or never" moment, given her deteriorating heart condition.

From the few letters Kyle sent her, she knew they had moved to California, where he took up a teaching job in a community college in the Bay Area. She took a bus to that neighbourhood, and checked into a small Holiday Inn close to the community college.

She wondered if he was still teaching there, and she felt ambivalent about seeing him again after all those years.

First, she needed to find out if he was still there before she could decide on her next move.

After a light dinner of soup and salad, she went for a walk in the neighbourhood to snoop around. She became tired and breathless after a short walk, so she stopped by a nearby pub to sit down and rest.

Everyone seemed to know everyone else there, except for her. She felt out of place, and was ready to call for her tab and leave when the receptionist of the Holiday Inn came in and sat next to her without invitation. The receptionist had orange hair, and was dressed flamboyantly. She was also the friendly and busybody type, and she wanted to know everything about Mary. They started to chat.

Mary told her she came to visit the fabulous Bay area landscape and architecture, and to experience the world famous California hospitality. She told Mary she had come to the right place. When Mary mentioned a friend by the name of Sanders and the community college, she told Mary again she had come to the right place. She knew everyone in the neighbourhood, including all the teachers at the College. Poor Mrs Elizabeth Sanders, who used to teach journalism at the school, and such a nice woman, too, died of ovarian cancer one and a half years earlier. And Mr Sanders just couldn't wait to remarry, to a former student thirty years his junior. There were rumours that she was already two months in the family way when they took off to Mexico for their honeymoon last month. By the way, Kyle Sanders's favourite watering hole was the restaurant in the next street, where he had lunch every weekday between one and two.

Mary finished the half pint of apple cider and went back to the hotel to rest.

The next day Mary arrived at Kyle's favourite lunch joint half an hour before one. It was actually a restaurant-cum-bar, with the bar tucked in the back, and the restaurant area occupying the front and the sides. She asked if she could look around first. The bar was dark and stuffy, and stank of stale tobacco. The restaurant area was spacious, green, and bright from natural light. She remembered Kyle didn't smoke and hated the smell of it, so it was likely he'd pick a window seat in the front as far away from the bar area as possible. She chose a table at the back of the restaurant halfway behind a pillar, where she could see everyone walking in and yet people walking in couldn't easily see her. She ordered iced tea and a ham and cheese sandwich.

Kyle walked in right on time at one. He had a receding hairline and appeared shorter than she remembered him to be, but was still quite handsome. His eyes were still intensely blue. He seated himself at a small table by the window, just as she had predicted.

She was thinking: What if he didn't even remember me?

Unlikely.

She'd like to think she was the only underage Chinese girl he deflowered during his few years in Hong Kong. He worked full time, and he had spent all his spare time "doing" her. On top of all that, he also had a wife to go home to. He couldn't possibly find any more time to pursue other love interests.

She had to be the only one.

She debated with herself whether to approach the table when he was ordering food from the young waitress. Mary watched their interchange and detected definite flirting on his part – and this from a man who had recently lost one wife and gained another. Somehow, talking to him was not so appealing anymore.

Shakespeare said it best: "Sigh no more, ladies, sigh no more, Men were deceivers ever, – One foot in the sea and one on shore, To one thing constant never."

She thought perhaps she should simply let him remember her as a bright-eyed fresh-faced pretty young thing, like that young bubbly waitress waiting on his table, and not the sickly "old lady" she had become.

Mary sat there reminiscing about her childhood and teenage years, and the days of being wild, including those spent with a man who used to be more than twice her age, whom she hadn't seen for more than twenty years and now sitting less than twenty feet away.

She watched Kyle until it was almost two o'clock when he called for the tab and abruptly left after paying.

11

Mary took the next bus back to San Francisco, and put the finishing touches on decorating her new apartment. She put in place some of her personal items, including a group photo of her and all the other graduates from Po Leung Kuk, taken at their high school graduation. The rest were Jason's valediction and graduation photos, and a collage of his photos growing up.

She wondered if looking at those photos would make Jason's life in the US less homesick, or more.

Looking at those photos made her a little homesick. It had been fewer than ten days in the US but she missed Hong Kong already. She especially missed Jason. She had her return ticket back to Hong Kong for the next day. For the rest of the time, she spent with Judy shopping for daily necessities for Jason's use. She didn't buy anything for herself, and Judy asked her why? Mary said it was because she hadn't made up her mind yet whether to come with Jason to live in San Francisco. Deep inside she was wondering: Will I live long enough to make a second trip back here?

She was prescient.

The plane ride on her return from San Francisco was particularly crowded. It was early June, and many university students were going back home to Hong Kong for the summer. Mary had a window seat and a large man who had too much to drink at the airport took up the aisle seat. He tried to engage Mary in an obnoxious conversation about the greatness of the British Empire, and she wasn't feeling well.

The big man fell asleep soon after take-off, and Mary didn't feel like waking him up to get out in case he'd launch into another diatribe. She was having cramps in her legs and she was hoping to stretch her legs walking around a bit but instead she stayed in her seat and slowly massaged her calves until she too fell asleep.

She woke up with a dull ache in her chest and much difficulty in breathing. She pressed the help button. It took quite a while for the flight attendant to show up.

By then Mary could hardly speak. Even in the dim cabin light, her face appeared ashen and her lips purple.

A medical doctor on board came over to help. The big man was asked to move and Mary was able to rest her legs on the empty seat next to her.

The doctor, after getting the medical history and a brief physical examination, diagnosed Mary as having severe heart failure, possibly complicated by a blood clot from her leg that went to her lungs – a medical condition known as deep vein thrombosis leading to pulmonary embolism. The blood clot that went to her lungs aggravated her heart failure beyond control.

The plane was two hours from landing at Hong Kong's Kai Tak Airport, and all they could do was to give her an oxygen mask and additional doses of Digoxin and Lasix.

The pilots radioed ahead and an ambulance would be waiting on the tarmac upon landing.

They sent someone to meet Jason at the arrival gate, and he was told to go the hospital to see his mother.

The ambulance took Mary directly from the airport to Queen Elizabeth Hospital, where the medical staff knew her well.

Jason rushed to be by his mother's side in the emergency room. She had so much to talk to him about, but she was so breathless she could hardly finish a sentence without gasping for air. She saw tears in Jason's eyes. She reached over to wipe them away. She hated to see him sad.

The staff pushed Mary's stretcher into a large cubicle specially equipped for cardiac emergencies and they ordered Jason to wait outside. Mary wanted Jason to be with her because she knew her time was running out. She protested, in vain. The ER staff pulled the curtain to the cubicle shut and the last Mary saw of Jason was a lanky bespectacled young man with messy brown hair straining his neck to peek at his dying mother.

He looked worried and helpless. Mary was heartbroken. They had each other for so long and yet not long enough; and she didn't want him to be ever alone.

At that moment, Mary was worried sick about him, even though she should have been more worried about herself dying.

The specialists at the hospital agreed with the diagnosis made by the doctor on the plane. They worked frenetically to save Mary, but her heart just couldn't cope with the extra burden of having a blood clot blocking the circulation to her lungs.

When Mary's heart stopped beating, the "code blue" was announced, and a whole team of cardiac arrest experts started to work on Mary.

They tried for almost half an hour, before the physician-in-charge at the emergency room who led the CPR team ordered a halt to the resuscitation efforts. They had tried everything, including injecting adrenalin directly into Mary's heart twice and applying the defibrillator three times. The nurse who was giving the cardiac massage was exhausted. Mary's chest wall was bruised and crushed from fractured ribs – a common complication from prolonged and overzealous cardiac massage. They pulled out all the tubes and needles from her. A nurse then pulled up a clean white sheet and covered her from head to toe.

The physician-in-charge asked for the patient's chart and wrote on it: "All resuscitation efforts failed. Patient pronounced dead at 23:13 hours. Provisional cause of death: Cardiac failure secondary to pulmonary embolism and chronic rheumatic heart disease. Coroner's office to be notified."

Someone who died at that relatively young age, after becoming morbidly sick while traveling on an airplane would definitely be required by law to have an autopsy to document the cause of death. That formality was of no concern to Mary, who was dead way before they stopped all those futile resuscitation measures.

Mary felt no pain or discomfort after her heart had stopped and her brain had ceased to function. She was up there looking down while a group of people congregated around her bed making a fuss over her. She could "see" them covering her closed eyes with a white sheet. Soon she felt like floating in air as she moved further and further away from the emergency room scene and all the noises there. In her solipsistic view, she had always wondered – when she died, would the whole world die with her? Because every time she fell asleep, the whole world went to sleep with her, did it not?

However, there were dreams when she slept and dreams were supposed to be associated with specific brain activities in tandem with the telltale neuromuscular phenomenon known as rapid eye movements (REMs).When people are dead, so are their brains; hence, there should be total darkness without dreams or REMs, complete unconsciousness, absolute exclusion from worldly affairs, and forever.

However, Mary continued to exist. It was not like dreaming. It was a different kind of existence. She lost her physical presence and power, but she was aware of what was going on around her without the conventional five human senses. She could see without eyes, hear without ears, and communicate without her voice. She also retained her memory.

Not long after she passed away, there were frequent flashbacks of her life.

The harsh years in the Po Leung Kuk Orphanage brought back only warm feelings, especially those related to the camaraderie she shared with best friend and fellow orphanage dweller Jane Chan, but no bad feelings of the hardships there.

She thought of John MacFadzean, Jason's father and the love of her life. He was the melancholic and debonair type, tall and handsome, and so drop-dead gorgeous in his three-piece suits made by the famous Indian tailor Ravi in Tsim Sha Tsui and his silk ties from Gieves and Hawkes.

She cherished those wonderful nights John came to her flat and made love to her tenderly. She used to read over and over again John's letters and postcards he sent from Scotland where he and his other family spent every summer and Christmas.

There were many memories with Jason in the picture. They used to practice pronunciation together while listening to BBC news on the radio. Jason was just so much smarter. He nailed the accent and the nuance of the BBC tongue within months. How excited Jason was every time she promised to take him to the library to look up science questions neither one of them had answers to. They talked about everything while hiking in the country parks around the Lion Rock. All the teachers at King George's Secondary School where Jason attended had nothing but good things to say about him. She was so proud of him. She remembered every word of Jason's high school valediction speech. She could still hear the applause resonating in the background.

She missed Jason so much. She started to pray. She never believed in any gods, not since her teenage years when all her dreams were unfulfilled. But like everyone else, she prayed when desperate; and she was desperate to continue to care for Jason.

No gods showed up; Mother Nature did.

Mary was new to her bardo, but she was not timid or shy when it somehow involved her son. She immediately complained to Mother Nature about her hard life before she died, and the hardest part was having to leave her son to fend for himself before he became a mature person. Mother Nature said she knew all about it. The reason she was talking with Mary was to tell her she would be compensated for her unhappy life by the bestowal of three wishes she could use to foster a happier life for her son.

Mary was immensely grateful. That was the greatest gift she could ever hope for. Imagine – not one, but three wishes.

One particular song came to her mind: 'Three Coins in a Fountain'. In the original story, legend had it if one threw a coin into the Trevi Fountain and made a wish to come back to Rome, the return would be guaranteed. But in the story only one of the three coins had worked.

Mary was thinking: If I make all three wishes to come back to life, maybe one of them will work?

Then, Mother Nature's instructions were clear. Apart from using the wishes only for specific events related to Jason and not harming anyone else, also the law of nature must not be contravened. Mary was dreaming when she thought she could come back to life using the three wishes. Mary was a big dreamer when alive. Once a dreamer, always a dreamer.

When she stopped dreaming, she had to face reality, which was to agonize over Jason for a large part of his adulthood because of his vulnerability. Jason was what the Americans would call "a straight arrow". He was a meek and gentle soul. He had great integrity, generosity, kindness, and grace, and probably all the other virtues known to humankind. But that caused him problems – he became a soft target for bullies and people seeking to take advantage of his extraordinarily good nature.

Mary had another worry in her afterlife – that Jason would be alone and desolate when he became old. She was an orphan and he was the only child; hence, he had no relatives to speak of. And he was not inclined to make close friends. It would soon become quite clear that Jason was a diehard asexual; hence the chance of him having children was close to zero.

Not long after death, Mary was already under constant pressure worrying about her son's well-being.

The three wishes from Mother Nature were precious, and squandering anyone of them would be much regretted. That turned out to be quite a challenge for Mary in her afterlife. With Jason's life in the US full of trials and tribulations, she had to resist the impulse to use them whenever Jason was in any distress. She had to choose the occasion wisely and the timing had to be perfect. She knew she had plenty of work cut out for her ahead.

12

Mary took a break from her ongoing worries and remembrances, when she became aware it was the day of her funeral. She wanted to be there. She wanted to know how Jason was coping.

"Always go to your own funeral, otherwise no one else will." Was it Yogi Berra who said that?

She descended among the crowd around her grave in the Catholic cemetery located in Lai Chi Kok in West Kowloon. The people gathered there were mostly friends from Po Leung Kuk and King George's. Jane was there directing the traffic and setting the agenda. Judy and Andrew had taken leave from their restaurant to attend the funeral. Some of Jason's classmates from King George's came by to pay their respects. Many of the teachers were there, too.

They were about to cover the coffin with soil. Fifty or so people stood around with their heads bowed while the minister delivered the eulogy. There was not a dry eye there and Andrew was wailing. Jason stood in the front facing the minister. Tears streamed down his cheeks. Mary knew what he was thinking: Mother has devoted herself to raising me and now that she is gone, I am on my own. And worst of all, I can never reciprocate the selfless love she has given me throughout my life.

"Regrets could be the greatest source of misery for humankind," someone wise once said.

Mary wanted to tell Jason not to be sad and that she was still around, but he could not hear her. Jason's hair was a mess, and she tried smoothing it out, but her phantom hands could not touch him.

Mary was overwhelmed with grief witnessing her son's distress.

"What do I have to do to be able to communicate with my son?" she pleaded with Mother Nature.

"Let me live a few more years, please," she continued. "Wait until Jason has become a grown man, and then I can die a thousand deaths. Let that be my first wish."

There was no response.

She should not have asked for anything that contravened the law of nature. She had already died. Nothing could be done to reverse that.

Mary came to her senses quickly. "Sorry. I shouldn't have…that was stupid, it won't happen again," she said while sobbing.

Among many reasons to be sad, Mary was particularly not pleased that, on her death, Jason qualified as an orphan because technically he was still a minor and both his parents were gone. Mary knew how being an orphan felt like, and she wished not the same ordeal and misery for Jason.

Unfortunately, orphanages seemed to run in the Lee family.

*

Jason was like a zombie for weeks after his mother's death. Jane took over his life. Jane consoled him as much as she could, when she was not breaking down herself. She gave him a copy of Mary's will, which stated that she owned many millions of dollars' worth of properties and stocks and she had left everything to him.

Jane insisted that from then on, she would be his de facto mother. Jason must not leave her out on anything he intended to do. She reminded him once again that she changed his diapers many times when he was a baby. Jason would turn seventeen soon – the age of majority by law, and theoretically, he could take care of his own finances and other matters. Jane suggested retaining the trustees Mary had hired to continue managing his finances, and Jane would make sure that they were all from reputable banks and accountancy firms. The most important thing for Jason was to continue with his brilliant academic endeavors. He could do his mother, and, for that matter, Jane and all his mother's friends proud by becoming a famous scholar.

It was almost time for Jason to start school in California. Jane helped him pack and made all the travel arrangements.

Weeks before, Malcolm – the lawyer who rescued Mary from the MacFadzean widow's lawyers – had sorted out all the probate matters. They were not sure exactly how much money Mary had left him, but it would be substantial since both the property market and the Hang Seng Index, an indicator of Hong Kong's stock market, had skyrocketed since Mary had inherited the fortune from John.

Jason wanted to leave their small Kowloon Tong apartment where he grew up in exactly the way it was, especially his mother's bedroom and belongings. Jane could take care of it while he was away. When Jason came back to town to visit, he wanted to stay in his old bedroom.

All that settled, Jason left for San Francisco to begin his long and lonely journey leading to a new life on foreign soil. Mary followed him, and watched him like a hawk. When to apply her wishes would be her biggest challenge.

The year was 1976.

13

Andrew and Judy met Jason at the airport.

Dragon Inn was always the first stop before going anywhere else – to have a meal, even though Jason was tired and jet-lagged and not hungry at all.

During the meal, Judy pointed out all Mary's favourite dishes: Grandma's pork, General Tso's fried chicken, Shunde fish, and butterfly prawns. That didn't lift anyone's spirit.

After the meal, they took Jason back to the apartment his mother had recently purchased. Jason kept Mary's room the way it was. He would use the spare room. The only additional furniture he needed was a giant bookshelf. His books, the vanity, and the wooden man zhuang were being shipped from Hong Kong, and would arrive in a month or so. Andrew showed up the next day to introduce the city to Jason. An interview with the dean of the City College of San Francisco was scheduled for the following Monday.

*

Students at the San Francisco College were mature and at least above average academically, all striving to obtain a solid education leading to a good career. Childish bullying was unheard of.

Jason picked pre-med subjects including biology, biochemistry, and other health sciences. He remained the selfless nerd who was more than willing to help his fellow students in their studies. The lanky Hong Kong Eurasian boy with the rumpled hair, big glasses, and the posh BBC accent fascinated all his classmates. Many were curious about him, and wanted to befriend him. He was polite to everyone but intimate with none.

He declined socializing with fellow students outside of school. He was afraid of having to deal with girls akin to Rachel.

During weekends and holidays, the hostel emptied as students returned home to visit relatives and friends. Jason also left, to seek solace in his apartment on Bush Street and he spent time reading and staring at the photos, or practicing kungfu with his sparring partner, the wooden man zhuang.

He also spent a lot of time at the Dragon Inn, to be with Judy and Andrew. He felt close to his surrogate parents because they reminded him of his mother, all Hong Kong orphans raised in Po Leung Kuk.

Jason spent his time reading in the bar area. Many Chinese restaurants all over America had bars, to milk more money from customers waiting for a table. Dragon Inn was so busy the bar area was always packed with customers. Jason felt bad doing nothing while everyone else was running around working like ants around cookie crumbs. He volunteered to work as a bartender.

Like everything else Jason engaged in, bartending became an academic exercise. Within hours, he memorized the recipes of all the drinks menu concoctions.

He turned out to be a good worker for Andrew and Judy. He was hardworking and courteous, and communicated well with the customers, who all refused to believe he came from Hong Kong and insisted that he was born and raised in England. How else to explain his BBC accent?

They loved to hear how Jason pronounced certain words the British way. They would call all their friends over and asked Jason: "Tell them what pills you take so that you don't get that funny headache."

Jason obliged every time. "I take vee-tamins in the morning to prevent having mee-graines in the afternoon," he said, with an exaggerated accent.

The customers howled in laughter and slapped their thighs before ordering another round of drinks.

Judy pulled Jason aside. "Don't let them laugh at you like that. I know you can say those words the American way."

Jason said he didn't mind a little harmless teasing. He was simply entertaining them by telling them what they wanted to hear. Moreover, it was good for business. Jason – always the sweetie pie.

Jason also found out the quickest way to become a popular bartender was to be more generous with the alcohol portion of the drinks. Whenever Jason was behind the bar, the tips box would be full before the night was over. Instead of pocketing the tips like other bartenders, Jason insisted on handing over all the money to his godmother at the end of each shift. The part-time job at the Dragon Inn was a diversion for Jason, not work.

Judy and Andrew had no children of their own, and they were happy to have someone like Jason to lecture and to pamper. They were not as bossy as Jane, but they were over the top in teaching Jason how to live his life in the US. Jason knew they meant well, and tolerated them and their endless lectures.

They thought that Jason might be homesick for Hong Kong, so they paid and arranged air travel for him to visit Jane the following summer with the understanding that he could help them in procuring some exotic Chinese herbs and spices and other special foodstuffs not readily available in America. They handed him a long grocery list to pass on to Jane. Jane would later pack up all the stuff they needed in a suitcase for Jason to carry back.

Jason had no close friends or relatives in Hong Kong or America, and his schoolmates were all studying in U.K., but at least he could consider Jane, Judy and Andrew family, and that was a small comfort for Mary.

14

Jason did miss Hong Kong, with all the hustle and bustle in Tsim Sha Tsui, and the tranquility of the hiking trails around the Lion Rock where he and his mother used to roam. He returned to visit two years in a row. In later years, he couldn't always pull himself away from New York, because of his numerous problems, and was able to visit regularly only when he became a much older man.

Whenever he visited in the earlier years, Jane took him to the trustees' office to receive a status report of his inheritance which grew significantly year after year. The properties he inherited were worth ten times more than when Mary first bought them years before, and the blue chip stock prices also increased in value many times. The rental income and share dividends were reinvested into property stocks, which were star performers among the blue chips.

Jane kept asking Jason if he had any girlfriends in America and teased him that many girls would want to marry him because of his money. Jason told her he didn't want to think about girls until he became established as a doctor. Little did she know girls were always furthest from Jason's mind.

Jason spent his summer breaks in Hong Kong studying in the Central Library and walking the Lion Rock trails. If Colin and Rachel happened to be in town, they would meet in Jane's bar, so that they could drink themselves silly and raise hell, and Jason could catch up on the latest with all their classmates and teachers from King George's.

Jane also had the chance to lecture him and mother him, just like in the good old days.

He enjoyed some solitude in his Broadcast Drive apartment, where he stayed in Mary's bedroom to read, and went back to his own bedroom to sleep.

*

When he was in his last year of junior college, he talked to many people to help him decide where to go and what to do next. Most students, especially the Chinese from California, preferred Berkley or UCLA, to be close to home. A few Jewish students were applying to attend the Yeshiva University in New York City. They bragged to Jason that it was the best university in the world. Jason dug out extensive information on the Yeshiva University from the library and thought it suited him perfectly.

Yeshiva University had separate colleges for its male and female undergraduate students. Men went to the Yeshiva and women went to the Stern; hence no need to worry about sex being imposed on him. It had highly selective and secular postgraduate schools including the Albert Einstein College of Medicine, which ran a fast-track medicine program requiring only three years of pre-med studies followed by three years of medical training. It suited him because he was terribly bored of the slow pace of the junior college curriculum. The academic environment also suited him because many of the students were orthodox Jews, who were unlikely to organize toga parties or be involved with frat-boy shenanigans.

His mind was so set on studying there that he took the trouble of studying Torah Umadda, the orthodox Jewish philosophy closely associated with the Yeshiva University, so that during the prospective interview he could at least show his deep interest in and respect for the University.

He got his interview with Yeshiva, showed off his knowledge of Torah Umadda, and his application was successful. He chose to major in psychology.

His life became hectic the moment he relocated from the Old Gold Mountain to the Big Apple.

He brought with him the wooden man zhuang and the vanity.

The main campus of the Yeshiva was in Washington Heights in upper Manhattan, home to academics, artists, bohemians, and many new immigrants, especially those from the Dominican Republic.

For the first year, he lived in a hostel. His roommate was Leroy Katz, a star wrestler for the university team. The jock was the opposite of Jason, all brawls and no brain. He was heavily drenched in testosterone, so much so that he often had to sneak girlfriends into their room, as he put it, to let off some steam. To give him privacy, Jason would spend the night in the hostel's all-night study room. He studied for half the night and slept on the sofa there until dawn. When other hostel residents saw Jason with a stack of books and a toothbrush heading towards the study room, they all knew Leroy was having some action that night.

Leroy felt bad about making Jason spend numerous nights on a sofa, and offered to compensate him by arranging a session of group sex in their room. Jason didn't know whether to cry or to laugh at his offer, and declined the favour in a hurry.

Jason was definitely "different", staying in the hostel all year round with no social life to speak of. He studied hard, followed a routine and never did anything wrong or exciting.

Mary was watching over him, but often slipped away to some bijou cinemas to watch re-runs of old movies, or to Las Vegas to listen to some old crooners singing golden oldies. Her taste in music and cinematography remained stuck in the fifties and sixties. Her body died, but her passions lived on. She still relished watching re-runs of Hollywood classics such as *West Side Story*, *Gone with the Wind*, *The Sound of Music*, *Casablanca* and all the other Bogart movies. And all the Hitchcock and old James Bond flicks. Nevertheless, she preferred watching just about any movie over Jason with his books.

Jason was still celibate. Many students studied hard all day long, but they all managed to have a bit of sexual relief. The Stern College for Women was only a few subway stops away, and the students from Yeshiva socialized with Stern students often, but not Jason.

Albert Einstein College of Medicine was not easy to get into. To improve on one's chances, one had to be an insider – children of alumni, and those deeply religious in the Jewish faith, or somehow involved in the Yeshiva community. Jason only had the option of doing volunteer work in one of the faculties in the

Yeshiva network. He opted to volunteer in the Psychology Department.

One of the professors was Leona Koch. She taught a course in dementia. Jason enrolled in her course and found her knowledgeable and articulate. She was older and matronly, kind and gentle. He decided to volunteer for her. Was Jason subconsciously looking for a surrogate mother?

He approached the Professor and asked if he could help her in any of her research projects. Professor Leona Koch was happy to have some free labour and arranged to have Jason participate in a project in which elderly people were screened for early signs of dementia. That was how he first developed an interest in Alzheimer's disease.

There is a pre-ordained blueprint for everyone's life. Jason was destined to go to New York City, study at Yeshiva, volunteer for Professor Koch who happened to be a researcher on Alzheimer's disease, and later, Jason would study at Albert Einstein College of Medicine and research on Alzheimer as well, and because of his research success, become entangled in a legal wrangle which would cause him misery and frustration for more than ten years of his professional life, and consume a large portion of his inheritance money. Nothing could change the blueprint, or any of the seminal events in his life.

Also in the blueprint was where he chose to live. His neighbourhood was where he met someone special who later became his lady friend.

Jason decided to buy his own place after the first year at Yeshiva. He needed privacy and more room. He could rent, but property prices in the city were rising fast, and he knew he would be in New York City for the long haul.

Leroy the wrestler was getting more and more out of control. His hormone suppression sessions could last for days and Jason had no access to what he needed, for example, books and clean clothes. When he walked into their shared dorm room to get things, he would find two or more naked bodies engaged in carnal knowledge at different stages.

He called Jane for advice and Jane told him it was never wrong to buy a property if the buyer was going to live in it. Money from the trustees would be on the way.

He liked the Washington Heights neighbourhood, and picked a modest penthouse in a walk up low-rise building. He converted the upper floor into a study and sent for his books from Hong Kong and San Francisco, hundreds of them, and the lower floor became his living quarters. He placed Mary's vanity next to his bed, using it as his nightstand. That was odd for a grown man, but nobody had ever accused Jason of being normal. The wooden man zhuang went to a small exercise room connected to his study.

His downstairs neighbours were all academics and artists. No one in the building was a normal heterosexual.

The ground floor couple were lesbians. They bickered all day long like an old married couple. They owned a tattoo parlor down the street and they advertised their business using their own bodies as billboards. The younger one left Jason alone. The older one found out Jason was a pre-med student and she consulted Jason about her myriad ailments. Jason told her he was nowhere near having a license to practice medicine, and advised her to go to Columbia Medical Center nearby. She said she hated visiting doctors, but felt better just talking about her problems with someone. By the way, for his trouble, she'd give Jason a big discount if he was interested in having any tattoos, which she called body art. Jason said thanks but no thanks.

The second floor male gay couple were academics at New York University. Like most New Yorkers, they didn't talk to neighbours. They kept to themselves and never made any noise. They were always engaged in some kind of strenuous exercise: biking, roller-skating, going to the gym or on a ski trip.

The third floor resident was a tall black man with tits. He worked on Broadway, but nobody knew in what capacity. In the summer months, he liked to wear see-through sleeveless shirts, heavy make-up and a pair of bright red heels to prance through the neighbourhood. He winked at Jason every time they met, and Jason gave him a wide berth whenever they happened to be in the same area.

Having his own home at the end of his first year at Yeshiva College was timely because the second and third years were crucial in his acceptance into the medical school. All at once, he had privacy and no distractions, allowing him to concentrate on his academic pursuits. Not only did he need to excel in his undergrad studies, he was also expected to hand in a dissertation paper of some substance.

In spite of his tight schedule, he continued his volunteer work with Professor Koch in designing an algorithm to diagnose early senile dementia associated with Alzheimer's disease. He spent a few hours a week in her clinic. He also spent time interviewing elderly attendees at the Social Center for senior citizens in Washington Heights and collected data from them for Professor Koch.

The volunteer work required a lot of patience and organizational skills, personal traits Jason was born with. It involved asking old people questions and recording their answers according to a pre-set protocol.

Professor Koch was happy with Jason's work and was impressed with his ability to amass a huge amount of information in a short time. His volunteer work within the Yeshiva network would gain him brownie points when it was time to apply to Albert Einstein College of Medicine after three years of undergrad studies. It also helped his grades, and his dissertation on Alzheimer's disease.

15

Alzheimer's disease is possibly the most malicious malady afflicting humanity.

With it, you lose your memory. You also lose your dignity, intellect, free will, capacity to have fun, and physical independence. You impose insurmountable hardship on your devoted family members. More often than not, though, there is nobody devoted enough to care for you long term, and eventually you are likely to be abused and humiliated, cheated out of your money and other valuable belongings, before you are neglected and left to die a slow, lonely death.

It is a fascinating disease to study, though, because memory and its loss are the least understood natural phenomena in humankind. Jason became intrigued and fascinated by it while having contact with many Alzheimer patients taking part in Dr Koch's research.

Instead of picking an easy subject to do research on, as would most undergrad students, Jason chose a difficult one. Like most asexual people, Jason was eccentric to the max.

Jason wanted to make Alzheimer's disease his life-long study, and he realized that if he wanted to truly understand Alzheimer's, he needed first to crack the code on the three stages of memory: encoding, storage and retrieval, before he could discover how it could be lost.

The title of his dissertation for his pre-med studies was: Changes in the patterns of ionic signals generated by neurons' membrane potentials in the limbic system of the human brain and their relationship with memory loss in Alzheimer's disease.

Academics like to use difficult technical terms and phrases to scare and impress lay people. The same dissertation in lay language could have been: Loss of electrical signals in the midbrain is related to loss of memory in Alzheimer's disease.

The dissertation was forty thousand words long and full of technical details.

He first described the relationship between memory loss and Alzheimer's disease, and summarized the theories of memory retention available from the scientific literature. He then proposed his own theory of memory retention, and in theory, how memories could be extracted from the brain by electronic equipment and a computer.

*

A simple way for doctors to diagnose the disease is to test the patient's memory by asking him or her simple questions. The more demented the person, the more outrageous the answer. It's not unusual for some senile old chap to think today's leader is still Mao Zedong or JFK. That is how the doctor knows he has a serious case of Alzheimer's on his hand.

The gradual decline of memory is part of aging. Memory ability peaks in one's twenties, levels off, then declines steeply in one's eighties.

For Alzheimer patients, the decline occurs at a much younger age and at a faster pace.

The onset of memory loss in Alzheimer's disease is accompanied by anatomical changes in the brain. A harmful protein called the amyloid starts to accumulate among the brain cells, forming what the neuroscientists call tangles and plaques because that's what they look like under the electron microscope. They replace normal tissues, and as a result, the brain shrinks, and its normal functions including memory retention are severely impaired.

The memories to go first are generally the most recent ones. In the earlier stages of the disease, Alzheimer patients can actually recall events from their teenage years, even though they cannot remember what they had for lunch a few hours ago.

How memory is encoded, stored, and recalled has baffled scientists for centuries.

While it is easier to correlate brain structures and their mechanics to many tangible human activities such as moving an arm or seeing an object, it is always a challenge to correlate the brain's anatomy and physiology to abstract functions such as emotion, logic, intelligence, and the most intriguing of all, memory.

Some scientists theorize that the brain is holographic when it comes to memory retention, that is, it is first recorded, and then reproduced on demand by reconstructing many tiny bits put together into the whole picture, like a hologram. This theory is based on experiments done on primitive creatures such as the salamander. Scientists slice and dice its brain and then put it back into its original space in its head, and the salamander can still remember simple tasks it had learned before the experiment. It would be hard to imagine the same can be applied to the human brain, though.

Some scientists even go as far as saying that all memories are stored in a universal bank outside the brain, like the computer-age concept of storing data in iCloud or Dropbox.

This theory was partly based on anecdotes of young children who recalled "previous lives" in another community, and quoted well-documented events and names of persons from bygone days that were far too accurate to be discounted as guesswork or coincidence.

For example, a six year old boy in a small village in India told a visitor from another village 200 miles away that he used to be Ravi, the oldest son of a rich man named K. K. Abuja in the same village the visitor came from, and a few years ago he was strangled by his younger brother and buried behind their grandmother Tilo's grave, and that was why he disappeared one day. He had not fled in shame because he stole his mother Nina's jewelry box – his brother's version of the story. His brother had also buried the jewelry box near his body, planning to dig it out after Abuja Sr. died, when the younger brother would inherit everything.

The visitor remembered the case well from ten years before, and the names of the family were well-known. When he went back to his village, he related what he heard to the police chief, and they started digging and lo and behold, discovered the body and the jewelry box just like how the young boy described it. Some people believe stories like that are definitive proof of reincarnation.

These children tend to lose their memories of their "previous lives" when they grow older.

However, some scientists theorize that there are pockets of memories "floating around" and certain people are susceptible to incorporate these errant memories into their own memory bank. Proponents of this theory think the so-called evidence of reincarnation based on memories of a "previous life" is merely a re-hash of old memories from a universal memory bank trapped accidentally in a random person, especially the kind of person inclined to take in such errant memories, such as a small child.

*

There are numerous other theories related to memory encoding, storage, and recall.

The fact that there are so many theories to explain how memory works is proof that we don't know for sure how it does.

*

Other intangible functions of the brain, such as love, hate, anger, logic, intelligence, wisdom are usually used one-off during separate events, but memories can be recalled repeatedly, sometimes a countless number of times, and considering the vast range and depth of one's memory bank, the capacity for their storage must be huge.

Memories are known to be imperfect – easily lost, skewed, biased, mistaken, and faded with time. Yet all humans need this ability to survive.

Despite the obscurity of this poorly understood mental function, there is no doubt that human beings need certain anatomical parts of their brains to remember things. Scientists have figured out the physical sites in the brain responsible for memory by default. If a disease destroys a certain part of the brain, or if a disease requires the surgical removal of a specific structure of the brain, and as a result, deprives the patient of the ability to remember things, then the significance of that particular part of the brain for memory retention becomes obvious. All the available evidence derived from such experiences points to the fact that the brain's memory functions are carried out in a part of the midbrain called the limbic system.

The limbic system is located at the lower border of the cerebral cortex. It consists of three main parts: the hippocampus, the basal ganglia, and the amygdala.

The hippocampus is important for remembering events; the basal ganglia for remembering skills, such as swimming or riding a bike; and the amygdala for remembering emotional encounters, such as those marked by sadness, happiness or fear. That is why damages to different parts of the limbic brain can result in different kinds of memory loss.

*

Jason presented his own hypothesis as to how memories were stored. He surmised that the way the brain worked to retain memory was analogous to the working of the computer. Facts, events, and images were stored as bundles and stacks of data encoded by various combinations of positive and negative ionic charges which were emitted by the membrane potentials on the surface of neurons, the main cells of the brain.. These messages could be recalled deliberately or spontaneously by a trigger centre located in the limbic brain. The capacity of the neurons for this particular function is huge, since the human brain has 100 billion of them.

There were basically two types of memory – long term and short term. Short term memories lasted for eight hours or so, and were erased unless converted into long term ones. The hippocampus was the centre where all memories were processed before storage – a process known to scientist as consolidation. Memories deemed short-term were deleted and the ionic signals were wiped out in the hippocampus by neutralizing ionic impulses. Memories deemed worth saving (long term) were encoded and the signals were stabilized and protected by a shield of crisscrossing energy, encasing the matrix of neurons in the limbic system. Given that memories could be recalled at the speed of light, these encoded data must have been stored superficially on the cell surface of the limbic system and not buried inside the neurons. Memories were coded long sequences of ionic charges tethered to, and not fixated onto neurons or other cells in the system, hence should be retrievable by conventional electrical impulse receptors.

*

Jason's dissertation was well received and he was awarded a gold medal for it.

His hard work was rewarded further when he was accepted into the Albert Einstein College of Medicine at the end of his three years of pre-med studies at Yeshiva, earning a B.Sc. in the process.

16

The Albert Einstein College of Medicine was located in Eastern Bronx, where there were two affiliated teaching hospitals – the privately owned Albert Einstein Hospital and the public funded Bronx Municipal Medical Center.

The hostels, lecture halls, offices and research centres were all close by. Medical students were required to stay in the hostels. Jason was somewhat relieved that he could go back to his Washington Heights home on holidays and during short breaks to have a change of scenery and to unwind. Of course, Jason's idea of unwinding was a leisurely stroll in the neighbourhood, spending a little time talking to the older lesbian tattoo lady about her purported medical problems, waving back at the black transgender neighbour from across the street while ignoring his wink, or having an exercise session with the wooden man zhuang.

He had no one in the city to spend time with, but at least he had a place he could call home.

The medical curriculum for the fast-track programme was the same as the conventional four-year programme. It was crammed into three years so that the entire week was packed with lectures, tutorials, and hospital ward rounds in which medical students learned how to obtain a medical history from a patient and how to conduct a proper physical examination. They followed the interns and resident doctors around and learned from them how to make diagnoses and treat diseases, and many other finer points of the healing art.

There were no summer months off. All the medical students worked long hours and there was little or no social life, which suited Jason fine.

Jane and Judy called occasionally, to make sure he was eating right, and exercising regularly. Every year around October, they called to see if he could have a few weeks off around Christmas and New Year, and could book a flight back to Hong Kong via San Francisco to spend some time with them. Some years he made it, some years he didn't.

They were worried that Jason would be burnt out from studying too hard. They obviously did not know Jason well enough. Jason was having a great time learning all the different subjects of medicine, from anatomy to embryology, obstetrics to pediatrics.

Jason liked all the subjects but he particularly had a strong interest and background knowledge in neurology and psychiatry because of his exposure during his pre-med years majoring in psychology, and helping out with Professor Koch's research. He spent all his elective rotations in the Neuroscience Department, attending all the seminars, meetings and clinical rounds there.

He did nothing but study medicine. He never socialized with anyone. He didn't make any friends, with men or women. He would die a lonely man. Mary, watching him, knew she must do something about it, sooner or later.

Jason's three years of medical school were one of the most boring periods of Mary's afterlife. Following Jason's discourse with his colleagues about the pathogenesis, prognosis, and treatment modalities of diseases was like listening to a broken Pat Boone record. Mary escaped to watch reruns of old movies, or go to concerts where old crooners sang golden oldies. She was glad Jason's medical school days were finally over after three long years.

The year was 1984; Jason was twenty-five years old.

Then every graduate had to do one year of internship before taking the National Licensing Examination. After they passed the exam and were awarded a license to practice medicine, each had to choose a specialty to go into.

Jason decided not to do any clinical work – not surprisingly, considering his aversion towards physical contact with other human beings.

He discussed his career options with the medical school Dean Dr Gene Lewinsky, who pointed out to him it was a natural progression for him to do neuroscience research, and he highly recommended their own Neuroscience Department.

Albert Einstein College of Medicine had one of the strongest Neuroscience Departments in the world. It boasted of the best and biggest, in its buildings, laboratory space, equipment, and federal grants and other endowments. It attracted the largest number of world-class scientists and researchers.

The chair professor and head was the formidable Dr Harold Stein, who came from a wealthy and influential Jewish family in Chicago. Jason joined the Department based partly on Dr Stein's reputation, and it was a big mistake. The man did not deserve his good name and he turned out to be Jason's nemesis.

17

Jason spent four years in Harold Stein's department doing research. During that entire period, Dr Stein talked to him exactly twice. Nothing personal; Stein was a big man on campus, and extremely busy.

The first time was Jason's first day at work, in Dr Stein's grand office.

The man behind the big mahogany desk wore gold rimmed glasses, an expensive three-piece suit, jade cuff-links, and a colourful bow-tie. His build was average, face perennially tanned, eyes dark blue and piercing, hair light brown with frosty side-burns neatly combed back. He carried himself as if he was a royalty, expecting men to bow and women to curtsy when he walked by. Yet when he broke into a smile, however rarely, the whole room lit up.

Jason was in awe. He stood in front of the desk until he was offered a seat after Dr Stein was finished with a phone call. They spoke for about three minutes. Stein asked Jason what he was interested in. Jason told him about his undergrad work with Alzheimer's disease and his dissertation on memory retention. Dr Stein nodded in acknowledgement, and smiled. He then picked up his phone to call his secretary. He gave instruction to have Jason see Professor Saul Shapiro, who would be his mentor.

End of conversation.

Jason subconsciously bowed slightly before he made his exit.

They spoke again four years later, after which Jason ran into some serious trouble.

Jason had gone to see Dr Shapiro, who was then fifty-five years old but looked and acted much older. He was supposed to be an expert in Alzheimer's disease and was showing signs of the disease himself. He was a difficult person to deal with, a bitter man who blamed his alleged failures on everyone and everything but himself and inclined to repeat the same long-winded grievances to anyone who was polite enough not to walk away from him. Jason left his office a frustrated man. They met on a few other occasions over the years, and Dr Shapiro had difficulty remembering Jason's name, calling him John or Jack instead. Jason dreaded dealing with him. He pretty much preferred working on his own.

He shared an office and a large laboratory with ten other junior researchers.

For four long years, he toiled over one scientific issue – how to capture and interpret the ionic signals stored in the limbic brain, the epicentre of memory.

Jason surmised that metals were usually better conductors of all kinds of signals in nature. His first mission was to find the best metal for the task. With the right metal, his ensuing steps were to find ways to capture, record, and store the signals. Interpreting the signals would be the ultimate goal of his research project.

Based on his undergraduate dissertation theory, the membrane potentials of the neurons in the limbic brain could emit ionic signals. All Jason needed was a transducer to convert them into electronic waves, which could be amplified, recorded, and stored in any standard electronic equipment. The Albert Einstein Neuroscience Department had a sophisticated engineering section where Jason could easily find expertise, assistance, and electronic parts to custom-build whatever he needed.

As to finding the best metal conductor, the only way was by trial and error.

The Pathology Departments of the two teaching hospitals were able to provide a constant supply of freshly dissected brains from autopsies for the neuroscience researchers to work on.

It took him a few months to construct the electronic set-up to record and store the electronic signals. It did not take him long to discover that titanium could transmit the best ionic signals. Then he had to detect distinct patterns in the signals and compare them to what the owners of the brains did in their lives.

Interviewing the patients' family members and recording their departed loved ones' major events in life was the most time-consuming component of his research.

The patterns the titanium probe collected were analogous to electroencephalogram (EEG) tracings, except that they were more varied and complicated because peoples' memories are more varied and complicated. There was no doubt, though, that the patterns representing life events were subtly distinctive and unfailingly consistent.

A good computer program was required to interpret such subtle and complicated distinctive features of the electronic patterns efficiently, accurately, and quickly. Computer programming was a fledgling science, and Jason enrolled in a course at New York University to learn the tricks of the trade.

It took Jason many months, but he was able to write a basic computer program to assimilate the signals received and translate them into a meaningful language.

*

The Neuroscience Department held numerous academic meetings all year round, but the Research Breakthrough Meeting (RBM) was the highlight of the month. Not everyone had the opportunity to present his or her research results in the monthly RBM. The researchers had to submit their data in advance to a screening committee Dr Stein chaired. He allowed only papers he deemed worthwhile to be presented. There were usually only two to three papers scheduled each time, out of dozens submitted. The lecture hall had a capacity of 500 seats, and it was always packed to the point of standing room only for every RBM.

The star scientist in the department was Dr Henry Williams, whose research on Parkinson's disease and epilepsy had garnered accolades from the scientific community and admiration from his peers. Naturally, he was Dr Harold Stein's golden-haired child.

Dr Williams had more than his share of presentation time in RBMs and he always brought the house down with earth shattering discoveries in his area of research. He worked on the pharmacokinetics of epilepsy and Parkinson's disease, and the discoveries he made were important in the basic understanding of the diseases and the tremendous potential in terms of commercial application. Drug interactions at the cellular level, and the molecular genetics of the two diseases were too esoteric even for most neuroscientists to comprehend. Scientists present at the RBMs were in awe of Henry Williams's erudite and bedazzling presentations. They simply clapped and nodded at appropriate intervals.

Pharmaceutical company representatives were routinely there in the audience, to watch the star researcher with dollar signs in their eyes.

Dr Stein stood up and spoke each and every time after Williams's presentation, making sure that everyone there knew he was part of the winning team.

Jason looked forward to the day he could be as successful. He returned to his lab with a newfound vigour after listening to Henry Williams's talk.

The ten young researchers Jason shared an office with often discussed research projects they learned of during RBMs, and all thought Dr Williams was the most efficient researcher in the world. Then they hurried back to their own research, trying to catch up.

Jason didn't socialize with any of them outside the office. The Korean Ph.D. student whose desk was right next to his took a shine to him, partly because her name was Lee Jae Soong, sounding almost like Lee Jason. She started conversations with Jason regularly, but Jason made sure it was only about work, and nothing about personal lives. He never gave her a chance to be more intimate.

Jason plodded on with his time-consuming and tedious research. Progress was slow, but thankfully, steady. Mary had had no doubt that given time, he would have a breakthrough.

Four long years later, Jason thought he had enough data to make a presentation at the RBM. He submitted his findings to the screening committee, and to his great delight he was granted a slot in the monthly RBM, albeit one following Henry Williams.

Jason knew the subject well. He first gave a background summary of memory retention, similar to what he had described in his undergrad dissertation, and then presented his own theory as to how memory was retained in the limbic system. He described how he, by trial and error, found titanium to be the best conductor to capture the micro-electrical signals from the limbic brain's neurons, and the engineering behind his electronic device. His work in the past four years was mainly collecting encoded messages from the limbic brain's hippocampus and matching them with the notable life events of the brains' owners, with the help of a computer program he wrote.

His presentation was solid and the scientific data convincing. It should have elicited great interest from the neuroscientists in attendance. The only problem was – presenting a scientific paper right after Dr Henry Williams was like performing in a rock concert right after Jimi Hendrix had just played Purple Haze. The audience was already so drained of ecstasy and enthusiasm there was nothing left for the act that followed. Half the people left the auditorium after Henry Williams finished, while the rest trickled out the door gradually during Jason's presentation. Even Dr Saul Shapiro, his supposed mentor, who had never shown any interest in what Jason was doing to start with, left soon after Jason began talking.

Jason was grateful Dr Harold Stein stayed until the end.

After Jason concluded his presentation, there was some subdued polite applause from the few people left, and no one asked any questions.

Jason didn't feel very good about himself after that presentation, and was surprised to get a call from Dr Stein's secretary the next day. The big boss wanted to talk to him in private the following Monday first thing in the morning.

Jason was excited that weekend, thinking that his hard work was finally to be rewarded with recognition from none other than Dr Harold Stein, the Department Chairman and celebrity in the field of neurology. Little did he know that this second meeting with Harold Stein would be his last and the onset of misery for years to come.

When Jason showed up in his office, Harold Stein shook his hand and greeted him warmly. Stein commended him on his good work, and wanted to know more about it. Could Jason bring in his electronic tools, together with his computer, to demonstrate to his boss how he did it? His secretary had a trolley ready and she could help him move everything to the Chairman's private laboratory located on the same floor as his august office.

Jason was flattered. All those months no one paid any attention to his work, and now the Chairman of the Department was granting him a private audience.

Dr Stein's laboratory was huge, and furnished wall to wall with fancy instruments that Jason had never seen before.

The secretary told Jason to arrange all his gadgets and his computer on an empty bench to be ready for the Chairman.

Dr Stein returned twenty minutes later, apologizing for the delay. He brought with him a freshly dissected brain from a patient who had died the night before.

The Chairman was in a good mood. He toyed with Jason. "I won't tell you what this man died of. I want you and your clever computer to tell me, by playing with his brain," he said.

"I'll try my best, sir," Jason replied.

He then proceeded to show the Chairman his technique, step by step.

First, he applied the titanium probe to the hippocampus and it picked up signals that were transmitted via a transducer to a receptor. He recorded as many signals as possible by moving the needle to cover the whole hippocampus. That was the easy part. What to make of all the recorded signals was the essence of Jason's research, and the answer was in Jason's computer. He turned the computer on.

Dr Stein casually asked Jason what the password of his computer program was. Jason answered "marylee", and coyly added that it was his mother's name.

Jason's unreserved trust in fellow human beings could be a virtue, but giving out a password was outright stupidity in most cases. He was overwhelmed by Dr Stein's authority, personality and aura, and had too much trust in someone with such impressive academic credentials. He made a mistake, and he would pay dearly for it.

There were good reasons why his mother Mary was always worried sick about him.

After typing in the password, the computer program came into view, and Jason showed his boss the catalog of all human activities that he had deciphered in the past many months. With the click of a few more keys, the man's brain signals found a match. According to Jason's computer program, the man had had chest pain and shortness of breath before he collapsed, and he was singing when he started to have chest pain. Heart disease was the commonest cause of death in the US, and Jason had had enough experience of the specific signal pattern derived from his work on many other cadaver brains. Singing was also quite a common human activity, and his computer had that pattern recognition in his program as well. So Jason concluded: The man most likely had died of a heart attack, while he was singing.

The Chairman was obviously impressed, because he clapped loudly for almost half a minute. He told Jason the man was an actor on Broadway and he indeed had died of a coronary blockage, based on the autopsy findings supplied by the pathologists.

Jason also noticed there was another distinct signal pattern before the singing that the computer could not recognize, and he shared that information with his boss. If they talked to the people who were with the actor during that period, they could find out what he was doing, and they could add that new pattern to the vocabulary of his computer program.

Dr Stein slowly nodded in appreciation and told Jason to leave his equipment in his lab for a few days for him to look at more carefully, and he was thinking of moving Jason to a larger office because he was doing such good work.

Jason was full of joy and satisfaction when he left Dr Stein's office. He treated himself to an expensive dinner in his Washington Heights neighbourhood that evening.

However, his happiness did not last long.

18

Two days after he spoke to Dr Stein, he walked into his shared office to find his desk and other personal belongings missing. A security guard was on stand-by waiting for him, to notify him Dr Stein had assigned a different office for him. He followed the security guard to a storage facility which was quite remote from the centre of activities of the Neuroscience Department. He was to share the office with a clerk and a custodian. He found his old desk in the corner of the small dark room. His few personal belongings were on the desktop. The only thing missing was his notebook in which he penned all his research designs, results, and remarks.

He hurried back to his old office to find his notebook, and by then all his co-workers had returned. No one knew the whereabouts of his notebook, and most of them avoided eye contact. The Korean Ph.D. student Lee Jae Soong said that she was working late the night before when Dr Stein came into the room to direct some menial staff to remove Jason's desk, and she thought she saw Jason's notebook in Dr Stein's hand on his way out. She asked Jason what was happening, but he told her he had no idea.

The security guard showed up again and told him he had come back to escort him out, and from that moment on, his old office would be off limits.

Jason rushed to Dr Stein's office. The secretary informed him the Chairman would be tied up with meetings the whole day, but she would make sure Dr Stein called him back as soon as possible.

Jason sat in his new office facing a blank wall, wondering what was going on.

No one called for two days. Jason did not sleep for two nights.

Jason went back to Dr Stein's office. The secretary gave him the same runaround. He sat in the waiting area and told the secretary he would not leave until he had a chance to see the Chairman.

The secretary called an extension, nodding and saying 'yes'. She called another extension and whispered excitedly.

Two heavy-set security guards showed up. The secretary whispered to them. They approached Jason, and the older one asked him sternly to follow him out.

"I'm waiting for Dr Stein, and I'm not leaving until I see him," Jason said, firmly and politely.

"Sir, don't make me take out the handcuffs. I will if I don't see co-operation from you," said the older guard. He also said Jason was persona non grata in that building and he had orders from the administration to ban him from being there.

Jason refused to move.

The two guards reached out to grab Jason. Jason shook them off and stood up on his own. He tried to make eye contact with Stein's secretary but she was busy burying her head in some paper work behind her desk.

The two guards marched him to the lift lobby, and insisted on taking the elevator ride with him to the ground floor, staring at him until he exited through the front door.

Jason was beginning to get the picture. He was so humiliated and furious he was shaking all over. He walked around the campus deep in thoughts. Who could he possibly turn to for help?

The Dean, perhaps?

At the Dean's office, he was not locked out. Instead, Dr Gene Lewinsky welcomed him into his office right away. Jason asked for ten minutes of his time. With his hand on Jason's shoulder, he said that he could have all the time in the world.

All it took was a small act of kindness for Jason's floodgates of pent-up anger and despair to open. He burst into tears.

Crying was rare for Jason. Mary could not remember him ever crying as a young man, until he saw her dying in the Queen Elizabeth Hospital emergency room. In her afterlife, he cried twice, during her funeral, and when Harold Stein ruthlessly betrayed him.

He cried for a couple of minutes before he became composed enough to tell Dr Lewinsky what had happened. The Dean appeared sympathetic but if he was surprised, he didn't show it.

He pulled open his drawer and produced a letter for Jason to see. The letter was addressed to the Dean written by none other than Dr Harold Stein. He reported to the dean that he found the work of his young researcher Dr Jason John Lee patently unsatisfactory. Above all, Jason was not a team player. His continued employment could jeopardize the morale of other workers in the Department.

Harold Stein had dated his letter two weeks before Jason's presentation at RBM. Jason was left speechless at Stein's ruthless lack of integrity.

The Dean told Jason he didn't know what was going on. All he knew was that Dr Stein did not want Jason in his Department. His fatherly advice to Jason was to take up another specialty. He, being the Dean, was in a position to offer Jason a job in any of his other departments: surgery, gynecology, pediatrics, or whatever else he fancied.

Jason wanted to know why the Dean was so unperturbed by a faculty member in his school stealing the research work of someone else.

"Well, theoretically everything in that Department belongs to Harold Stein," the Dean said.

While Jason was sulking, the Dean put his hand on Jason's shoulder again, and urged him to take a week off to think about it. Then he could come back and they could discuss Jason's future.

The Dean was quite the diplomat.

Jason left his office not feeling any better. But he listened to the Dean's advice and took a few days off. He was not going back to that storage facility – that much he was sure of.

Jason went back to his Washington Heights home, his sanctuary, to think. The more he thought it over, the more frustrated he became. The worst part was that he was helpless in the situation. He took his frustration out on the wooden man zhuang, and went at it until his forearms were red and raw.

He then took the subway to Lower Manhattan's Chinatown to look for an herbal medicine shop. He found one and bought a large bottle of medicinal wine that he could use to rub on his arms. He applied it himself. His eyes moistened just thinking of the days when his mother had done it for him, the days when he was not all by himself, helpless, betrayed, and frustrated.

19

There was one other person whom he could possibly turn to for help – psychology professor Leona Koch. She was matronly and soft spoken, and seemed to have integrity. She had always been kind to Jason and had given Jason full credit for helping her with her research on Alzheimer's disease. She had written a glowing recommendation letter for his medical school application. They had kept in touch over the years, and Jason sought her advice occasionally on research methodologies.

Dr Koch was flabbergasted at Jason's misadventure. She was genuinely sympathetic with Jason, but admitted her powerlessness over any situation involving heavyweights the likes of Harold Stein and Gene Lewinsky. By the way, did Jason not know Harold Stein was Gene Lewinsky's son-in-law?

After realizing that Jason did want to continue with neuroscience research and not switch career paths, she recommended Jason see a friend of hers at the Columbia Medical Center.

That was the best news yet for Jason. Her friend was Dr Victor Vasco, a pathologist, who might be able to offer Jason a job. She would call him in advance.

Jason made an appointment, and went to see Dr Vasco.

Victor Vasco's office was crowded and messy. He kept bottles of specimens soaked in formalin – his prized collection of organs afflicted by rare diseases, dissected from autopsies, which he intended to study closely for research but never got around to them.

Dr Vasco was short and balding. His nose was the most prominent feature of his face. He dressed sloppily and looked scruffy. He talked fast in a heavy Brooklyn accent, and was quite liberal with the use of a few choice words in both English and Italian to make his point.

Jason liked him already. He spilled his guts in the pathologist's office.

Victor Vasco happened to know Harold Stein well, and he was not a fan of the neuroscience superstar. They had done their neurology fellowship at Harvard Medical School together, and Stein had apparently shafted Vasco more than once. He agreed to help Jason, no doubt because of his strong dislike of Stein. Jason didn't care why Dr Vasco was willing to help. At that moment, he could use any help he could get.

Victor Vasco was nobody's fool, though. He knew he was declaring war on Stein if he took Jason in, and there could be repercussions, given that Stein was in a position of power. He wanted to make sure he could easily distance himself from Jason should a difficult situation arise. He offered Jason the job of a Visiting Fellow, a permanently temporary position renewable on a yearly basis. The post came with a low salary, and no benefits or tenure. The School could dismiss him on a day's notice. He would be given an office, a laboratory space to do research, and access to the dissected brains that came through the autopsy room. In return, Jason would contribute to teaching by helping with lectures and tutorials for medical students and trainees in neuropathology.

Jason took the offer, and sent Dr Gene Lewinsky's office a memo tendering his resignation, and the address for his last paycheck.

Jason's office was small and windowless, and the furniture a disgrace. Dr Vasco apologized but that was the best he could come up with because Jason's position was not on the official payroll roster. The good pathologist was using his federal grant money to pay Jason's salary. He had to vacate a storage room next to the morgue to provide space for an unexpected addition to his staff.

Jason spent the following weekend cleaning and painting the room. He bought some furniture, including a laboratory bench and computer stand. He planned to acquire a new computer and some top-of-the-line electronic equipment. He also bought a safe, which he bolted to a hidden wall in his study at home. He would use it to store his future experimental data and results, having learned his lesson in Bronx.

Dr Vasco's Department had no budget for any of the expenses, not even the enamel and brush to paint over the moldy walls of Jason's pigsty of an office. The "Mary Lee Trust" picked up the tab for all those plus all materials and other expenses to support his ongoing brain research.

*

Jason called Jane to air his grievance about what Harold Stein had done. Jane freaked out. She cursed Harold Stein for what seemed like an hour. How could anyone be so crooked and mean? And all that from someone who was an academic, a doctor, and professor. She asked whether Jason wanted her to send someone over to talk to that prick. Jason firmly refused her help. He told Jane that in America, people settled their disputes in the court of law. Jane was used to settling her disputes with customers or other bar owners using triad thugs on her payroll.

"Then sue that prick," said Jane, before hanging up.

Jason did considering suing. He went to see his old roommate Leroy the wrestler, who had become a lawyer and was practicing in the neighbourhood.

In spite of his continuing addiction to sex, Leroy seemed sensible, honest, and competent. He told Jason divorce was his specialty, intellectual property rights was not. But it seemed to him Harold Stein was holding all the trump cards, and any lawsuit involving intellectual properties could be lengthy and costly.

He didn't charge Jason for the consultation.

"I owe you," Leroy said with a wink.

He also advised Jason to apply for a patent for his technique. Jason thought his technique was far from fully developed yet, and it might be premature to talk about a patent.

Jason put the lawsuit and patent ideas behind him and concentrated on his research project, starting from scratch.

It wasn't exactly from scratch. By then, Jason's brains were fully packed with information and ideas about his pet project. It should be much easier the second time around.

He wanted a more sophisticated electronic system. He went to Columbia's Engineering Department to put in his request. No one paid him any attention until he offered a chunk of money for services rendered.

As the Chinese saying suggests: With enough money, one can persuade a ghost to work on a gristmill.

A team of engineers came together and tailor-made for Jason a speedy transducer, a powerful amplifier, and a super-sensitive receptor with a huge capacity for storage. The receptor could send coded messages to the computer in the digital form instead of the analog model he employed in his old office in Bronx.

Jason knew the computer program was the key to his invention, and he started to write a new and improved program. He continued to enroll in computer programming courses at New York University, to stay abreast of the latest developments in computer technology and programming techniques.

The Pathology Department in the Columbia Medical Center provided a good work environment for Jason. It was not as cutthroat competitive as Harold Stein's department, he being the only neuroscientist doing pure research in Dr Vasco's Department. Jason's polite manners, British accent, and down-to-earth disposition easily endeared him to his colleagues. The pathologists working in the autopsy room also respected his extensive knowledge on the central nervous system and often sought his counsel on matters of the brain. They reciprocated by letting him work on the freshly dissected brains as long as Jason did not disfigure them. Jason was careful and always returned the brains intact.

There were no obstacles to his research work. He only had to report to Dr Vasco, who made no secret of his dislike of Harold Stein, and his wish for Jason to succeed was only so that Harold Stein would fail.

20

His work progressed steadily and within three years the number of human activities interpretable by the patterns of the captured coded electronic signals in his computer program was more than double what was contained in his old computer in Stein's possession.

A scientist needs peer reviews of his or her research for validation. One automatically gets a review when one submits a paper on the research to a scientific journal or presents it in a seminar. Most scientists do both. Jason was no exception.

He tried his hand first in a small conference held in Texas, not exactly the epicentre of neuroscience research and academia. The audience reacted more positively to his presentation than in Harold Stein's monthly RBM in Bronx.

Encouraged by the response, he submitted a manuscript of his research to the venerable *New England Journal of Medicine*. The editors of that famous medical journal rejected it within weeks. He went to Dr Vasco for advice. Dr Vasco told him to forget about sending his manuscripts to any of the major medical journals, because Harold Stein sat on the editorial boards of most of them.

Jason had no choice but tried submitting it to the Texas Medical Journal, and the magazine published it a few months later. This small provincial journal became Jason's main publication venue in subsequent years because it seemed to be out of reach of the long arms of the omnipotent Harold Stein.

As it turned out, publishing his work in the rinky-dink *Texas Medical Journal* did Jason a whole lot of good. It actually paved the road to his academic redemption years later. Karma worked in a mysterious way.

When Lee Jae Soong found Jason had moved to Columbia Medical Center, she tracked him down and called him occasionally to find out how he was doing.

She regularly updated Jason on all the gossip regarding Harold Stein. After Stein reviewed Jason's manuscript submitted to the *New England Journal of Medicine*, he had a fit.

From the data Jason presented in his paper, it was apparent that Jason's research results had leap-frogged what was stolen from him more than two years before, in spite of the fact that Stein had hired two researchers to replace Jason to work on "his" new project in his private laboratory. The two new researchers had made scant progress in the ensuing many months. Stein was heard screaming at the two researchers, threatening to fire them. He handed them each a copy of Jason's manuscript and gave them a deadline to catch up or resign.

He rejected Jason's manuscript on behalf of the editorial board of *The New England Journal of Medicine* because of the lack of detail in the methodology and computer program in the submitted manuscript, which Jason purposely omitted to prevent plagiarism. Despite that, he knew Jason's results were genuine; that was what irked him.

Even though no one discussed it openly, many of Jason's old colleagues knew what Harold Stein had done to Jason and many had resigned for fear of suffering the same fate.

Stein did not realize he had squandered the most valuable aspect of any project – the human resource. Had he kept Jason, he would have been able to convince Jason to collaborate with him, and Jason, being a generous person, would have been more than satisfied to do just that. He would have included his name in all his publications, as Henry Williams had done for him.

Not too many researchers had Jason's intellect, tenacity, diligence, and creativity. The two new researchers replacing Jason did what they could, but were handicapped by their lack of talent.

In subsequent years, Jason kept making new advances in ideas and techniques that Harold Stein could only drool over.

After waiting in vain a few more months for his two researchers to come up with something that could catch up with Jason's memory project research, he realized it was hopeless. He fired them and hired three new researchers with higher qualifications and more experience, at twice the original salary for each.

He also moved on to plan B.

Harold Stein had no qualms about walking into a law firm and asking them to file a vexatious lawsuit against anyone who happened to be blocking his way to fame and fortune.

He went to a law firm that specialized in intellectual property and asked the lawyers there to sue Jason on his behalf for the theft of the technique, which he claimed, was an intellectual property of his Neuroscience Department.

He also applied for a patent for the memory retrieval technique and machinery.

He instructed his lawyers to petition the federal district judge to order an injunction to stop Jason from using the technique in any shape or form, effective immediately. As usual with lawyers, they also sued the employer of the defendant, in this case, Columbia Medical School.

The day the bailiff handed the writ to Jason was another terrible day for Jason. The Dean of the Columbia Medical School also received a writ at the same time.

Jason went to see Dr Vasco and told him about the lawsuit. Dr Vasco reminded Jason that his position was that of Visiting Fellow, and he was employed as a temporary member of staff. He told him the Medical School might have to dismiss him to avoid the lawsuit. Jason promised to make sure his lawyer would understand the relevance and significance of his employment arrangement.

While they were talking, the Dean's office called. Vasco shook his head and told Jason the bad news. The Dean was adamant that Jason be dismissed immediately, so that the medical school could avoid a major lawsuit.

Jason would have to go the next day. Victor Vasco reminded Jason once again of Harold Stein's evil nature.

Stein was the brainy, evil type. His desire for fame, fortune, and power overwhelmed every virtue he might have, including his conscience. He must have rationalized his behavior by claiming he was doing it for the good of Albert Einstein College of Medicine, which was in constant competition with other famous medical schools in North America. The more powerful he was, the more evil, unconscionable, and dangerous he could become.

Jason went home dejected and demoralized. He worked out, using the wooden man zhuang, for two hours, followed by a medicinal wine rub.

He called Hong Kong around midnight. It was noon in Hong Kong, but Jane was still in bed. He gave Jane a couple of minutes to get a cup of coffee and light a cigarette before he told her the kind of trouble he was in.

As expected, Jane swore like a truck driver at the "prick" for almost half an hour, and insisted on sending someone to do the "prick" in.

Jane's swearing was typical of a Hong Kong Cantonese, who was inclined to target not only the intended subject, but also his or her family members. After cursing the "prick", Jane moved on to Harold Stein's mother, whose reproductive organs were in such poor shape no man should want to touch her. Harold's father was next. His reproductive organs were so useless he couldn't even get laid in a brothel. Herald's son was born a eunuch; and his daughter, well – Jason got her drift.

Jason calmly let her rant for as long as she desired, and when she took a breather, asked her for the trustees' telephone numbers. He was going to need mucho money.

Jane was still fuming. "Why can't you forget about your god damned brain research and become some other kind of doctor, a surgeon or a gynecologist, or whatever?" she stridently asked. "Wouldn't that be less troublesome and also make you more money? You are just so..."

Jason gently but sternly told her he needed to pursue the case, because it was more important to him than all the money in the world.

Jane didn't understand her godson, but knew that in spite of his meekness, he could be like a mad dog – one that would never let go of its bite.

Jane finally calmed down. She sighed, and admitted that the money was his, and he could spend it whichever way he deemed appropriate. She would fax him the names and telephone numbers of all of the trustees as soon as she got back to her office.

Mary was as mad as Jane. She wished Harold Stein dead. But Mother Nature's instruction was clear. She could not use any of the three wishes to do harm to another human being. All Mary could do was to watch from a distance, and wait for the right moment to help Jason.

Jason went to Leroy Katz again for advice. Leroy shook his head in disbelief. And he predicted, correctly, that Stein must have already filed for a patent, and advised Jason to do the same.

The National Patent Office was in the process of evaluating Harold Stein's patent application for the memory recall technique when Jason submitted his. The Office informed both parties of the co-existing applications.

The law firm Jason used for his patent application recommended Levy and Associates, a firm specializing in intellectual property rights.

Mr Levy asked for two hundred thousand dollars as retainer and told Jason to be ready for a long drawn-out legal battle. Mr Levy asked Jason about his financial situation. Jason told him he was in the process of selling all his inherited assets from Hong Kong, except his childhood home, and they added up to about three and a half million US dollars. He also had a modest apartment in San Francisco and another in New York, where he was living. He was hoping he would never have to sell any of those properties.

Mary was shaking her head, watching all this. That Jason; how naive could a man be? Wasn't it great his lawyer now knew exactly how much cash he had, so that he could continue to bill him until it became all his, before he dropped the case? Jason was such a hopelessly guileless geek.

Mr Levy advised Jason to resign immediately from Columbia Medical Center, and Stein's law firm would most likely leave Columbia alone until its position became clear. Jason told him they had already fired him. Meanwhile, Jason had brought his equipment and computer home to work from there.

Mr Levy understood Jason's research results were much better than Stein's; and in a way, they could use that as a defense, because in general the rich had no need to steal from the poor. He told Jason the best way to tackle this case was to be aggressive. Countersuing would be a good tactic.

Mr Levy seemed competent and knowledgeable. Jason had no choice but to follow his advice.

They countersued Dr Harold Stein and Albert Einstein College of Medicine for the theft of the technique, and the notebook chronicling all the research Jason conducted during his tenure at the College. Not that the notebook was of any value for the research project at that stage, but bringing attention to its existence would add credence to Jason's version of his ordeal. That could be the reason why it was missing to begin with.

The patent office noted that two parties were suing each other for theft of the technique, and decided to wait for the outcome of the lawsuits before considering granting any patent.

A court date was scheduled for all the suing and countersuing, for eighteen months later.

The year was 1990. Jason was thirty-one years old, unemployed, but working from home.

He had retrieved enough data from the brains of dead people, and had collected an enormous amount of information from his tedious interviews with more than a hundred families of the owners of those brains. All he had to do was to work on the computer to continue his program to match the brain signals collected when they were dead with things they did when they were alive. That he could do on a computer from home.

He had also developed ideas on how to collect memory data from live subjects, and he would start on the new project as soon as he was finished with what he needed to do with data from dead people.

By then he had also acquired advanced programming skills, gained from work experience and attending many computer-programming workshops at New York University. He worked day and night at building the perfect computer program for memory recognition.

21

Throughout all those years of frustration and despair, Jason remained celibate and socially desolate. No surprise there, for a diehard asexual.

Creating anomalies of all kinds is an immutable law of nature. Like all other sexual anomalies, including all kinds of sexual orientation and gender identity, asexuality was a creation of nature, not reversible by the most advanced psychotherapy, behavior modification or hormonal treatment.

There is really no need to change any of these anomalies, unless the person is engaging in immoral or illegal activities.

Many famous people in history are thought to have been asexual; most, like Jason, grew up to become great scientists. Isaac Newton was reputed to be one, as were Nicola Tesla, Glenn Gould, John Ruskin, H.P. Lovecraft, and Paul Erdos.

At that stage, Mary had no problem with her son being asexual, except the thought of him all by himself in his old age without anyone by his side was not what she wished for him.

The only people close to him were Mary's friends, and they were all much older than he was. After they died, Jason would be left with no one.

*

Then a young woman came along, who became physically and emotionally closer to Jason than anyone else since his mother's death.

It happened when Jason was thirty-two years old. The timing was good because he was then recently fired from Columbia, unemployed, and mired in lawsuits. He had really needed a friend.

The young woman was Juanita Mertz. Like Mary and Mary's mother, Juanita grew up poor, and was practically an orphan. The three women had a lot in common. They were all widows and single moms at one time.

She was a decent and hardworking woman, no doubt borne out by poverty in her formative years.

"Growing up poor is worth a thousand pieces of gold," is a popular Chinese saying. Poverty does build character. Juanita never took anything for granted, and always worked hard.

She was born in Puerto Rico. Her parents were of German Jewish and French extractions. She was the youngest of four children. When her mother ran off with another man, her father had no choice but to send the younger children to live with different relatives. He sent young Juanita to his cousin in New York City. She was then six years old and it was the right age to start grade school in the US.

The aunt lived in the Spanish Harlem section of Manhattan. She was a kind but weak woman, bullied by her domineering police officer husband. They had no children of their own. He was strict with Juanita until she reached puberty, when he became meddlesome and sometimes overly affectionate.

Juanita knew what he was up to when at the age of thirteen he put her on his knees and talked to her when they were alone, but immediately pushed her away when someone approached the room they were sitting in.

Juanita grew up to be pretty and foxy. A brunette with smoky hazel eyes that could talk, lips pouty and nose pointy, and complexion as smooth and milky as porcelain. And the way she walked stopped traffic wherever she went.

Life was not always easy for a girl who looked like that. Men automatically assumed she must be good in bed, sort of like Susan George in Straw Dogs in which every man in the neighbourhood wanted a piece of her. Susan George had bared her big breasts from an open window for the whole neighbourhood to see to have the desired effect. Juanita never had to do that. She tried to cover as much of her body as possible, but her fully clothed but curvaceous body and the way she moved about still drove men crazy.

Also, she spoke English with that exotic Hispanic accent that many men found sensuous.

She spent her teenage years fending off predators – men twice her age or older. She learned to be street smart and was able to balance not giving anything away but not offending anyone.

One day when the aunt's husband put a hand on her knee and then moved it up to squeeze her inner thigh, she knew he had crossed the line and had to be stopped right there and then. She gave him a stern dressing down followed by a peck on the cheek. He left her alone after that.

She was not interested in school and her only passion was dancing. Her aunt could not afford to send her to ballet school, so she picked up classical and modern dancing from watching TV and audiovisual instructional tapes she borrowed from friends. She was a natural and could have won dancing competitions had she been old and rich enough to enter any of them. Every chance she had, she would practice her moves. On the way to and from school, she would run, jump, and cart-wheel to make her legs strong and her body nimble. Unfortunately, the school she enrolled in did not have an extra-curricular program for dancing. She could not go any further than the occasional school performance during Christmas.

In her late teens, her aunt's husband did all he could to make her feel unwelcome in his household so she had no choice but to leave home as soon as she turned seventeen. With her aunt's help, she moved to a small apartment close by and found a job as a waitress in a restaurant in the Bronx owned by her aunt's friend, Mrs Gonzales.

Her ordeals with older men continued. She was popular with male customers in the restaurant but had to repel aggressive advances, and put up with the constant stream of dirty jokes and lewd remarks coming her way.

One customer was different. Michael O'Malley was a 25-year-old car mechanic who worked in the Bronx not far from the restaurant and was one of the rare residents in Spanish Harlem with an Irish last name. He was polite around her and was protective of her. He took the trouble of traveling daily to the restaurant around closing time to offer her a ride home, so that she would not have to use the not-so-safe public transportation in that area. She was not short of suitors but found this young man to be the most devoted and trustworthy. She started dating him and moved in with him soon after.

Michael O'Malley was hardworking, honest and loving, but not immune to the culture of Spanish Harlem. One Friday night, after some serious drinking, he got into an argument with some gang members, and ended up dead from gunshot wounds.

Juanita was heartbroken, not only because she had lost a man she loved, but also she was three months pregnant with the man's child. She was Catholic and decided to keep the child, but had no choice but to subsist on welfare.

After seven years of leading a low life depending on food stamps and Medicaid, and waiting for her monthly welfare check, she woke up one morning in her dilapidated apartment and found her seven-year-old son Mike on the kitchen floor crying. He was hungry and the cookie jar was empty. She tried looking for food elsewhere but the refrigerator was empty and there was no money in her purse. She broke down in tears. She was barely twenty-five years old and she did not like the direction her life was heading in.

She once had dreams of being a professional dancer. Now she dreamed only of getting rich quick so that she could get out of this jam. She prayed each night that a white knight would appear and take her away from the dump she was living in. She desperately wanted a better future for herself and her son.

But she was levelheaded. She knew that a white knight coming into her life was a pipe dream, and she had more of a chance at a better life from her own hard work.

She again sought assistance from her aunt, who gave her some money and helped her move out of Spanish Harlem, get off welfare, and find a job as a waitress in a diner in Upper Manhattan's Washington Heights. She struggled to make ends meet but was determined to make it on her own.

The diner she worked in was across the street from Jason's apartment.

22

Jason took breaks from his computer only for a quick meal and a slow walk in the neighbourhood. One of his favourite restaurants was Frank's Diner, where Juanita worked.

The owner of the diner, Frank, was too old and frail to work anymore and he hired a manager to run the place. They served the usual diner food, and had a daily special: meatloaf Monday and Wednesday, lasagna Tuesday and Thursday, fish on Friday, and steak N' eggs for the weekend. Jason regularly went there for most of his meals. No need to cook, or wash dishes; plenty of time left for him to do some more work in his study.

Jason preferred the back of the diner. The front section housed mostly young blue-collar workers, firefighters, police officers, and truckers. They were typical rowdy young men who talked about women and sports all day long. The entire left section was non-smoking and catered to families with young children.

In the back section of the diner, Jason often found himself among old folks who talked slowly and ate even slower. This section was Juanita's section and she had always been curious about this lanky man with impeccable manners and a funny accent. While most men would flirt with her, usually at first sight, this one never seemed to notice her, and when she took orders from him, his gaze would focus on her face and not wander off to other parts of her body.

They exchanged pleasantries and nothing more until one day Jason overheard her arguing with the manager Sean Griffin. It appeared that Sean was rather mean to Juanita.

Sean ordinarily had the demeanour of a maître d', ceremonious with studied courtesy, and always charming and efficient when smoothing things out for irate customers. His butler-like persona was accentuated by the portly physique, the thinning red hair parted in the middle, and a handlebar mustache.

He usually kept an expressionless face, but that day when he was arguing with Juanita, he lost his cool. He looked vicious when he said if she didn't like it, she could quit.

Juanita said she needed the job to support the little man at home, and all she was asking for was equal opportunity.

When Juanita came over to take orders from Jason, she was holding back tears. Jason waited for most customers in the section to have left, before he asked for the bill.

"You don't mind my asking – I couldn't help overhearing you and Sean, what was that about?"

Juanita looked at him. This gentleman seemed truly concerned, and not trying to hit on her.

"I want my turn to work in the front section. Every other waitress has had a turn many times and I've had none for months and months," Juanita replied.

Why was it important for her to work in that section? Well, that was where they usually got the most tips. All she had to do was to smile at those young men, call them handsome, and they would flash their cash. In the back section where Jason liked to sit, everyone was nice, but the tips were either ten per cent or in the case of the pensioners, only the small change.

"My son is going to be ten soon, there is no way I can survive on minimum wage."

"Why doesn't Sean let you have your turn?" Jason asked.

Juanita gave Jason the kind of look usually reserved for someone totally clueless about the ways of the world.

But he seemed sincere. She sighed. That was because Sean had been trying to get into her pants and she wouldn't let him – so that was her punishment.

Jason honestly did not understand why men had to go through so much trouble to get into women's pants, but he realized he was the exception and they were the rule. He couldn't think of anything to say. He apologized for not tipping more. He was never a big tipper; ten per cent was his norm. He left a five-dollar tip for a ten-dollar meal that evening.

After what Harold Stein had done to him, nothing bothered Jason more than injustice and betrayal. He felt deeply for Juanita because of the unfair treatment she was suffering in the hands of her superior. He returned the next day and quietly asked Juanita if she would like a part-time job doing domestic work in his house. Hours would be flexible. Not much to do, really, a little cleaning, vacuuming, and laundry.

As for the pay, about how much would she need for her son's schooling expense? Five hundred dollars a month. Okay, she got herself a deal, and it would be tax-free.

Juanita promptly started the part-time work the following week, and spent an hour or so three days a week at Jason's place doing housework while he worked in his study upstairs.

*

She found out that Jason led an incredibly simple life. The kitchen was spick-and-span because nobody ever used it. He had a small and simple wardrobe. A few shirts had missing buttons, and socks had holes in them. The furniture was simple and basic. All he had plenty of were books.

There was one piece of furniture that caught her attention – a vanity normally used by women to sit in front of to do make-up. It was quite fancy and out-of-place among Jason's other household items.

She couldn't help but ask Jason about it. Jason told her it was his late mother's and that was one thing belonging to her he brought all the way from Hong Kong to New York. That piece of furniture meant a lot to him, because his mother used to let him sit next to her while she did her make-up when he was a toddler.

He told Juanita he had had a great mother and he missed her a lot. While on the subject of motherhood, he complimented Juanita for her diligence, and her determination to give her son a good education.

The last thing Juanita expected from a man she was flirting with was for him to talk non-stop about his mother.

She was usually wary of men doing her any favour because there could always be some kind of repercussion, but this time it seemed different. Unlike Sean Griffin the sleaze-ball, Jason was such a gentleman. The part-time job was much needed and timely, and it didn't appear to be a ploy to get her into the sack. Jason was not exactly her type, but she was willing to go out with him if he was interested. And if they became an item, she would make sure that Sean knew about it, too.

*

Sean and Juanita had a complicated relationship. They used to be good friends because Juanita's son Mike and Sean's daughter Virginia went to the same schools in Spanish Harlem. They were the only two kids with Irish last names, and both had light hair. They did look somewhat alike and were thought to be siblings, twins even.

Mike grew up thuggish, getting into fights almost every day. Some fights were started because Virginia was harassed and bullied by some boys in the school. She was pretty and they just wouldn't leave her alone. Virginia had to patch up Mike's wounds and bruises so often she kept a first-aid kit in her school bag. The two young ones had camaraderie, like siblings.

Sean was a divorcee and a single parent like Juanita. The ex-wife was a drug addict who disappeared somewhere down South after the divorce. Juanita and Sean became friends because of their children, and they used to help each other out, such as giving them rides to school and school functions. It was a good relationship until Sean started to make passes at Juanita. A pat on the buttock, a kiss too close to the lips, unwelcome touches to many parts of her body, hugs that lasted too long – general lecherous behavior that made Juanita's skin crawl. Juanita was capable of dressing down her uncle when she was thirteen, so handling someone like Sean when she had become a grown woman was not a difficult task.

After the confrontation, Juanita made it clear she would not tell the children about it, so that their friendship would not be affected.

She was hoping Sean would take it like a man, but Sean's creepiness continued. Juanita was already working in Frank's Diner, when Sean successfully applied for the manager's job. He didn't forget or forgive being spurned. He punished Juanita by not giving her the more profitable tables, and made it clear things could change if she was more amenable to his demands. Juanita kept her promise and never told Mike anything bad about

Virginia's father. She remained polite to Sean in front of the children, but privately she couldn't stand him.

Compared to Sean, Jason was a breath of fresh air. She had had a string of lovers in the past decade or so. None of the affairs had worked out because most of her lovers had wives. Jason was not exactly her type; but now that she was older and had had her share of Romeos, Casanovas, jocks, and braggarts with movie star good looks, she wanted someone like Jason – down to earth, modest and kind, educated and rock solid in character.

But it didn't look like having an affair with Jason was going to happen any time soon. Juanita tried different ways to encourage him to ask her out or make some kind of advances. She even encouraged him by being coquettish with him, something she almost never had to do with men. She didn't lack knowhow when it came to getting a man's attention. When she took his orders, she leaned close so that their bodies touched. Instead of groping her, Jason backed away from her.

She repeatedly hinted to him that she was bored out of her mind after work, hoping Jason would offer to take her out. Instead, Jason encouraged her to go to the library to read books. She even put on extra cosmetics and perfume for him, and hung around his table a lot. But he didn't seem to notice her extra effort to make herself attractive.

Jason's favourite topics of conversation remained his mother and the virtues of books. Tips were now regularly five dollars after every meal.

Juanita started to wonder about this man. What was wrong with him anyway? Did he not know all the male customers in the front section were dying to date her? From what she heard, there was a competition: The first to take her to bed would win prize money plus the title "Champion Lady-Killer".

She was wondering if Jason was gay, but from her experience, even gay men liked to befriend her, as they had repeatedly assured her, gay or not gay, men were fond of the companionship of attractive women.

She also wondered if she had lost her touch with men.

23

Juanita thought of a way to get close to Jason. She knew his routine.

Jason's penthouse was in the heart of Washington Heights, where small art galleries and quaint shops thrived amid its bohemian streets, and food markets and restaurants inundated ethnic areas dominated by Dominicans.

He enjoyed walking around his neighbourhood but did enough of that on weekdays after dinner. Every Sunday, when pedestrian traffic was light, he preferred long walks all over Manhattan similar to the long hikes he shared with his mother around the Lion Rock in Hong Kong in his youth.

Juanita asked Jason if she could join him in his Sunday walks; she needed the exercise, and she was afraid to walk alone because Manhattan was not exactly a safe city. She would swap off-days with another waitress, who was more than happy to do so because Sunday football on TV usually guaranteed heavy drinking and big tips from the customers for the shift.

Jason happily agreed. In spite of his asexuality, he needed companionship, and some emotional if not physical intimacy. Someone to talk to, although not to cuddle with.

He was depressed, and anything to cheer him up was welcome. It was always pleasant to have Juanita around.

Juanita was not a morning person, but managed to show up at Jason's door at eight o'clock every Sunday morning.

They walked towards the Upper West Side, before crossing over to Fifth Avenue and following it downtown instead of staying on the West Side, where some neighbourhoods in midtown and further downtown were too edgy for his liking. Fifth Avenue provided access to many museums and places such as the Lincoln Center and Central Park where they could watch children skate or fly a kite.

Jason was someone who put a high premium on knowledge. Therefore, he usually picked one Big Apple landmark to visit on any given Sunday and researched that destination so that he could tell stories to entertain Juanita, no matter whether she was interested or not. With Manhattan's rich heritage, he never ran out of landmarks.

They frequently walked as far as Houston Avenue before turning into The Village, where Jason would tell Juanita the life stories of some of the writers, cultural icons, and artists known to be frequenters of the grooviest urban oasis in the world. They normally finished the day with a meal in Chinatown.

The weather was getting cold. One morning, Juanita said to Jason: "Can you hold my hand? It's cold."

Jason blushed. He took off his gloves and handed them to Juanita.

Juanita was mad. She threw the gloves back at Jason. "I don't want your damned gloves. We've been going out for months, and you have not touched me yet," she said. "Not even my hands. What the hell is wrong with you?"

Jason smiled awkwardly at her. He didn't know what to say.

Juanita didn't talk for the rest of the day; not even a goodbye when Jason walked her home.

She didn't show up the next Sunday.

Jason continued to have meals at Frank's Diner. Instead of just once a day, he went there for meals during all of Juanita's shifts.

Juanita took orders from him as usual. No small talk, though. When Jason tried to engage her in a conversation, her responses were monosyllabic. Jason yearned to continue the congenial relationship with Juanita, but he did not know what to do to make up with her. He was not exactly a smooth operator. All he knew was to be polite.

Juanita was still mad. She was a lot more experienced in "relationships" than Jason. Most people were. And she knew sometimes a little jealousy could work the magic. So she became extra friendly with a few other male customers in front of Jason. Jason looked forlorn when Juanita flirted with other men, asked for his tab, and left hurriedly.

She continued to clean house for him, getting paid.

Juanita soon got tired of all the men she became friendlier with trying too aggressively to woo her and to know her better, in the biblical sense. Some already started to grope her. She missed the prudish and boring Jason; the hardworking nerd, who wouldn't hurt a fly, with his oversized glasses, messy hair, and unfashionable clothes; who lived like a monk, and was kind enough to pay her a good salary to clean his house even though the house didn't really need that much cleaning.

She finally broke the ice, and asked if it was alright to show up the following Sunday for the walk. And she promised not to make him hold her hand – that was meant to be a joke, which of course Jason didn't get. Jason was obviously pleased but offered no repartee. Juanita rolled her eyes.

"Maybe we'll visit the Guggenheim again," said Jason, rubbing his chin and thinking hard.

Juanita made a gagging gesture, behind his back.

*

They walked and talked. The weather was still cold. Jason suggested that Juanita could put her hand into his coat pocket to keep warm. Juanita giggled at the suggestion, and took the opportunity to show the world they were a couple, alternating her left hand and right hands into Jason's right and left pockets. Jason felt a little awkward at first but got used to it after a while, grinning all the while like a child who had found a solution to a difficult puzzle. He even put his hand in the same pocket she had her hand in, with his glove on.

Juanita had a million things to tell Jason; such as what Sean was up to in recent weeks, and how she would love to cut his balls off. With that Hispanic accent, "balls" rolled off her tongue so vividly they seemed to be visibly dancing on the floor in front. She also shared with Jason her numerous problems with her unruly son Mike. Why couldn't he be more interested in books? Why was he not interested to become a doctor or a lawyer when he grew up? She wondered if Jason might have a positive influence on him if Jason could spend some time with him. He was only ten years old, but already built like a bull, and as stubborn as one.

Mike's first few years of life were spent in Spanish Harlem, and it seemed that he had never left there. His preferred neighbourhood was still the Spanish Harlem even after Juanita had moved to Washington Heights since she started work at the diner. He went to school in Spanish Harlem and all his friends were from there.

He was never interested in school. His only passion was baseball. He and his friends played street baseball all day long, when they were not watching it on TV, or talking about it.

Jason wanted to please Juanita, so he offered to tutor Mike in his school work. Juanita thought that was a brilliant idea. She would try to make Mike come to Jason's house an hour or so once or twice per week. Juanita wanted to hug Jason to thank him, but hesitated. She wasn't ready for another rejection from her "boyfriend".

Juanita asked why Jason didn't work in a hospital like other doctors, and Jason shared with her his legal problems with his ex-boss. However, he never harped on his frustrations and hardships. He thought Juanita had enough problems of her own. At such difficult times, Jason's mettle shone through.

*

There were talks of Frank wanting to sell the diner. He had plans to move to Florida. The weather in New York was killing him.

Sean Griffin was definitely interested in taking over the diner, and he tried his best to come up with the money. He called upon his friends and relatives to pool together the capital. He talked to banks about a loan. All that took time, but Frank was in a hurry to sell.

An idea hit Jason. He could buy the restaurant, and give it to Juanita to run, instead of her having to work under somebody like Sean Griffin. He hoped Juanita would be agreeable to his idea. He asked. Juanita thought he was only joking, and responded flippantly: "Sure, sure, sure, why not?"

Jason wasn't joking. He never joked.

He was then flush with money, having just asked the trustees to send him millions of dollars to be ready to fight the legal battle Harold Stein had started.

Jason went to his friend Leroy Katz again, and told him what he wanted, and he wanted it done quickly and quietly.

Leroy wondered why Jason should help this woman. Jason said she was a good friend. Leroy left it at that, sparing Jason any further questions, which would be embarrassing only to someone like Jason.

Leroy said he would try to bargain down the asking price by five per cent, and he succeeded. The deal was sealed within a week.

Leroy also drew up a contract between Jason the new owner of the diner, and Juanita the new manager, to protect both parties' interests, especially Jason's. Jason and Juanita were invited to his office, as Leroy proceeded to explain to them the finer points of the contracts before they signed it. Jason guaranteed Juanita a base salary, which was higher than what Sean Griffin was getting. In addition, Jason's holding company would give her a percentage of the net profit, calculated pro rata at an exponential rate when the profit exceeded certain benchmarks. It was a generous offer, but Jason reserved the right to dismiss her on one month's notice.

Jason pulled Leroy aside. "Is that last part about dismissing her at such short notice necessary?" Jason asked. "It seems cold and harsh."

Leroy put his hand on Jason's shoulder, and said: "I'm telling you as your lawyer and your friend – don't ever trust a woman completely, especially a good looking one."

Leroy quoted American author William Scott Downey: "The more beautiful the serpent, the more fatal its sting". And the line from a B-movie actress: "Don't underestimate me, darling, I can go from lady to ghetto in 2.5 seconds."

*

Another week later, Frank spent all day frolicking with young cocktail waitresses in Miami Beach, and Sean resigned on his own after he had found out the new manager was going to be Juanita.

Juanita couldn't believe it at first, and was wondering why someone like Jason, who didn't even own a car, nice furniture, or fancy clothes, could possibly have that kind of money. He did not even have a real job. But the deal came through, and Frank got his money and signed over the restaurant to Jason in the lawyer's office, and Jason handed over all the keys to Juanita. Her dream of a white knight came true, although not in the usual fairy tale kind of way. She went over to Jason's house, and said: "I don't care whether you like it or not, I am going to give you a big hug." Jason stood there red-faced, his body stiffened. At least, he didn't recoil from her. After he calmed down, he gathered his courage and admitted intimacy with his lady friend, sort of.

"You are a good friend and I want to help you," he said. "I want you happy."

Sometimes, an understatement is the most powerful way to deliver a message. Jason downplayed his generosity, and Juanita was all the more overwhelmed with gratitude. She was moved to tears, and her whole body trembled. She was hoping Jason would come over and hug her tight. It didn't happen, but she felt protected and loved by Jason, nevertheless.

She couldn't thank Jason enough, and hinted to him they might as well get married, since she already told everyone, especially Sean, that her fiancé had purchased the restaurant for her to run. Jason blushed and clammed up.

"I'm only kidding," Juanita quickly added.

*

Juanita needed to learn how to run a restaurant. She sought assistance from her old boss, Mrs Gonzales, owner of the Bronx restaurant Juanita used to work in before she became pregnant with Mike.

She led Juanita through every step. Juanita first applied for a line of credit from a bank, so that she wouldn't have a cash flow problem. The bank manager approved it after a phone call from Dr Jason John Lee, who used the same bank to deposit millions of dollars from his Hong Kong trust. She then retained the services of an accountant on Jason's behalf, and asked Jason's permission to renovate the diner to make it cleaner and greener, upgrade the IT system for the cash register and the accounting, install state-of-the-art technology for ordering food and drinks, and modernize the kitchen.

She asked Jason if they should re-name the diner Jason's. He vehemently insisted it should be called Juanita's Diner. With a name like that, Mexican food naturally had to be included in the menu. She hired a Mexican chef, and lucky for her, it was a good move because Mexican food was becoming all the rage in New York City. She retained most of her co-workers and their regular customers, and soon the business was more profitable than ever.

Juanita told Jason she wanted to continue to come over to his house to clean. His house didn't need cleaning more than once a week, and there was no need to pay her. Juanita wanted to be part of his life, and doing laundry for him was as personal as she could think of with Jason. They saw each other at least once a week and talked on the phone often. Juanita felt for sure that he cared about her, just not touchy-feely like all the other men in her past. And no sex. By then, Juanita was too busy with the diner to think too much about it. They were like an old married couple before they were even close to being lovers.

He went to Juanita's diner a few times right after the renovation, and was impressed with its new décor and clean environment. He complimented Juanita on the improved service and efficiency of the place. He seldom returned because Juanita insisted on not charging him. Also, some of the old employees were eyeing him funny. Some asked about the big day – the anticipated wedding, enough to make Jason feel awkward and uncomfortable. Jason did not mind eating somewhere else. There were enough bistros, diners and Chinese chop suey joints in the same neighbourhood for him to choose from.

24

With a medical degree from a prestigious medical school, and plenty of expertise in neurology, Jason was unemployable. No neurology department in North America was willing to take him in with the lawsuits hanging over his head. He continued to work from home.

The profit from Juanita's diner just about covered his monthly expense, but lawyers' fees were eating up his bank account rapidly. Juanita was making more money than he was. Juanita knew that, and brought him food often, and household supplies. She bought him clothes. He returned most of them, and gave Juanita back the refund. He didn't need them and they were not his style. Juanita threw up her arms, and shook her head. She felt like hitting him, but soon, just like the few people he was close to him before her, she got used to him and let him be.

Mike was made to come over to Jason's apartment two afternoons a week. It wasn't easy. He was only ten years old but rebellious as hell.

"I don't want to be taught by that stupid boyfriend of yours."

"He is not stupid; he is extremely smart; he's a brain doctor."

"He looks stupid; and he's got that stupid accent."

"Have some respect. He owns the diner I'm working in. And the job pays for the house you live in and the food you eat. And your allowance. If you don't go, you get no allowance."

The only reason he dragged himself to the nerdy doctor's home to be lectured for two hours was because otherwise he wouldn't get his weekly allowance. Juanita had a temper hot enough to match the chili served in her diner, and when she was mad, even Mike was scared.

Mike showed absolutely no interest in anything except baseball. After trying for a couple of weeks, Jason changed tack, and decided to impart in Mike some book knowledge using baseball as a tool. Jason went to the library and borrowed books on baseball, about its history and the rules of the game, how its stats were calculated, and the biographies of many baseball personalities, past and present. That finally caught Mike's attention, since he strived to know everything about America's favourite past-time. He learned history, mathematics, and vocabulary that way.

Jason was not exactly his idea of an idol, or a surrogate father, but he could feel Jason's integrity and kindness. In return, he was honest with his tutor, and over the years, never took advantage of Jason's good nature.

When Mike turned thirteen, he became a walking encyclopedia on baseball, and Jason had nothing more to offer that would interest him. They had an honest discussion. And they agreed to part ways. Mike thanked Jason for all his good intentions and time and effort, and told Jason formal education was not for him, and not everyone was as brainy as Jason. Mike just wanted to play baseball, the same way Jason just wanted to read books. Could Mike make Jason play baseball and talk baseball all day long? Jason understood. The two teamed up to convince Juanita to send Mike to a baseball training camp. They did their research and found a baseball training boarding school in Florida. It would be expensive, but Mike would be like an aquarium fish getting to live in the ocean. Juanita had to spend long hours at the diner, and there was no one home to supervise her wild child. Sending him to a boarding school was decidedly a sensible option. Mike got what he wanted, and he had Jason to thank for it. He gave Jason a hug, and Jason let him. Juanita looked on, tears filling her eyes. She smacked her son jokingly and said, "Do you know how lucky you are? I never ever get hugs from him." Jason bowed his head and shuffled his feet.

*

Juanita called Florida at least once a week, to make sure her son didn't get into any trouble. Mike would return to New York City for a break during summer and Christmas every year.

*

Juanita made an effort to wake up early every Sunday to walk with Jason, until noon at least, before she returned to the diner to work and left Jason to continue his walk by himself. She then joined him in Chinatown for a late meal at night.

*

Jason's research progressed steadily in spite of working solo at home. Whenever memory recognition made any significant progress, he would present it in the Annual Texas Neuroscience Conference, and the *Texas Medical Journal* regularly published the abstracts of his papers.

*

Earlier, Lee Jae Soong had called to say goodbye. She had completed her Ph.D. thesis, and was soon to return to South Korea to work for the Seoul Medical University. She filled Jason in on all the latest goings-on in Harold Stein's department.

Stein confided in Dr Henry Williams, his favourite researcher, that he and his lawyers had hired a private detective to find out all about Jason, and they determined that Jason owned a modest apartment in Washington Heights, and had limited cash in the bank. He surmised Jason would avoid the lawsuit for fear of financial ruin, and would soon quit brain research all together.

Henry Williams had a big mouth. Soon, many people in the department knew.

That would have been accurate information at the time of the gumshoe's investigation. Had they waited a few more weeks, they would have learned that Jason had three and a half million dollars in his bank account, and Harold Stein would not have been so cocky.

Lee Jae Soong wondered if Jason had the stomach to fight such iniquity. Jason told her he'd fight until the day he died, and she would be the first to be informed of the outcome.

Harold Stein's friends and family had organized a fund-raising dinner to support him, selling plates at two thousand dollars each. It raised nearly a quarter of a million dollars, to supplement the legal costs required to defend the "scientific integrity" of Dr Stein.

The Albert Einstein College of Medicine also agreed to pay part of the legal costs.

Another tidbit was about Dr Henry Williams. GenePharma, one of the biggest pharmaceutical and biotech companies in the world, offered him an obscene salary to take on the helm of its Research and Development Department, but he turned it down. Instead, he accepted a position at Cornell Medical Center as the Chair Professor of Neurology.

By the way, all the young researchers were still talking about Jason's missing notebook. It had become an inside joke, at Harold Stein's expense.

*

The lonely years Jason spent in his apartment working on the computer were most heartbreaking for Mary. He was on the verge of cracking up. The only things that kept him sane were the wooden man zhuang he used almost daily; the annual Texas Neurology Seminar which he looked forward to; and his Sunday walks with his "girlfriend" Juanita.

Life was so frustrating and monotonous even his neighbour, the older tattooed lesbian's frequent waylaying him on his return home after dinner followed by her long-winded discussion of her purported medical issues, was a welcome digression. He was not a medical student anymore, but a licensed doctor, and he could honestly advise her that all her problems were psychosomatic. But she said even hypochondriacs could come down with real serious diseases. They argued until Jason excused himself to go home to sleep.

His other neighbour, the tall black man with breasts still waved at him excitedly like a kid seeing Santa Claus in the window of a department store, and winked at him as soon as he got Jason's attention. But Jason wouldn't go as far as befriending him. He was just too weird.

Juanita brought him diner food often late at night so that he could have a snack, and she could see him. He cared about

Juanita enough not to burden her with his problems. But seeing her and talking with her made life more bearable for Jason.

Even though Jason never talked too much about his problems, Juanita knew about his lawsuits, and his frustration working alone from home. She wished Jason would just let off steam by having sex with her, as most men would do. But it didn't seem like it was going to happen. The most intimacy Jason allowed himself was her hand in his pocket. A kiss on the cheek was also a routine. A kiss on the lips was never attempted by either. Juanita could feel that Jason was not ready for that kind of intimacy. She didn't understand it, but she accepted it. She had decided that Jason was to be her white knight for life. She used to want someone suave, full of élan, debonair, and witticism, and a fantastic dancer. Jason was exactly the opposite, but she wanted him.

*

Jane called now and then, so that Jason could bring her up to date with the latest developments of the lawsuits. She never failed to complain that all the doctors she knew in Hong Kong were making big bucks, and why couldn't Jason come back to Hong Kong to practice and forget about his god damned brain research? Jason told her firmly he was not going anywhere until he beat Stein in the court of law, and if not there, at least in the court of medical opinion. His reputation as a neuroscientist was slowly gaining credibility because of his presentations in Texas.

After numerous tries, Jane knew Jason would not give up the fight. She eventually stopped nagging him about how other doctors were getting richer and he was getting poorer by the day. She let him be.

25

The court date finally arrived. Jason was then thirty-three years old, but looked much older.

He was there for twenty full days listening to arguments from both sides.

Lawyers like to split hairs. The crux of the matter was who invented the technique and owned it, and whether it could be monopolized at all? Could other people use the technique freely?

Instead, lawyers from both sides argued over every little detail of the memory recovery technique and machinery, which they did not even fully understand.

Jason was called for questioning for one day, and Dr Stein was called for the next. He did not look in Jason's direction once, and he lied through his teeth. He claimed he ordered Jason to carry out the experiments, and all the ideas originated from him. He denied any knowledge of Jason's notebook.

He called on Saul Shapiro to testify on his behalf, to tell the judge that Jason was not productive at all during his time at the Neuroscience Department in Bronx. Saul Shapiro was the Alzheimer expert assigned by Dr Stern to mentor Jason, but never did anything useful during Jason's four years there. It did not take long for the whole court to realize that Dr Shapiro was a sorry senile sinecure. He still could not identify Jason by his correct name, alternatively calling him John and Jack. Mercifully, the judge quickly dismissed him.

No one else from Einstein College was available as a witness for Stein, and Jason could not produce any witness, either. He worked on his own all those years. In the end, it was Jason's word against Harold Stein's.

They had to wait three weeks for the judge to pass judgment.

When it was finally issued, it was a twenty-page document. She ruled that there was no proof of theft on either party, and in the scientific community, scientists always enjoyed academic freedom; hence, there was no need for any injunction to stop any party from using the technique to do further research.

The judge advised the National Patent Office to proceed with the patent application procedures, and if they were successful, co-ownership of the patent would be considered.

Stein instructed his lawyers to file for an appeal, assuming that Jason should be running out of money by then.

Stein and his lawyers also proceeded to re-apply for a patent for the use of titanium to retrieve electronic signals from the limbic brain, and two other separate patents, one for the electronic signals collection technique and another for pattern recognition of the signals by the customized computer program.

Jason's lawyers advised him to re-apply for the same patents.

Jason was not someone who would idle, not even for one day. While in court, Jason thought it would be brilliant if criminal suspects could be proven guilty or not based on their memory records.

The day after the last court date, he went to Dr Leona Koch's office and asked if he could use her patients to do some tests. The tests would be non-invasive and completely harmless, and most of all, they could benefit her patients by giving them some mental exercise. Dr Koch's patients had all signed consent forms to undergo all kinds of mental tests, and Jason could simply piggyback his experiment onto hers.

He wanted to try titanium probes attached to the scalp, and see if he could detect signals from the whole limbic system through the skull, analogous to electro-encephalograms routinely used in hospitals around the world. The limbic signals, of course, would require a more sensitive electronic system to detect because of the skull barrier, and the interpretation could be more complicated, given that signals could come from all three parts of the limbic brain at the same time; namely, the hippocampus, the basal ganglia, and the amygdala. It also meant he would require a more sophisticated computer program.

Dr Koch was emeritus professor, and in her last year or so of employment before her complete retirement from the academe. She was fearless; even Harold Stein could not hurt her. She agreed to let Jason use her clinic until she retired.

By then, no one in the world knew more about the science of memory than Jason did. From working with cadaver brains, he learned memories involving skills and emotions were not well preserved after death, no matter how fresh the brains were. Skills and emotions were integral parts of many memories, and they were intact only in the brains of conscious people.

While the hippocampus is the main centre of memory, the basal ganglia is the centre of memories for skills and the amygdala is that for emotions. They become inert when the person becomes unconscious, from sleep, general anesthesia, or death. Jason was sure he could retrieve more memories from conscious people because of signals from the basal ganglia and amygdala.

To collect the maximum amount of signals from the limbic brain, Jason designed a titanium headband that surrounded the forehead and middle of the skull, sitting above the ears.

The band resembled the irremovable headband the Monk made the Monkey King wear in the epic novel, *Journey to the West*, favourite reading for every Chinese child. In the novel, whenever the Monkey King got out of control, all the Monk had to do was to say a special prayer, and the headband would inflict such headaches that the Monkey King would roll on the ground in agony, begging for mercy. That was how the Monk controlled the rambunctious Monkey King and made him obey him and carry out all his orders.

Interestingly, in just the way the Monk tamed the Monkey King, Jason's titanium headband would bring many criminals to their knees in later years.

*

Hair might add to the interference in signal transmission. To avoid having to shave anyone's scalp, an invasive procedure, Jason selected only bald men attending Professor Koch's geriatric clinic, and there was no shortage of them.

Jason's emphasis was on the seminal events of his subjects' lives, especially those related to violence and felony of any kind, since he was thinking of his technique's use in solving crime.

Testing Professor Koch's patients for memory was not a walk in the park, because many of them, though not senile, were curmudgeons. But it was rewarding because at the end of ten months Jason had collected so much data and had records of so many memories from the patients as well as from their families that there was enough for him to work with from home for years.

Jason had had to modify his computer program significantly. With his superior programing skills, he developed an algorithm to synchronize and integrate all the signals coming from the three main centres of the limbic brain: hippocampus, amygdala, and basal ganglia, and the patterns that emerged were more distinctive and multiplex than when he had signals solely from the hippocampus.

He realized what set apart his new technique from the original one he invented while he worked at Albert Einstein College of Medicine was his computer program. To avoid having his computer program stolen again, he had to guard it securely. And he must have a backup. The latest version of his program was always updated onto a CD-ROM and put into his safe. Opening his program required two sets of complicated passwords, one of which he changed at intervals. He also installed an anti-theft program.

He thought about re-applying for a patent of his new and improved computer program but decided against it. There was no rush. Let the Patent Office decide on their original applications first. He preferred keeping the holy grail of the memory recovery technique a secret until the time was right.

Year after year, Jason presented the progress of his research at the Annual Texas Neuroscience Meeting. The meeting organizers knew of the legal battle between Jason and Harold Stein, and they were willing to overlook the lack of a clear description of his method used, especially the details of his computer program. They were interested only in his results. They were all too willing to be spectators of a legal drama unfolding in front of them year after year, and they were secretly rooting for Dr Jason Lee.

There must have been a spy or two from Harold Stein's Department at the Texas meeting because before long, the Albert Einstein College of Medicine team would be presenting something similar in other conferences, with titles like "Memory

Recovery of Crimes". They also used a titanium plate applied to the scalp of living subjects. They didn't use a head band; using that would make their copying Jason look way too obvious. However, their results were never as good as Jason's. Never in a million years would Stein's team know that they had to include signals from the basal ganglia and the amygdala to produce the optimal results. Even if they did obtain the signals from these brain structures, they still would not have known how to use them unless they had the ingenious algorithm written in Jason's computer programming.

One could never fool the scientific community, not for long anyway, because there were simply too many smart people around. It did not matter what Harold Stein said or did, in the neuroscience community, most people knew Jason's research findings were always years ahead of Stein's. Major conference organizers began to contact Jason in advance to invite him to give talks regardless of Stein's objections.

The ten junior researchers who shared a room with Jason in the Neuroscience Department at Albert Einstein College of Medicine later found jobs in neuroscience institutions scattered all over the world, and they all spread the word of how Jason was shafted, and Harold Stein's invention was actually the brainchild of Dr Jason Lee.

Dr Harold Stein's clout and influence were waning by the day. He was hoping that he could prevent the slide by obtaining exclusive patent rights. But it didn't look like it was going to happen anytime soon.

The National Patent Office needed time to decide on who should be granted the patents. Each side took many months to provide evidence of originality. Again, it was Harold Stein's word against Jason Lee's.

The patent officials had to consult literally hundreds of experts on the technicalities of the memory recovery machinery, and the computer programming. After three and a half years of deliberation, they finally reached a decision.

They rejected the patent application for the use of titanium for both parties, based on the argument that what was naturally occurring was not patentable; only techniques and devices invented by men were. For example, Isaac Newton could not patent gravity or the apple that fell from the tree, while Steve

Jobs of Apple could patent the company's iPhone and the iPad because they did not grow on trees.

The Patent Office also found the technique to capture electrical signals from the limbic brain was simply a law of nature; hence not patentable. The electronic equipment used was commonplace and the reception and transmission of electrical signals were basic concepts of physics; hence not patentable.

The computer program was man-made; hence potentially patentable. However, the Patent Office rejected the application for the computer program which Jason wrote years ago, because it was not unique and original enough. There were numerous computer programs out there for pattern recognition of all kinds, using artificial intelligence.

Jason was in fact glad that none of the patents were granted, otherwise there was a good chance Harold Stein would be named as co-inventor. He was also wondering – had he applied a patent for his new computer program, would he be granted one?

All those years, Jason could not share his invention with other scientists because of the ongoing lawsuits; hence, progress in the field was greatly impeded. Details of his methodology and computer program were undisclosed because he was afraid of plagiarism, especially by Harold Stein. Other scientists could not replicate his work, and major journals wouldn't publish his work.

He didn't want to complicate matters by revealing any details of his methodology and his computer program, knowing Stein's ruthlessness and lack of integrity. He could not publish freely and his scientific papers appeared only in the *Texas Medical journal* because their editors followed his research and his lawsuits, and also paid attention to his oral presentations.

They had faith in him.

26

While Jason was mired in lawsuits, Juanita also had to deal with lawyers and the court of law – because of her son. Mike O'Malley got into big trouble back in New York during the summer of 1999, when he was eighteen.

The five formative years Mike spent in Florida not only made him a better baseball player, the total freedom he enjoyed also nurtured him into a full-blown thug.

The Florida sun made his hair lighter and his skin darker. The daily workout did wonders for his body. He became six feet two, 190 lb., all muscles, ruggedly handsome, and a hunk like his father. Unlike his father, he was moody and calculating. When provoked, instead of acting like a hothead, he would walk away brooding and planning his next move.

He became a figure much feared among his peers. There were people who crossed him and later ended up with broken bones, and would not talk about what happened to them. No one seemed to have gotten away with offending Mike. The police in the Florida area where the baseball academy was located all knew him well, because he got into plenty of scrapes as a juvenile. And he was the main suspect in some of the assault cases, in which the witnesses and victims refused to talk. But he managed to stay out of serious trouble over the years in Florida, until he returned to New York.

He rushed back to the City because of Sean Griffin's daughter Virginia, his childhood friend and soul mate.

Virginia was a good student. She was offered a scholarship by the University of Pennsylvania in her senior year. Blue eyed and blonde, she had the face sought after by model agencies and the unblemished complexion of a young Celtic lass before the sun and aging ruin it.

Mother Nature has a way of deciding on anyone's genetic make-up. It's random but not necessarily fair for individuals, like being dealt a hand from a thoroughly shuffled deck of cards. Most hands are a mixture of good and not-so-good cards, but some rare hands have all the good cards. Not only beautiful and smart, Virginia was vivacious and sweet, and everyone's darling.

But that didn't exempt her from evil intent and natural disasters. Mother Nature gives everyone equal opportunity when it comes to random acts of violence and unforeseen accidents. Everyone, regardless of the genetic make-up, is equally susceptible to bad luck.

Virginia's trouble started on her prom night.

The prom – what an awful American invention. Social interaction in a dance hall is so passé for the American youths of today's generation. Proms have generated nothing but poor self-esteem, teenage angst, vanity, jealousy, and commercialism. How many youngsters on a prom night had wished they had the look that could kill like that possessed by Carrie in Stephen King's eponymous novel?

Proms were intended to create opportunities for teenagers to interact with the opposite sex in a festive social context, but they often ended up creating less wholesome opportunities, such as getting hopelessly drunk or recklessly losing their virginity. Or both.

The prom was scheduled for the last Saturday of May. Virginia had on a strapless violet blouse, revealing the creamiest of shoulders, cleavage, and a pair of long legs.

She was going through the usual teenage problems with her father Sean Griffin.

The dress she was wearing was a little too revealing for her father's peace of mind. But he knew better than to say anything. He simply went to her closet and picked out her favourite shawl and told her to take it along, in case they cranked up the air-con in the dance hall.

She knew exactly what that was about, and played along by wrapping the shawl around her shoulders in front of her father, covering most of her décolletage.

Sean kissed her forehead and couldn't help but repeat his mantra about the lascivious nature of men in general. He ought to know. He himself had been lusting after young women for years.

Sean did have a point. Virginia's "problem" was that men of all ages lust after girls like her, pretty and innocent-looking at seventeen – a strong aphrodisiac.

In a way, beauty in a woman is a blessing and a curse wrapped in the same package bestowed by Mother Nature; with it, you win some, you lose some. Virginia had lucky breaks in her young life because of how she looked, but on that fateful prom night, she paid dearly for it.

The theme of the prom was discotheque, channeling Saturday Night Fever, with Bee Gees music, strobe lights and the whole cheesy retro shebang. Virginia was a good dancer. Several boys in her class danced with her by turns, and sometimes all her girlfriends did a group dance with her. Somehow, Virginia always ended up in the centre, doing the female version of John Travolta in that 1977 disco movie. Everyone simply loved to watch her dance, and marvel at her moves.

The chaperones closed the venue at ten, but all the revelers were naturally high and many arranged follow-up entertainment to continue with the partying. Virginia wanted to dance some more, and she talked her friends into heading towards a nightclub called The Stars in the Forest Hill neighbourhood in Queens.

There she ran into a man who would change her life forever. His name was Kelly Mackenzie.

*

Kelly Mackenzie was a piece of work.

The whole world learned of his wickedness only after he was murdered a few months later. The police retrieved from the bank vault all his self-produced audiovisual tapes, which documented all his sex crimes. He was a serial sadistic rapist.

The media had a heyday with the case. For months, feature articles were written with new angles or new leads. Sages and gurus were interviewed for their pontifications on such heinous evil and depravity.

According to a psychologist interviewed, a human being's moral compass is guided by a triad of counteracting forces, namely: desires, virtues, and rationalization.

Desires prompt us to do bad things to satisfy our own primal urges; virtues deter us from doing them; rationalization is for our peace of mind if and when we stray.

The truly psycho-violent type has not the slightest qualm in satisfying their desires at the expense of others' sufferings, and they sleep well without any need for rationalizing their misdeeds.

Serial rapists and murderers, men who keep young girls as sex slaves in dungeons, pædophiles, and parents who abuse their own children belong to this psycho-violent subclass.

*

Kelly used to be a detective with the Nassau Police Force in New York's Long Island, but resigned from the post after he became a prime suspect in a string of cold cases of rape in Long Island. He happened to be in the picture in every one of them.

He had a remarkably charmed life growing up, adored by both parents and his two younger sisters. He was used to getting what he wanted. He wanted sex as young as thirteen years old, and he got it from his younger sisters' babysitter. She was sixteen and did him the favour because he was a handsome boy and also she thought it was cool that a boy would always remember her as his first. Every time the parents were enjoying a night out, the babysitter would babysit Kelly's two young sisters for half a night and take care of Kelly the rest of the time. Kelly got hold of a compendium on all known sexual positions and methods, and went through it from cover to cover with the babysitter. He also tried a few of his own inventions, which always involved some sadistic components. Even at that age, he had a penchant for kinky violent sex.

After one particularly violent session, in which Kelly tried to sodomize her against her will and almost succeeded, the babysitter told him she wouldn't do it with him anymore. He begged and begged, and promised to behave.

He did behave, for a while.

Then when she was ready to enter college at eighteen and babysat for one last time, Kelly let her have it.

By then he was fifteen and almost a head taller and much stronger than the babysitter. After tying her up, he forcibly sodomized her three times, before he sent her to the hospital with multiple injuries caused by his having beaten her senseless.

Before the ambulance took her away, Kelly had whispered in her ear while sneering: "Don't forget to tell the police I am a juvenile, and you are an adult."

Kelly was already in his thirties, but with his baby face, boyish charm and "hip" fashion sense, he wouldn't be out of place among a throng of students in a college campus. His well-groomed and clean-cut appearance and a swagger typical of many cops surely added to his appeal to the opposite sex. But Kelly hadn't had a steady girlfriend for years.

He had his last steady girlfriend when he was seventeen. She got pregnant and refused to have an abortion. It had caused him a lot of grief.

But Kelly had always been lucky, and never more so than when the girl miscarried a couple of weeks later. Kelly paid her a perfunctory hospital visit, not so much to comfort her but to affirm the miscarriage. He then dumped her faster than a schoolboy with his cigarette when caught smoking by the headmaster.

Not having steady girlfriends did not mean he wasn't interested in sex; he lived for it. Even though picking up girls and getting them into the sack was never a problem for him, the women didn't always agree to his brutal and rough kind of sexual requests. Worse still, many of them became too clingy and demanding afterwards.

Then he discovered flunitrazepam, better known by its trade name, Rohypnol, and Ropy in the street.

He read about this date-rape drug in some newspaper feature story and in an instant felt as if the sea had parted for him.

He went to a dodgy clinic in Chinatown and coaxed a prescription from the old doctor there for purported insomnia.

He tried the drug on his subservient lovers and it worked in the way that tabloid news article had described. In their semi-comatose state, they acquiesced to his every demand and indulged all his cruel whims, no matter how rough. And they remembered very little of the ordeal the next morning.

Kelly determined that the ideal dosage for an average-sized woman would be two and a half tablets of that dull green medicine. The victim would be knocked out in a reasonably short period of time, and yet wouldn't be totally unconscious. She could still be able to moan and groan in response to his brutal treatment.

Next, this wily creep put what he learned in the police academy to good use. Raping a woman in his own home would not be a good idea, and love motels were equipped with CCTVs. Instead, he bought a van and modified it so that the back of it became a small windowless bedroom. There were rugs and pillows, lots of pillows. He also installed spotlights and audiovisual equipment.

He set out to cruise all the bars and nightclubs in his Long Island neighbourhood looking for sex slaves. With his handsome face and courteous manners, he could easily chat up any single woman. When the time was right, he slipped two and half tablets' worth of the pulverized drug into her drink unnoticed, and waited. At the first sign of the drug taking effect, Kelly would quietly escort the woman out to his van. After driving to a deserted location, they would climb into the back and he would have one to two hours of fun before dumping his victim by the roadside.

He was obsessed with leaving some scars behind, a kind of signature on his 'artwork'. He preferred leaving bite marks. He had in his possession numerous sets of dentures used for props in Dracula movies. As part of his foreplay, he sank his fangs into the woman's upper arms, breasts, inner thighs and buttocks. He was especially brutal with his victim's genitalia.

He always switched on his sophisticated audio-visual set-up in his van before he started his "performance".

He was meticulous in cleaning up the woman and the inside of the van after each encounter. The videotapes went into a bank safe deposit box, to be taken out occasionally for his home entertainment.

Most women kept quiet after the ordeal even though they knew they had been violated, with such outrageous bite wounds sometimes requiring medical attention, but they simply didn't know what to do because they had no recollection of what had happened. And often they were too embarrassed to show the bites to friends and family.

A few did make police reports, after some urging from family or friends who saw the wounds, or from the doctor who treated them. But investigations hardly ever yielded substantial evidence for the police to take further action. There were never enough body fluid residues for the crime lab to work on. Of the few cases with some clues, all pointed to Kelly being the last person seen with the victim.

After a few years and countless women, the police finally caught up with him and raided his home. They found nothing to incriminate him. They searched his Toyota, which he ordinarily used to commute. They did not examine the van closely, which was parked at the back of his house and made to look abandoned. It was covered with dirt, and the rear end was resting on bricks, its two hind wheels having been removed and hidden in the basement.

Kelly proclaimed his innocence vociferously and resigned from the force in protest against his treatment by his fellow law-enforcement officers.

He soon started his own private investigation agency, specializing in documenting spousal disloyalty.

When he restarted his nocturnal activities, he took the precaution of moving to a new turf, in Queens and other Boroughs instead of his Long Island neighbourhood.

Two weeks previously, he had visited The Stars and to his delight, found the nightclub swarming with young co-eds because of the kind of music they played, and ID checks were perfunctory at best. He spotted a cute blonde and zoomed in on her. After chatting her up for almost an hour, the blonde's boyfriend returned from an errand, and was extremely hostile towards him. He made it manifestly clear that it was time for Kelly to get lost. Kelly had to change tack and target another girl who would have been his third or fourth choice, whom he managed to drag into his van at one o'clock in the morning.

Kelly returned to The Stars that night, hoping to see the blonde again and to have another go at her if her protective boyfriend wasn't around.

27

Kelly spotted Virginia on the dance floor. She was with her friends doing a group dance. Kelly had earlier scoped the place thoroughly for his next victim. There were many pretty girls in the Stars that night, but no one was nearly as young and innocent-looking as Virginia. When she twirled, her violet dress lifted up like Marilyn Monroe's white skirt in that famous photo, revealing incredibly shapely and creamy legs.

And that face. Kelly swallowed hard as he immediately conjured up the image of Virginia's angelic face contorting in pain. That immediately brought on twitchiness in his groin.

He moved closer to the group, pumping his hips and swinging his arms to the beat of the music. His dance moves were in sync with Virginia's. He could really dance well – such is the banality of evil. Soon enough he was dancing with her in the centre, with other dancers on the floor retreating to the periphery, many only watching and clapping along. They sure were a spectacular dance couple.

Kelly looked over to the table where Virginia's girlfriends had returned, and saw also four or five boys of high school age, sharply dressed, who talked and walked confidently like they owned the world. Kelly thought that could be a problem; he would have to play it by ear.

When the DJ took a break and the music stopped, he leaned over to Virginia and asked: "How about a drink?"

"No thanks. I will have to wait quite a few more months before I can have the hard stuff in public," Virginia said, exaggerating her age.

Kelly was buying time. "How about orange juice?"

Virginia looked into those smiling eyes and thought this guy seem harmless enough. She agreed to have some orange juice.

Never let the face fool you. One of the most sadistic serial murderers of all time in the US was nicknamed the Santa Claus, because he had a white mane, rosy cheeks, and smiling eyes like Kelly's. This psycho Santa's shtick was to stab ice picks into young girls' inner ears to hear them scream, and to leave their mutilated bodies at the entrance of their high schools so that he could watch their classmates' horrified reactions when they bumped into the gory displays. One wonders whether the Santa Claus serial murderer can send shudders through those listening to the song, 'When Irish Eyes Are Smiling'. That psycho has totally ruined a very lovely song.

On the way to the bar, Kelly with the smiling eyes whispered to Virginia that if she had never had a real drink before, he wouldn't push, but if she could handle it, he could add a little vodka to the orange juice from his hip flask. Virginia felt challenged by the offer, hesitated for a few seconds, and then nodded in agreement.

Accepting booze from a stranger was not a smart thing to do, but what teenager would admit to never having tried alcohol at the age of seventeen? And Kelly really did seem like such a nice guy.

Kelly lowered the glass of orange juice below the counter and asked Virginia to shield the glass from the bartender while he poured the vodka from his flask. That maneuver gave him a chance to "accidentally" brush Virginia's thigh with his hand. He wanted to know if it felt as smooth as it looked.

There was a sudden loud bang at the other side of the bar. One of the bartenders was practicing his fancy mixology tricks by tossing a bottle over his left shoulder and trying to catch it behind his back without looking. He missed and the bottle hit the sink, causing quite a ruckus. Kelly knew that he had to act fast because this "baby" probably had a curfew even though it was Saturday night, so the distraction was welcome. He quickly reached into his pocket for a homemade dispenser, and with one smooth squeeze, the desired amount of the dull green powder was dumped into the orange drink, while Virginia turned towards the commotion.

She took a sip of the drink and nodded towards Kelly in acknowledgement of the added vodka. After a few more minutes of chitchat, Virginia thanked him for the drink and told him she'd better return to her friends.

While Kelly was plotting his next move, there was another commotion in the area towards which Virginia had headed. The crowd around there was getting bigger, and someone yelled: "Move away, give her some air."

Kelly went over to look, and broke out in a cold sweat. There on the floor was Virginia, pale as a ghost and struggling to breathe.

Virginia's friends were in shock. Luckily, an older boy named Ramon regained his composure quickly and promptly took control of the situation.

He screamed at the crowd gathering around: "Stay away, give her some air, and someone dial 911 for an ambulance, like right now!"

Ramon and his friends then moved a row of chairs to form a barricade around Virginia to keep the crowd away. He then went outside to wait for the ambulance men, to show them the way as soon as they arrived.

The ambulance arrived in less than five minutes. By that time, Virginia was semi-conscious and her breathing was labored and wheezy.

Virginia was quickly placed on a gurney and transported into the ambulance.

There was no hospital in Queens capable of handling such an emergency. The closest major hospitals were in Manhattan. Traffic along the Long Island Highway and Midtown Manhattan was congested in spite of the hour because of a traffic accident. The driver of the ambulance made a snap decision to take the Whitestone Bridge over to Bronx and follow the highway to reach upper Manhattan. An ambulance man suggested Columbia Medical Center, and the driver thought it was as good as any other option. He phoned the emergency room staff there to alert them of the dire case they were bringing in.

Virginia's friends were able to reach her father and tell him what had happened, and that the ambulance was on its way to Columbia Medical Center.

They tried to administer first aid to Virginia in the ambulance but they failed to put in an intravenous line because her blood pressure was so low all her veins had collapsed. One ambulance man placed an Ambu-bag over Virginia's mouth and nose, and every few seconds he squeezed the bag to try to force air into her lungs. The ambulance driver knew a real emergency when he saw one. He drove like a madman with the siren blaring, and was able to reach the hospital in a matter of minutes.

28

Dr Lyons, the chief resident at the emergency room, took one look at Virginia and knew she was suffering from asphyxia – a lack of oxygen. To assist her in breathing, he needed to place a tube through her throat down her windpipe.

He barked out orders like the pro he was for the nurse to bring the endotracheal tube. He lifted her chin and using the laryngoscope, pushed her tongue aside so that he could look down her throat. He noticed that the flap over her windpipe was swollen beyond recognition, and the vocal cords and the surrounding tissues were red and swollen as well. The tube would have to be forced in. He tried three times, causing some bleeding in the throat region, but the vocal cords were clamped tight.

The only alternative to get air into her lungs was to cut an opening in her windpipe through the middle of throat – a tracheostomy.

Dr Lyons shouted again, with even more urgency, this time for the tracheostomy surgical set. By then, Virginia had turned blue.

He made a small but deep incision with the scalpel and immediately reached the trachea. The cartilage ring supporting it required a little more force from the scalpel but not too much more. As soon as the tracheal wall was punctured, air rushed into Virginia's lungs and a slight hissing sound was audible. Dr Lyons inserted the three-way valve into the aperture he made in the trachea, adroitly connected it to an Ambu-bag and started pumping air into her lungs.

Dr Singh, the second year surgical resident was able to put an intravenous line in her ankle region by making a surgical cut and fishing out a large vein. The EKG monitor was hooked up, and as soon as air started to fill the lungs, the heart began to beat regularly. However, the blood pressure was only 70/40. Dr Singh wasted no time in infusing one liter of Ringer's Lactate solution into her circulatory system followed by intravenous Dopamine in titrated doses to raise and maintain the blood pressure.

Colour returned to Virginia's face, but she remained unresponsive to all kinds of stimuli. It was anyone's guess as to how long she had been deprived of oxygen.

Dr Lyons took enough blood from her to send to the clinical laboratory for all the routine tests, and also saved enough for prospective tests that might be deemed necessary when more clinical information became available.

Judging from the presenting symptoms and the gross appearance of her larynx and vocal cords, Dr Lyons thought there was no doubt that Virginia had suffered a severe allergic reaction that could cause shock and severe swelling in many parts of the body, especially the upper respiratory tract. The only question was: what had caused it?

Dr Lyons first had to talk to the anxious father. The nurse pointed at Sean, who was pacing the floor in the waiting area.

They shook hands and Dr Lyons gave him a run-down. As soon as her condition stabilized, and as long as there was no multiple organ failure or systemic infection, Dr Lyons would ask Dr Richard Schwartz from Neurology Department to see if there was any permanent brain damage. He wanted to send a blood sample to an old associate working in Stanford University, who had in his lab the world's most powerful Mass Spectrometer.

Seeing Sean's arched eyebrows, Dr Lyons added that the Mass Spec could detect all possible drugs and toxins in the world that would have caused the severe allergic reaction.

Dr Lyons then spoke to one of Virginia's classmates, and determined that the last thing she took was the orange juice in her hand when she returned to their table in The Stars after dancing. He made a note of that. Later, when he talked to the police, he suggested they search for a glass of orange juice.

Dr Lyons then transferred Virginia to the ICU, where she could be closely monitored.

29

When Mike heard about Virginia's mishap, he rushed back to New York, driving in his Camaro like a man possessed. When he reached town, she was still in the hospital. After being comatose for seventy-two hours, she started to come around, and breathe on her own without the respirator. She still had the tracheotomy and couldn't talk easily. When Mike tried to communicate with her, she wrote on a piece of paper, "Go ask Ramon."

Mike found out from Ramon what happened that night, and Dr Lyons told him the blood test from Stanford University confirmed Rohypnol in Virginia's blood. Since Virginia never touched that drug, Dr Lyons thought her drink must have been spiked, and that poison was the most likely cause of the hypersensitivity reaction that almost killed her.

Mike was enraged, but not showing much emotion. No one would have guessed he was ready to kill, if he could get away with it.

He intended to stay by Virginia's bedside while she was still sick. But as soon as she was well enough to go home, he would set out to find the bastard, and he already knew what to do with him when he found him.

Virginia's tracheostomy was sealed off in a week; then she was transferred out of ICU. She was discharged after another two weeks, alive but traumatized. Mike took Virginia home, and then he hit the road, looking for the perpetrator who poisoned his sweetheart.

Mike had a few friends in the police force. One of them was a detective with the Fifth precinct in Queens, which was involved with investigating a few cold cases of rape involving Rohypnol in their jurisdiction.

It did not take Mike long to find out that Kelly Mackenzie had been a prime suspect on similar cases in Long Island and more recently in the five boroughs.

Videotapes from the CCTV showed Kelly on the dance floor with her but there was no evidence that he had anything to do with spiking Virginia's drink. The police never found the glass of orange juice, and samples of juices from the jugs in the Star's refrigerators were cleared of any kind of contamination.

Mike's detective friend said he was almost 100 percent sure Kelly was the perpetrator, but catching him might be difficult because he was just too slick.

Mike stole a mug shot of Kelly, and also a copy of the police report. He found out where Kelly lived.

Every evening for two weeks, he drove to Kelly's house in Long Island and stayed across the street overnight watching Kelly's every move.

He was nervous the first night there because the Camaro he drove from Florida was modified into a *gangsta* set of wheels. It might have blended in easily in the streets of Spanish Harlem, but in the middle class Long Island neighbourhood, it stood out like Yao Ming in a kindergarten playground.

The next day, he rented a grey mid-size Ford sedan and parked it at a different spot a few houses away from Kelly's home. No one paid him or his car any notice.

He watched Kelly arriving home from work. Whenever Kelly jumped into his car to leave the house again, Mike followed him at a safe enough distance so as not to arouse suspicion. During the two weeks, Kelly did not go anywhere further than the supermarket. Mike stayed up all night to watch Kelly's movements about the house with a binocular. There was nothing suspicious. He did not go out much and he turned off his house lights before midnight.

When Kelly left for work in the morning, Mike tried to break into the house but found Kelly's security system for the house worthy of a drug lord's residence. There was this dirty van parked in the back of the house. Its two rear tires were missing, and its rear end supported by bricks.

After two weeks of surveillance, Mike was not getting anywhere. He thought of different ways of hurting Kelly, but none would guarantee success without risking police arrest. He could also tell that Kelly was vigilant when he was out and about, and he also suspected that Kelly always carried a gun.

Breaking into his home was not an option; he did not want to alert Kelly to the fact that he was being followed.

The only thing he could possibly break into was the broken down dirty van, so he decided to give it a go. It turned out to be all that was needed to nail Kelly.

Using the skill he acquired in the streets of Spanish Harlem, he worked on the car lock, and in minutes, broke into the van without leaving any trace of forced entry. When he got into the back of the van, he discovered Kelly's dirty little secret.

The next day, he went to a specialty shop and bought what was needed to track a moving car. He returned to Kelly's house and installed an electronic device on the van's underbelly. When the van was on the road, a signal would be sent to a receiver Mike carried. It had a global positioning system (GPS), making it easy to track the van whenever Kelly drove it.

After the Virginia incident, Kelly lay low, and did not use the van for a long time. Mike patiently waited for him to make another move, never letting the receiver out of his sight.

One night, after watching a movie on TV about a haunted house in which scantily clad teenage girls ran around scaring one another and screaming loudly, Kelly went to his basement to fetch the two missing wheels to put them back onto his van, recharged the battery, and hooked up the audio-visual equipment in the rear compartment. He then packed some of that green powder and a new set of "teeth" from his stash in his underground dungeon, before he set off to New Rochelle, an upscale suburb in the Westchester County near the Bronx – one county in which he had yet to rape any woman.

It was a Thursday night and the bar he went to was packed with young co-eds from a nearby small college. He slowly sipped from a tall gin and tonic while he watched the young revelers dancing and getting smashed. It seemed that all the young women were accounted for. He was contemplating a move to another bar when a dark-haired girl came up to him and started a conversation. She was cute enough and had a nice body. She would do, he thought.

The girl was quite inebriated and probably would have agreed to have sex with him without the Rohypnol, but that wouldn't be enough fun. He followed his modus operandi and slipped the routine dose of the green powder into her next screwdriver. By the time he helped her to his van, she was semi-comatose. He put her in the back, and already had in mind a spot where he could do whatever he wanted to the girl without being disturbed, in City Island, about ten minutes away.

The place was a parking lot for trucks. It was dark except for streetlights from the access road. He parked behind a row of trucks so that his van would be shielded from passing cars, even though he doubted anyone would be using that road in that hour. All the truckers should be home sleeping or getting drunk somewhere. He shut off the engine and got out of the front seat, ready to climb into the back of the van to have some fun.

He was loosening his belt by the van when someone whacked his head from behind. He passed out cold.

Mike knew how to use the exact amount of force to knock someone out without killing him. He was good with a baseball bat. While Kelly was on the ground, he swung his bat at his knees with all his might a dozen times each. When he was done, the sight wasn't pretty. He would have continued if the bat had not been broken in the middle. He was satisfied that Kelly would be wheelchair bound for the rest of his life.

He then reached down to yank off the electronic tracking device. He did not bother with the broken-off piece of the bat but picked up its handle. He planned to dispose of it when he was far away enough from the crime scene.

While driving, he glanced at his watch. It was one thirty in the morning. In a few hours, truckers would be arriving at the depot and after they called the police, TV news crews should be broadcasting from the scene around nine. By then, he should be drinking coffee at his favourite diner in Spanish Harlem.

He made a detour to Chinatown in Lower Manhattan, stopped by a garbage dump and ditched the baseball bat handle in it. He still had time for four to five hours of sleep and a shower before he drove to the diner ten minutes away from home.

The local TV news station WYNN took pride in being the first to get to any crime scene, before any other news media. On a few occasions, they managed to arrive there even before the police did. The woman reporter at the scene was frowning and looking grim as if all the problems of the world were on her shoulders. She was talking fast and breathing even faster.

Mike was surprised she was constantly referring to the parking lot as the murder scene. What murder? She was reporting on the condition of the young woman found in the van at the murder scene. Mike listened on and finally got the whole story. Apparently, the driver of a truck found a dead man lying next to a dirty looking van around seven o'clock in the morning. He had messed-up knees and a plastic bag over his head tied to his neck. He also heard noises coming from the back of the van. He opened the back door and found the incoherent young woman. He called 911.

Mike was dumbfounded. He did not use the plastic bag. So who did?

Two days later, police showed up at Juanita's house with an arrest warrant for Mike. They found the missing piece of the baseball bat in a garbage dump in Chinatown. The break at the end with the handle complemented perfectly with that at the end of the other half of the bat found at the murder scene. They later confirmed Mike's fingerprints were on the handle.

Everyone marveled at the efficiency of the police, and the extraordinary odds of finding the missing baseball bat handle in one out of hundreds of garbage dumps in the city. The Bronx police chief's only comment on the matter was that they got a tip-off from an anonymous source.

The young dark-haired woman with large breasts recovered and had no recollection of the ordeal. She was lucky Mike got to Kelly before Kelly got to her.

Police searched Kelly's home and found the dungeon where he stored his numerous sets of dentures and the stash of pulverized Rohypnol. They also raided his bank deposit box where all his crimes were documented.

The case was sensationalized to the extent that even Juanita's Diner became famous. Many people in the city touted Mike as a hero, and petitioned the Mayor for his pardon.

During the trial, Mike admitted he had used the baseball bat on Kelly, but vehemently denied he had used the plastic bag to suffocate him. The trial was wrapped up in five days. In spite of all the moral support from many people in the metropolis, and the legal defense by one of the best criminal lawyers in the city, who volunteered his service, he was found guilty of murder, and sentenced to twenty-two years in prison.

Virginia was the most heartbroken. Mike had to suffer for trying to punish the bastard who intended to rape her, and had almost killed her.

Mike told her he used the baseball bat but not the plastic bag, and Virginia believed him. Mike would never lie to her.

Mike did the crime, and should serve the time. But the punishment did not fit the crime if indeed he hadn't used the plastic bag.

Jason accompanied Juanita throughout the trial. After years of stability and relative bliss, her life suddenly turned topsy-turvy. She blamed Mike for being a bad boy. She blamed herself for being a bad mother. She needed moral support, and she got some from putting her hand in Jason's coat pocket. Jason was there in court with her throughout, but his mind couldn't help wandering off frequently, pre-occupied with the use of his memory retrieval technique in solving crime.

30

Before they sent Mike "up the river", Juanita and Jason had a chance to talk to him. Juanita cried and screamed at Mike. Mike screamed back. Jason had to separate them and calm them down.

To ease the tension, Jason brought up the possibility of using his invention to help Mike. That caught the attention of both mother and son, and they stopped quarreling to listen to Jason. Jason briefly explained to them how memory recovery worked, and he knew for certain it was accurate, and in theory, it could exonerate any innocent person even though there would be legal obstacles. But first, Mike had to be innocent of the murder before the test could help him.

"Did you use the plastic bag?" Jason asked Mike.

Mike said no, looking Jason squarely in the eye. Jason looked at him sternly, and asked again. Mike shook his head. Jason nodded. That was how they'd always communicated.

Jason went over to Juanita, and, to her big surprise, put both his hands on her shoulders, firmly. Juanita could be imaging it, he was also massaging her shoulders to ease her tension. "He didn't do it," said Jason quietly, looking at Mike.

The warmth of his hand transmitted from her shoulder to her heart. Juanita thought: I know you care about me, and you are my man, for life.

"I love you, Jason," Juanita blurted out.

Jason blushed and mumbled something incoherent.

After a short silence, Jason regained his composure.

"My invention may be able to get Mike out," Jason said. "But first we need to find a lawyer who is willing to take a chance with me."

*

Virginia was the first person to visit Mike in prison.

The maximum security prison was located in upstate New York two hours' drive away from Manhattan. She used Mike's car to get there.

The last thing Mike did before the police handcuffed him was to throw his car keys at his Mom.

"Let Virginia have my car, Mom."

Mike loved his Chevrolet Camaro. It was all souped-up. The car's silver body was decorated with gangster's graffiti. The tires were wide and high, and the sound system was worth almost as much as the car.

With a car like that, she drove at a normal speed, not too much below and definitely not over the speed limit, so as not to draw attention from the highway police. She timed her drive so that she could arrive there half an hour before the start of visiting hours. She wanted to be the first in line. All the other visitors seemed to have the same thing in mind. The bumper-to-bumper queue of cars started at the exit ramp to the prison facility, all the way to the parking lot. Virginia had to settle for a parking spot ten minutes' walk away from the entrance. The line of visitors in front of the entrance gate waiting to get in was half a mile long.

Most of the visitors were women and children, and they wore clothes seemingly bought from the Salvation Army Surplus outlets. Virginia made a mental note to dress as modestly as she could on her next visits.

All the prisons in the US must have used the same architects. Surrounding the entire mammoth low-rise grey buildings were twin layers of glittering razor-wire fences, each taller than a basketball hoop. The ten feet deep space between the inner and outer fences was piled high with loose razor-wire coils. Tall watchtowers were set apart every hundred feet or so encircling the whole compound.

The visitation area was huge. Visitors were unexpectedly subdued and well behaved. They communicated in whispers, rendering the place quiet enough to allow echoing whenever someone slammed a metal gate shut somewhere.

The guards were grim-faced but efficient. They followed a protocol. First, the registration, followed by people walking through metal detection hoops and their possessions passing through X-ray machines. Each party was issued a number. When the number was called, the party was led to a double-door tunnel. The first door had to close firmly before the second door could open. The tunnel led to a private cubicle. Each cubicle connected to an identical cubicle on the other side separated by a thick slab of bulletproof glass. Conversation was possible only through intercom wall phones, one on each side. Physical contact was out of the question. If objects were to be passed on to the prisoner, a guard nearby needed to closely examine them first. Virginia brought along a photo of herself, and a carton of cigarettes.

Mike came out after a short delay. He had on a standard orange prison garb. He looked pale and gaunt. Virginia's tears welled up at the sight of him. She promised to visit and write regularly, and to supply him with as many cigarettes as allowed. Mike told her not to worry and that she should take care of herself and not get into any trouble, go meet guys, get married and have kids.

That was enough to make Virginia burst out crying. Mike tried to calm her down by letting her know that other inmates in the prison paid him a lot of respect, and he promised not to get into any trouble.

Together with her photo and the cigarettes, Virginia also gave the guard one hundred dollars to put into Mike's account, the maximum amount allowed at any given time.

"Can I do anything else for you?" asked Virginia.

"Yes. Get me out of here. Talk to Jason. He is working on some science that makes people confess the truth."

"I'll also talk to a few more lawyers and see what they can do."

"I would rather you talk to Jason. My lawyers don't believe in me, even though they say they do. Jason does. And lawyers are useless."

*

Virginia could not help the tears from flowing while she walked back to the Camaro, thinking of what Mike had done for her over the years, and all she could do to reciprocate was to give him a hundred dollars and a carton of cancer sticks.

Virginia talked to Mike's lawyers. They had filed for an appeal, but were not too hopeful for a reversal of the verdict. She consulted a few other lawyers, but none had any novel approach to deal with the case.

She brought up Jason's invention with the lawyers. Most of them had never heard of it. If it was still in the experimental stage, they felt it could be 50 years before it could be proven to work and be admissible in court.

She talked to Jason about it. He was more optimistic. He thought it could be admissible in the court of law within years. What was needed first was a lawyer who was willing to boldly use his pioneering technique as a test case to exonerate a convict.

Virginia forfeited the scholarship given to her by the University of Pennsylvania. Instead, she busied herself going from one lawyer's office to another, trying to find one that would be interested in using Jason's technique.

None found.

However, very soon, there was a lawyer who was bold enough to take the chance with Jason's invention, and it succeeded in exonerating a murder suspect. However, it wasn't Mike.

31

Jason had been working from home for more than ten years.

His inheritance money had dwindled to the last eight hundred thousand, the bulk having been drained into his lawyers' pockets.

His lawsuits with Harold Stein had reached a stalemate. Even though he was making progress with his research, he was neither getting any formal recognition, nor was he getting any pay for his work.

No worries. He would soon be gainfully employed, finally, at forty-two years of age.

The lawyer for a Texas billionaire happened to have read about Jason's invention in the *Dallas Daily*, which on a particularly slow news day, covered one of the most celebrated Annual Texas Neuroscience Seminars.

The lawyer was Julian Cromwell, and his client, Horace Tate III, was charged with the murder of his third wife, who was rumoured to have slept with more than half of the adult men in the small town near Dallas where they lived. The fact that she had even had a fling with one of the billionaire's sons from a previous marriage apparently was the last straw for the billionaire. Her naked body was found in the woods about five miles out of town. The cause of death was strangulation. He was the prime suspect because a few days prior, in a drunken rage at the town's exclusive golf club, everyone there had heard him say that he wanted to kill her with his bare hands for her blatant promiscuity.

Around the same time a hiker found her body, Mr Tate was involved in a car accident. The Cadillac he was driving hit a tree on Route 67, and he suffered a head injury with loss of consciousness and subsequent post-concussion amnesia. He could not remember a thing about what he did in the twenty-four hours prior to the car crash.

Horace Tate III said that it was not in his nature to kill, but proving it would take more than a proclamation of innocence. If Dr Jason Lee's work was as good as they said it was, Julian Cromwell could prove his client's innocence through science, even though the evidence from the test would most likely not be admissible in court.

Everyone, including Mr Tate, wanted to know what happened during those twenty-four hours.

Julian Cromwell contacted the President of the Texas Neurology Association and asked him for advice. The professor told him only two persons in the world were capable of performing the test, and both were in New York. One was Harold Stein working in the Albert Einstein College of Medicine, and the other was Jason Lee, who used to work for both the Albert Einstein and Columbia Medical Colleges. He also told Julian Cromwell of the legal battle that was going on between them, and whispered to Julian that, off the record, Jason Lee was the real deal, and Harold Stein the pretender.

Julian discussed with Mr Tate all he knew about the test and the two experts available, and asked him to decide who to go to for the test.

In typical Texan fashion, Tate wanted both.

He said he had nothing to hide, and he believed in equal opportunity, adding that he also happened to know the Chairmen of the Board of both medical schools.

The chairman of the board of Columbia Medical School was eager to be of help to one of the richest men in the world. He called the dean of the Medical School and ordered him to take action. The dean scurried to Victor Vasco's office and asked him to do everything within his power to invite Jason back to join his staff, as soon as possible. They didn't wait for a positive answer from Jason, before they vacated and cleaned Jason's old office and quickly applied a new coat of paint to its walls. The Human Resources Department produced a contract in record time, and instead of a Visiting Fellowship, the school offered Jason the position of Assistant Professor of Neuropathology, which came with a decent salary, a full pension and other benefits.

Vasco only had Jason's home phone number, and he called every fifteen minutes until Jason finally answered close to ten o'clock at night. He was out that day to attend a computer programming workshop.

Vasco explained to Jason why he was suddenly so much in demand after nearly ten years in exile. He was polite enough to ask Jason to please consider coming back to work in his department. Jason should come back for the sake of helping a potentially innocent man, who happened to be one of the richest in the world. He would call Jason again first thing in the morning. He urged Jason not to let Harold Stein steal the whole show, purposely using the word "steal" to egg Jason on.

Jason hardly slept that night. There was just so much to think about. Close to daybreak, he made the decision.

A Chinese proverb says a good horse never turns around to eat the grass behind it. But that applies to people who have options. For Jason, whose career was in a rut with no prospects on the horizon, going back to an old workplace was certainly better than going nowhere.

When Vasco called the next day, Jason delivered the good news. He agreed to rejoin the Columbia faculty even though many of the head honchos of the School including the dean were obviously fair-weather friends. It was easy to swallow one's pride when one was down in the dumps. He also felt he owed Dr Victor Vasco some loyalty, and he genuinely liked the work environment there.

He did stress to Dr Vasco that there was no way he could work with Harold Stein again. Vasco said he understood, and he would make sure they would work on the case separately and independently.

Jason signed the employment contract and was back in his old office the next morning with all his gadgets and computer. Jason didn't even have the chance to arrange his office furniture before the dean summoned him. An urgent assignment was waiting for him.

The dean asked how soon Jason could be ready to perform the test on Mr Tate. Jason needed two or three days to set up his equipment, and more importantly, to do a test run on a volunteer before he could take on Mr Tate.

Harold Stein was clamoring to do the test first, and if Jason needed time to prepare, they would let him go first.

The dean warned Jason that it would a high-profile event, and a make-or-break occasion for Jason's career.

Jason was confident his test would be accurate, and it would be useful to the billionaire only if veracity was the outcome he desired. The billionaire had said he had nothing to hide. He'd already passed the lie detector test and was willing and ready for the memory recall machine to test him as well.

That settled, Jason returned to his office to get his system ready and to find a volunteer for a test run. The dean ran over to the Waldorf Astoria Hotel where a joint press conference was scheduled together with contingents from the Albert Einstein College of Medicine.

32

Harold Stein spoke on behalf of the Albert Einstein College of Medicine. He made sure everyone in the audience knew that the technique of recalling memories originated from his laboratory, and implied that he had the vision when he first started training in neurology years ago, years before some of the current neuroscience researchers had even finished high school. Everyone there knew which particular researcher he was referring to. He was eloquent and witty. If talk was the only game in town, Albert Einstein won the first round in the battle for scientific excellence between two of the best medical schools in North America.

The dean of Columbia Medical School spoke after Stein. He told the audience Dr Jason Lee had worked in Albert Einstein College of Medicine in the same years when memory recovery technology was first introduced and developed. He worked for Columbia Medical School on and off, and was currently a teaching staff there. He could not be at the meeting because he was too busy making preparations in his laboratory for the biggest test of his life.

He didn't mention Dr Jason Lee had been fired from Columbia years ago and was re-employed that very morning.

No one mentioned the ongoing lawsuits.

Both sides agreed to carry out the test independently, using politically correct phrases: no fear or favour, academic integrity and freedom, and so on and so forth.

They were going to do their tests under the close watch of the whole world.

*

Horace Tate III arrived in New York City with his entourage in his private jet. After checking into his suite at the Waldorf, he went to Albert Einstein Hospital to have a complete physical check-up. The technique employed by Harold Stein required a light general anesthesia, and he wanted to make sure Mr Tate was physically fit for it. The cardiologist who headed the medical team told the reporters waiting outside the hospital that Mr Tate was as fit as a man half his age and he would be ready for the test the next day.

The reason Stein required to sedate his patient heavily was that from his experience, a fully awake subject sent too many interfering signals through the titanium plate he used. He thought that was the smart thing to do.

Stein's personal laboratory was refurnished for the occasion. The aroma of an air freshener filled the room. Expensive paintings were hung on the walls to cover unsightly posters and stains. The most impressive pieces of equipment were showcased near the entrance. No one had been allowed to use the lab for three days prior so that it was pristine.

Stein had with him three assistants, all wearing white gowns and surgical masks. A cardiologist and two nurses also attended, along with the anesthesiologist Dr Rebecca Lange.

When brought in by wheelchair to Stein's laboratory at exactly nine o'clock in the morning, the larger-than-life billionaire was in a jovial mood. He looked, talked, and acted like a character straight from the set in that popular 1970s TV show *Dallas*, except that he was richer and louder.

He was a big man, six feet six and over three hundred pounds, pink from head to toe, and was so full of energy that he was frequently accused of taking a speed-and-cocaine cocktail for breakfast. But he never touched that stuff. He drank, though, lots of bourbon and rye, and vodka martinis. Everyone around him wondered how he could move his big frame so fast from point A to point B without causing a slight earthquake. He was seldom serene or pensive, always animated, or excited. He either scowled or howled with laughter. Never a dull moment with him.

With a booming voice and a thunderous laugh, he bellowed howdy to everyone as if he owned the place.

He turned to Stein.

"Hey Doc, goin' to hurt during the test?" he asked. "I ain't afraid of a little pain, but I welcome any excuse to go back to my suite to empty the mini-bar first." Then he roared into laughter.

Stein was extra respectful towards Mr Tate. For once, there was a larger figure than the great Harold Stein in the same room. He introduced Dr Lange, who was assigned to administer a light general anesthesia to Mr Tate. He assured Mr Tate that he would not feel a thing.

Tate took one look at Dr Lange, and then he feigned seriousness and told one of his private nurses to lock away his wallet securely.

"Last time I passed out with a pretty woman in the same room, I woke up buck naked and poorer than a pickpocket in a nudist colony."

He roared into laughter again, and everyone laughed with him.

Stein then proceeded to explain the entire procedure in detail, and discussed all the possible complications and risks associated with general anesthesia.

The big man signed the consent without hesitation. But he wasn't done with working the room yet. Again, he feigned seriousness. He pulled Stein close and suggested if the doc was to mess up his brain, the doc should make sure to do a thorough job, so that he could plead insanity to all the charges against him.

All the while, Dr Lange was preparing him and getting ready to put him under. Mr Tate was not finished yet. He winked at Harold Stein, and said, "Hey Doc, I'll pay extra if you can erase all my bad memories, especially those involving my three ex-wives." More laughs.

Dr Lange did not particularly enjoy his repartee. She quickly infused the sedative into his intravenous drip to stop him from talking further. He passed out in the middle of another joke. Dr Lange put an oxygen mask over his mouth and nose and fixed her gaze on the cardiac monitor.

Each one of Stein's assistants had a specific duty. One applied the titanium plate to Mr Tate's scalp corresponding to the hippocampus region, and made sure the plate had good contact with the shaved skull. They never copied Jason's titanium band because they didn't want people to think they were closely copying Jason who first introduced the headband in one of the Texas Neuroscience conferences.

Another assistant operated the electronic components of the machine; and the third manned the computer.

Stein himself stood there and watched.

The titanium plate continuously collected data from the hippocampus area. It was fed into the electronic system, and immediately relayed to the computer, ready to be recognized and interpreted by their computer program. The procedure was completed in three hours.

Mr Tate was then taken to the recovery room for observation, attended by his three private nurses. The first thing he asked for on waking up was a dry martini, stirred, not shaken.

Earlier, Mr Tate had recorded all the activities he could recall between his outburst at the country club and his waking up in the hospital after his concussion followed by his arrest and subsequent murder charge. His meetings with lawyer Julian Cromwell were also meticulously chronicled. All significant events could serve as milestones to extrapolate the timing of all the mystery events in that twenty-four-hour lapse in memory subsequent to his concussion.

*

It took Harold Stein and his assistants three days to finish examining all the data. Mr Tate's activities were mainly business dealings and his indulgence in big meals and alcohol binges. They recognized police questioning and lawyer visits. The car accident was also there. The twenty-four hours of memory lapse involved some drinking and was otherwise basically a lot of joyous events. They couldn't decipher anything definite. Significantly, it appeared that there was no evidence of physical violence; hence no murder. They were happy with the results, and were too eager to tell the world what they had found.

The original plan was to have both experts complete their tests and, depending on the findings, there would be a combined press meeting and a joint statement, making sure there would be no incriminating evidence against Mr Tate. But Stein insisted on holding a press conference on his own, right after he thought he had the answer from his test, before Jason even had a chance to examine Mr Tate.

Harold Stein's strategy to upstage Jason Lee was potentially brilliant. If Jason found something similar, Stein intended to say something to the media to insinuate that Jason copied his results. If Jason's findings were different, there was a good chance Tate's lawyers wouldn't use them, and Stein could trumpet Jason's failure.

Columbia University objected to Stein announcing his findings ahead of the originally agreed schedule; Julian Cromwell strongly advised against it; Harold Stein called the press conference anyway.

Harold Stein was in a hurry to steal the thunder, so to speak, from Jason Lee. He had already stolen the entire invention from Jason, so why not that as well?

During the conference, the great showman told the packed roomful of reporters he had worked non-stop for three days examining the data he had collected personally. He explained briefly the technical aspects of the test, in a condescending manner, and emphasized repeatedly the level of difficulty of the task. However, he had overcome the hardships, and produced the goods. He had found no evidence of murder in Mr Tate's memory bank. It was definitive. It was unequivocal. It was high drama.

He allowed questions.

"Will the findings be admissible in the court of law?" a reporter asked.

"I'm not a lawyer," Harold Stein replied. He paused to look around the room, in anticipation of chuckles from people who were not fans of lawyers, and admiration from everyone in the audience for his false modesty, and then he continued. "We live in a country deep-seated in the rule of law, and I'll let our court of law decide on that."

"Do you expect Columbia Medical School to produce the same results?" another reporter asked.

Stein shrugged without saying anything, as if he didn't care what the other scientist came up with.

"You claimed Mr Tate didn't kill anyone, but were you able to find out everything he did during his twenty-four-hour period of amnesia?" Someone asked – a good question.

174

For the first time in a long time, Harold Stein appeared flustered and sheepish. He carried on and on in a long-winded discourse on the science involving the limbic brain, the difficulties one could encounter working with it, and what he had done so far to counter those difficulties. He never really answered the question. At the end of the ramble, most people didn't remember what the original question was, and those who did were in no mood to ask the same question again.

*

Jason was scheduled to do the test the next day.

33

When Mr Tate walked into Jason's lab, accompanied by his legal team, his nurses, and the Dean of Columbia Medical School, he was surprised to find himself in a small rustic room with only a few pieces of small unimpressive machines and a single computer.

Dr Jason Lee was the only one there.

Mr Tate was glad there was no need for general anesthesia. His head needed to be shaved, but Harold Stein's staff had already done so.

Mr Tate was pleasantly surprised that he would be awake, and free to think or talk as he liked. No worries, no pain, and no inherent danger of any kind.

"Hey, I like your method already. No wonder they say you are the real deal, Doc."

When Jason produced a standard consent form, he asked where to sign without reading it.

Everyone else waited outside while Jason put the titanium band on his head and tightened it until it was snug against the scalp. Before long, the machines were humming, and data were flowing into the computer.

*

After Tate's murder charge, Julian Cromwell had hired a few hypnotists to work on him, to see if they could bring back memories from that twenty-four-hour lapse. They never got anywhere with Tate because he was one of the few people around that could not be hypnotized. But with his head under the tight clasp of Jason's titanium band, no memories could escape the memory recovery machinery.

Because he was wide awake, not only was the hippocampus active, his amygdala and basal ganglia, centres in the limbic system responsible for memories associated with skills and emotions, were also in full throttle, firing signals simultaneously into the computer. Jason's sophisticated computer program's algorithm was able to assimilate all the signals and formulate unique patterns recognizable as specific activities.

According to Jason's working theory, the contributions to memory recollection by the basal ganglia and amygdala were huge. For instance, with hippocampus alone, drinking alcohol could be recognized as just that. With input from amygdala and basal ganglia, a miserable, out-of-control, inebriated episode of drinking could be differentiated from a blissful, friendly, controlled kind of social drinking.

Many human activities, such as having sex or getting into a bar brawl, are associated with acquired skills and innate emotions. Sex is accompanied by lust and love, and its pleasure enhanced by skill; a bar brawl is associated with anger and fear, and any physical confrontation requires fighting skill. There are countless examples of human activities of this nature.

Jason took only one and half hours to complete the test, before he sent Mr Tate on his way to the martini bar. In that short period, he collected a few times more signals than his counterpart from Albert Einstein College of Medicine. Luckily, his computer program was much more advanced than Harold Stein's, and it could process the data ten times as fast; hence, he was confident enough to promise Mr Tate the results in less than three days.

Interpretation of Mr Tate's data turned out to be harder than what he had expected. His computer program was based mainly on the lives of old geezers in Professor Koch's clinic. Mr Horace Tate's life style was categorically different and immensely more colourful. For example, during that 24-hour gap in his memory post-concussion, there was much heavy drinking and happy bantering with different people. There was almost a brawl with another person, which was averted after some joyous toasting. There was quarreling but no physical violence, ruling out murder. In between drinking, Mr Tate was engaged in a few prolonged activities that were unrelated to violence or drinking, but were totally unfamiliar to Jason. He examined those signal patterns over and over again, and scratched his head.

He had worked non-stop around the clock until he lost track of time. He did not realize he hadn't slept for thirty hours, and he dozed off in front of his computer.

Mary was watching Jason's work closely and she knew what those signal patterns represented. She must find a way to tell Jason. It was time to use one of the three wishes granted to her by Mother Nature. What Jason was working on was the biggest test of his life. It could turn his career around.

Jason was then forty-two years old and had had sex exactly once, when Rachel gave him a blow job in high school. Sex was always furthest from his mind. Most people would have guessed correctly what a man like Horace Tate might have done after some serious drinking. Jason didn't get it.

While he was dozing off, Mary summoned all the afterlife energy she could muster and wished her son a dream. It was a simple dream. A woman was giving him a blowjob. He could only see the back of her head bobbing. It certainly reminded him of what Rachel did to him many years ago. It would have been a wet dream for other men, but for Jason it was a nightmare.

He jolted awake in the middle of the oral sex. He rubbed his eyes. In front of him was the computer screen showing a series of patterns he had been agonizing over before he dozed off. It clicked, finally. Could those patterns represent sexual activities?

In a separate data bank, he had signal patterns representing sexual activities of all kinds retrieved from his old pal, Leroy the wrestler. A couple of years earlier, Leroy had volunteered to be Jason's test subject. He was fully aware of Jason's research, after Jason told him all about his misadventures with Dr Harold Stein, while he was considering suing Stein and later when Stein was suing him.

He volunteered to be Jason's guinea pig when Jason brought up the prospect, because he relished the opportunity to re-live some of his wildest nights. The wrestler had an unbelievable memory in this regard, and was able to describe in detail all his sexual activities during a preceding twelve-month period. He got a kick out of relating to Jason his sex-capades for hours and hours, even though Jason flinched at each of the lurid details.

What Jason wouldn't do for science!

Jason kept data from Leroy in a separate CD-ROM in his safe at home. He had not incorporated it into his computer program yet because he was busy sorting out data from old geezers from Professor Koch's clinic, and those geezers had no recollections of recent sex at all. Jason intended to work on a few more sexually active individuals before he could formulate more definitive and consistent signal patterns to feed into his computer program.

He rushed home. He took from his safe the CD-ROM dedicated to the sexual memories of Leroy the wrestler, and returned to his lab to incorporate all the data on sexual activities into his computer. It took hours, but it was worth it.

Presto! The series of patterns he was scratching his head over were very much compatible with those of the wrestler's. What was extraordinary in Mr Tate's case was the sex had lasted for hours and it seemed to have involved more than one sexual partner.

Jason called the dean to tell him what he had found. The dean immediately called a meeting with Horace Tate III, and Julian Cromwell and his legal team.

Jason presented his findings, and was hoping Mr Tate himself could shed some light on the matter.

Mr Tate still couldn't remember anything.

Michelle Meade, one of Julian's assistants, was the most street-smart of them all, and she right away drew the correct conclusions.

Michelle told those present in the meeting that, at Mr Tate's age, with due respect, sex with more than one woman almost invariably represented commercial sex. Within a ten miles radius outside the metropolitan limits of Dallas, there were at least fifty licensed brothels.

Julian Cromwell would send someone right away to check on all of them along Route 67, where Mr Tate had his car accident, and see if they could come up with something.

Michelle Meade made a few discreet phone calls, and three assistants from the law firm were on their way to Route 67, carrying a photo of Mr Horace Tate III.

They all agreed not to make any noise until something substantial came out of Jason's findings.

The good news came eight hours later. They found a place called The Hot Pistol half a mile south of Route 67, and the people there remembered Mr Tate well because he acted like he owned the place and he showered people with hundred-dollar bills as if it were worthless "hell money" burnt in a Chinese funeral home.

According to their log book, on the day of his wife's murder, he came in early afternoon, polished off two bottles of Jack Daniels over time, ordered three girls all at once, and stayed there all night carousing.

At one point, he had a big row with the bouncer who complained about him being too unruly and boisterous. The owner of that joint intervened, brought him some more drinks and calmed him down. He left the place at dawn. And The Hot Pistol was fifty miles away from the scene of the murder.

Julian and his team wasted no time in flying down to Dallas, visiting the bordello and obtaining affidavits from the employees to verify his client's time there.

They asked the brothel workers why they never reported the billionaire's time with them to the police. Mr Tate was a famous man, and his murder charge was widely aired. Each worker had a different answer. Some said it was too dark in the brothel to be sure it was him. Some said confidentiality was their number one concern. Some claimed they'd never watched the news.

The owner was more candid. They did call Mr Tate's office twice, hoping for some monetary reward, but no one called back after Tate's people found out the calls were from The Hot Pistol.

Most of all, no one truly believed it was the same man, a billionaire, who had visited their lowly establishment.

34

How about that? Mr Tate had an airtight alibi he didn't even know he had. He was relieved and elated. He did most of the talking in the press conference, with Jason, the dean, and his lawyers by his side.

Harold Stein was not invited.

When Julian Cromwell announced the alibi to a roomful of reporters, he reiterated the fact that his client had no "memory fingerprinting" – a term he coined that would subsequently become the standard jargon for the test – of the murder, only the alibi.

When interviewed by CNN back in Texas later, the billionaire told the reporter since the whole world knew about it, he must make it clear that he was not a regular customer at The Hot Pistol or any other bordello. He was under extreme stress at that time and he simply wanted to go somewhere to relax and drink. He had had a bit too much to drink and things got out of control. He ordered three girls because he was a kind and considerate man. He wanted the girls to have a chance to take turns to rest.

Because of his alibi at The Hot Pistol, the prosecutors dropped the murder charge, and the police started to look for other suspects.

Horace Tate III rewarded Columbia Medical School with a one hundred million-dollar donation.

The Horace Tate case brought fame, prestige, and money to Columbia University. The Medical School rewarded Jason with an office three times the size of his old one, and promises of unlimited support in manpower and other resources for his future research.

Harold Stein got a slap in the face.

The dean of the Columbia Medical School got more media exposure than anyone else. He used "we" and "us" when he talked about Jason's invention, and prattled on about the leadership in the school that nurtured research resulting in Jason's invention and many others.

Jason remained low key. He knew he was lucky to have stumbled upon the bordello incident only because he had that nightmarish oral sex dream while he was struggling to find an answer to the unfamiliar signal patterns. He needed to perfect the program before he could use it with confidence. It could be a matter of life and death for those who relied on it to defend themselves against criminal charges.

There was wide coverage of Mr Tate's case and memory fingerprinting in the press, and Dr Jason Lee was fully credited for it. And the media never let Harold Stein forget his lackluster performance prior to Jason's brilliant discovery of Tate's alibi in a brothel.

Harold Stein made a fool of himself by insisting on an early press conference even though Mr Tate and his team of lawyers had planned a strategy in advance in which the two medical schools would hopefully produce a consensus indicating Mr Tate's innocence.

He tried too hard to upstage Jason, and got himself badly burned. It was no one's fault but his. However, people like him never blame themselves. He blamed his failure on his research assistants. He blamed Jason for not sharing his results with him and not inviting him to his meeting with Mr Tate. He blamed bad luck.

After saving Mr Tate, Jason was convinced his memory fingerprinting technique would be most useful for the judiciary system. He already had another project in mind when Horace Tate called to thank him personally after his acquittal.

Mr Tate asked what he could do for Jason to express his gratitude.

"Hey Doc, I owe you big time, you saved my ass," he hollered on the phone. "Let me do something for you, as a token of my appreciation. Anything, Doc."

Jason told him he wanted to help other innocent men and women by using memory fingerprinting to exonerate them. Before he could do that, he needed first to experiment with a lot of people who were actually guilty of all kinds of crimes to clearly define their memory fingerprints.

"I don't know how to get to them, and I don't know anyone important enough in the city to help me. Can you help?" Jason asked.

"The Governor of New York owes me a favour. I'll talk to him," Mr Tate said.

The Governor's people called on Jason within a week. Jason described to them what he had in mind. They in turn described to him the state's penitentiary system. The governor could first appoint Jason to be a member of the New York State Commission for Penitentiary Safety & Welfare, so that he could have unlimited access to any of the prisons and jails in the State of New York as an official.

After the briefing, Jason chose Rikers Island, because it was the most convenient facility for him to commute to.

On any given day, one could find more than ten thousand alleged perpetrators of serious crimes in Rikers, all locked up because they were either denied bail or couldn't meet bail.

The next week, the governor's staff drove him there to meet the warden. The warden had heard of Jason and the Horace Tate case and was pleased to meet him. Jason told him that he would like to interview one inmate per week. He could not handle more than one at the onset because he reckoned he would need at least a few days to analyze the collected data to make sense of it. When he became more familiar with the fingerprint patterns, he might want to interview more inmates per week.

Each interview would take less than two hours, and required the inmate to have the hair shaved above their ears. As a reward for their trouble, the inmate would be paid one hundred dollars. Columbia Medical School had given Jason a generous research grant, and he was using it for his latest project.

Jason also needed a locker for his equipment.

The warden was polite but seemed reluctant to help. He complained bitterly about the heavy workload and poor funding of his facility. At least one guard would need to accompany the inmate during the whole process, and they were already decidedly short on manpower.

Jason felt he was imposing. He turned to the governor's people, beseeching their help.

The governor's Chief of Staff winked at Jason and smiled. He turned to the warden and said: "Oh, I forgot to mention Mr Tate has agreed to donate one million dollars to your staff pension funds every year for the next ten years, to show his appreciation for your helping Dr Lee."

With money, one can convince a ghost to work on a gristmill, or a prison warden to co-operate.

The warden grinned like a moron for the rest of the afternoon, and personally took Jason to the personnel office to issue him an ID badge and a parking permit. He would assign a duty deputy to comply with Jason's every request during his weekly sojourn.

For the next year or so, Jason borrowed Juanita's car to drive to Rikers Island every Monday morning, and checked in with the designated deputy warden. First, he looked at their logbook for willing participants. As a routine, the warden briefed all the inmates and newcomers on the program. It involved no pain, no drugs, no physical hardship, no need to talk if they did not want to, and no coerced confessions. A licensed medical doctor would be in charge.

There were always enough volunteers. Prisoners often looked for diversions; anything was better than being cooped up in a small space with other prisoners. The warden also advised Jason to bring cigarettes to reward those who fully co-operated.

Jason's experimental design required populations accused of the same crime to be matched for age and race. Fortunately, crime in New York was equal opportunity, and there was never a shortage of criminals of different races and ages.

The first crime he elected to study was rape, mainly because he already had some solid data relating to sex, thanks to Leroy Katz and Horace Tate III.

Rikers Island had a protective custody facility for alleged rapists. For months, Jason was a regular there, testing and interviewing an alleged rapist every Monday, and analyzing the collected data the rest of the week in his lab. After working on thirty rapists, he nailed the memory fingerprinting for rape.

He discovered the pathos common among all alleged rapists. They all claimed innocence; and all found God while in jail. In a way, Jason's questionnaire before exit was useless because none of them ever told the truth about the rape. But sometimes they volunteered some wacky activities that could help Jason build up the vocabulary of his computer program.

The brilliance of Jason's research methodology was such that he was looking for a common pattern of signals from the limbic brains of inmates accused of a particular crime; so, as long as some of them did commit the crime, he should find a consistent and distinct pattern of limbic signals, a specific memory fingerprinting of the crime. In all likelihood, most if not all of the alleged did commit the crime and Jason could always find the answer, eventually.

For example, the thirty alleged rapists he examined all produced the distinct memory fingerprinting of rape even though all had denied the crime. At their trials, the court found twenty-nine of them guilty based on irrevocable evidence. The single man who walked was acquitted on a technicality, and had probably committed rape, too.

Another important finding was that there was no racial and age difference in the distinctive memory fingerprinting of rape.

Thinking of Mike and his promise to Juanita to try to exonerate her son of murder, he next studied convicts charged with murders and homicides. After that, he systematically went through the entire list of felonies.

Jason was not the only one working on improving the justice system in America. He got a call from Julian Cromwell, Mr Tate's lawyer, and co-founder of a non-profit organization called Justice for the Underprivileged, Indigent, and Coloured Individuals (JUICI). He wanted Jason to meet Marvin Green, the other co-founder of JUICI. They had something important to discuss with Jason.

35

The two co-founders of JUICI had quite different backgrounds. Julian came from a wealthy white Georgian family, and Marvin was a dirt poor ghetto black from New Orleans. Julian's father was a football hero from Atlanta. Marvin never knew his father.

Julian, though born and raised in Georgia, lost his southerner persona and accent, from spending a lot of years in, of all places, New Orleans. New Orleans had too many out-of-town residents to have a dominating accent or culture. He didn't try to lose the attributes of his heritage; it was simply a result of mingling with people from all over the States and other countries.

He wore his black hair long, and his glasses were black-rimmed. His friends teased him that he was impersonating Gregory Peck in *To Kill The Mocking Bird*, down to the actor's speech and mannerism. He had never even watched the movie, and yet the resemblance was uncanny.

Julian's father, Wayne Cromwell, played quarterback for the local high school, and later for Georgia Tech. He made it to the pros, playing first-string quarterback for a second-rate team. His football career was cut short after two years during a brutal post-season game in which his right shoulder was almost torn off.

After football, he joined a national insurance company as an executive, and with his movie star good looks and sunny personality, he soon rose through the ranks to become vice-president. He and a few friends jumped ship when he turned forty, and started their own insurance company. He was the CEO, and the company's major business was homestead insurance for Florida, Mississippi, Alabama, Georgia, and Louisiana.

*

Marvin grew up in a poor neighbourhood in New Orleans. He must have suffered from malnutrition growing up, because he had never reached the size of a normal adult. He was no taller than Sammy Davis Junior, and like Mr Davis, he didn't have a pretty face. Neither one of them would win in a beauty contest. He couldn't match Sammy's talent in music, but made up for it by being astute in business.

He and his younger brother lived with their mother in a small shabby bungalow provided by the Welfare Department. His mother couldn't hold down a job because of an undiagnosed illness that left her tired all day, every day. Marvin pretty much took care of himself and his younger brother starting from a young age. He hardly attended school, playing hooky so that he could loiter in the French Quarter, hustling tourist dollars by tap dancing, shining shoes, and cracking jokes. The money went to fast food for the family, as his mother was often too tired to shop, let alone cook.

While Marvin never had much schooling, Julian went to Louisiana State University on a football scholarship, and later attended Tulane law school.

However, the two had something in common. They both had developed a sense of outrage over injustice and inequality.

Julian's mother had died from complications while giving birth to Julian. His father soon re-married; he wanted a mother for the newborn.

The second wife was a blond beauty queen from Houston, and she treated Julian reasonably well - until Julian turned three and she became pregnant with her own son. The stepmother mentality set in, and her own son, Jay, got all the attention while Julian was neglected. Jay's birthdays were always major events while Julian's were hardly ever remembered.

His father had always been supportive of Julian, and told him more than once, that it didn't matter Jay got more gifts and stuff, Julian was bigger and stronger, better in sports and in school. God apparently had given him more. But the father was rarely home, and Julian had to put up with all the snide remarks and unreasonable disciplinary measures that came his way.

Growing up in that environment, Julian learned to be independent and mentally tough.

When he became a teenager, he stopped calling his stepmom mom. Their relationship turned from cool to icy. Julian left home at eighteen, and supported himself through college and law school by taking part-time jobs and student loans, declining any financial support from his father. He was able to obtain a football scholarship from Louisiana State University, playing quarterback like his father did. He wasn't about to follow in his father's footsteps, though; his heart was not in football. He talked the coach into letting him play reserve, so that his training schedule would not be as demanding as the first-string players. He needed time to do his school assignments well, and to take up part-time jobs to pay for food and board. He was a laboratory assistant in Charity Hospital in downtown New Orleans and a bartender in a hole-in-the-wall pub across the street.

Charity Hospital was a teaching hospital for both LSU and Tulane Medical Schools, and they took care of patients other hospitals would not touch. They were mostly patients on welfare and many came in with injuries from dealing with the police in downtown New Orleans. The hospital was where Julian gained first-hand knowledge of the plight of the minority and the underprivileged. Part of his job as a blood bank laboratory assistant was to take blood from patients for crossmatch. He met many alleged perpetrators of crime and victims of police brutality and heard stories from them. He was convinced many of them were innocent. That was when he decided to study law, so that he could try to help those poor folks.

The hole-in-the-wall pub he worked part time in was a favourite watering hole among the faculty members of the Tulane Law School. He made friends with many of them, and they helped him apply for and successfully secure a scholarship and student loan to study in their faculty after graduating from Louisiana State University with a degree in Sociology.

After finishing Tulane Law School, he felt he still had a lot to learn from his professors, so he stayed on to become a junior faculty member.

After a few years of research, he became a leading expert in the US penal system. According to his studies, up to seven per cent of those in prison were wrongly imprisoned because of the incompetence of law enforcement agents, forensic scientists or defense lawyers. As an academic, he published research papers and gave lectures far and wide.

After delivering one of his talks to a civil rights group based in New Orleans, Marvin approached him to state his interest in starting a charity legal centre to help the poor and underprivileged.

*

Throughout his childhood, Marvin had to worry about having enough to eat, because his mother was bedridden most days, and the welfare check never seemed to last till the end of the month.

His mother was actually a fantastic cook. On rare days when she felt better and stronger, she would prepare meals that would make Marvin lose his appetite for fast food for days. He developed an interest in cooking at a young age, and when he became tall enough to reach the stove, he badgered her to teach him to cook all the dishes he liked, especially fried chicken and barbecued ribs. Once he learned the basics, he experimented with spices and sauces and got all the flavors down pat.

In his early teens, he took over the household finances – the welfare check, as well as all the household chores, including cooking. Even the neighbours appreciated his culinary skills and often paid him to cook for them.

On his eighteenth birthday, he put on a clean shirt, picked up a bucket each of fried chicken and barbecued ribs, took a deep breath and marched into the neighbourhood bank where he was known as the kid who cashed his mother's monthly welfare check. He asked to speak to the branch manager.

The bank manager was too busy to see him that day, so he left him the food and his telephone number.

It took the manager four days to call him back. He asked for and was granted an appointment during which he spent two hours presenting his business plan.

With the taste of the chicken and ribs still lingering in his mind, the manager agreed to take a chance and grant him a small loan.

Marvin opened his neighbourhood BBQ takeout restaurant three months later. The bank's manager and staff were Marvin's only loyal customers for the first few months. Then the eatery's following grew, and he had to rent the space next door to accommodate the growing business.

He realized early on that the recipe for success in the food business was consistency and tastiness. He purchased the ribs and chicken from the same distributor and demanded the same high quality every time. The rotisseries and frying pans were custom made. The temperature and procedures for preparing his menu items were set in stone. His food's good taste relied primarily on the marinade whose formula was known only to him. He rented a warehouse in a secret location and manufactured it in bulk himself. Later, he would bottle the sauce and sell it in all his outlets and many supermarkets - purposely omitting one essential ingredient. The chicken and ribs in his restaurants were still superior. That secret missing ingredient was Chinese triple-distilled rice wine. No other wine would do the trick. When his operation became too big, he outsourced the sauce manufacturing to a factory in China's Fujian province. Asked on numerous occasions why his food tasted so good, Marvin said it was an ancient Chinese secret.

His business success did not exempt him from personal tragedies, though. Doctors finally diagnosed his mother's illness: She had been suffering from early-stage multiple sclerosis. Within a year of diagnosis, her condition went rapidly downhill and she died.

Her previous doctors missed the diagnosis because she was a welfare recipient. When a patient on welfare complained of being tired all day long, the obvious diagnosis was laziness. When Marvin took her to a private practitioner, the specialist took her illness seriously, listened to her complaints carefully, and gave her a thorough physical examination. He immediately arrived at the correct diagnosis.

Such was life, Marvin had learned; people with money can always buy better things, including healthcare. And legal representation, as he found out later.

That was not where his personal tragedy ended. His baby brother, then eighteen years of age, could not attend their mother's funeral because he was in jail. He had been in the wrong place at the wrong time, and even though there was no firm evidence against him, he was awaiting trial accused as an accessory to murder in a case of robbery gone wrong. He told the police he didn't even know there was a robbery going on when he stepped into that convenience store at one o'clock in the morning. He ran to get away from the sound of the gunshot.

He was so shocked and embarrassed at being arrested he didn't call Marvin for help.

The legal aid lawyer assigned to him was an old drunk who could hardly sober up to appear in court on the arraignment day.

When Marvin found out about his brother's trouble, he wanted to hire a well-known criminal lawyer in the city, but was told to get ready a quarter of a million dollars, with a hundred thousand up front as a retainer. Marvin had just opened up his sixth outlet. He had no choice but to put the whole business for sale on the market.

When the brother learned of Marvin's plan, he hanged himself in his cell.

Marvin was devastated. His brother was not only his flesh and blood, but someone he had cared for since birth. He would always remember that little boy with bright wide eyes and eager expectations running to him every time he came home from the French Quarter after a hard day of hustling. He always had food in his hand for his beloved younger sibling who probably hadn't eaten the whole day. He loved to watch him shove down the food. He'd let him eat first, telling him he'd already had his share. When the little one had had enough, he'd clean him up and put him to bed, and then eat any leftovers.

That little boy was the reason he'd never run away from home and his motivation for success. Now that he was gone, he had no reason not to run away, and no motivation to do anything. He became a recluse.

After a few months, his staff decided to do something about his self-destructive behavior. They literally kicked in the door to drag him out of the house to see a psychiatrist.

It took a year of therapy for Marvin to straighten himself out and get back to work. He came back with a vengeance. Within the next four years, he opened 50 more outlets. By age 32, he had more than 150 outlets in the South, with annual revenue in the millions of dollars.

When he attended one of Julian's talks on legal injustice in the US penal system, Julian impressed him with the eloquence and the correct dose of indignation in his speech. The image of his younger brother hanging in jail and the incompetence of the law enforcement agents and the lawyer involved ripped into his heart all over again.

He approached Julian afterwards and said he wanted to do something about it. Could Julian help? The two had numerous late night meetings and came up with JUICI, with the operating costs mainly bankrolled by Marvin. Julian was the free-of-charge lawyer-in-charge, recruiter of volunteers, and occasional fund-raiser.

*

When Marvin Green sold his franchise and his secret sauce formula to a big national food conglomerate owned by Horace Tate III, he received a large chunk of cash. He used one third of the money to set up a trust for himself, one third he invested in an Internet start-up and the rest he poured into his pet project, JUICI. He offered Julian the position of legal director at an annual salary comparable to his pay at Tulane. Julian jumped at the opportunity, and quit his academic post at Tulane on short notice.

Marvin Green's corporate headquarters was in Dallas, and he helped Julian set up a private practice office in a swanky part of town, and an office of JUICI in the ghetto of downtown Dallas. In a few short years, Julian Cromwell became well-known in the Dallas area as the go-to lawyer if the alleged was innocent. JUICI became a well-known charity for people who couldn't afford a lawyer.

*

Julian had kept in touch with Jason. He knew about Jason's ongoing research on crime fingerprinting using the criminals in Rikers. Julian was convinced that Jason's invention would be an ideal tool for JUICI's work.

Julian and Marvin met with Jason in New York, and explained to him in detail JUICI's vision and operation. They invited Jason to join them as their Scientific Director.

Jason accepted the honorary position. It was a perfect leadership trio – one had the legal knowledge, one had the forensic science expertise, and one had the money.

While Jason continued to perfect the memory fingerprinting technique, Julian gave lectures to the legal community on Jason's invention to familiarize lawyers and judges with the potentially potent legal weapon. Hopefully they would grow to trust it.

They would need a test case, a case actually sanctioned by the court of law. Jason had briefed Julian on Mike's murder conviction, and his staunch belief that Mike was innocent. They visited Mike in prison, and signed him up as a JUICI client, and the first in line to be tested by memory fingerprinting approved by the court of law.

36

Jason called Lee Jae Soong in Korea to tell her about Mr Tate's case, with much satisfaction. She updated him on Harold's Stein's other woes, with much glee.

She still had contact with former colleagues in Stein's Neuroscience Department. From what she had heard, things were not going well for Stein at all. He hadn't given up on monopolizing the memory fingerprinting technique he stole from Jason. He filed an appeal to the Federal Court again, but it declined to hear the case. The Board of Directors of the Albert Einstein College of Medicine announced that the school would no longer subsidize any Harold Stein lawsuits relating to his research. Stein had to pay out of his own pocket for the latest legal fee, amounting to many thousands of dollars. He had no idea why Jason had such a deep pocket. His wife had had to cancel a fund-raising dinner at the last minute because of poor response.

That was the least of his problems.

His star protégé Dr Henry Williams, head of the Neurology Department at Cornell Medical Center was not doing so well, either.

Scientists from GenePharma, with their humongous research budget, tried to replicate Dr Williams's research findings and not only had they failed to reproduce similar results, many of the outcomes were contradictory to his claims. A whole team of scientists gathered to scrutinize the data presented in all the papers Henry Williams had published over the years, and they found numerous inconsistencies. They also found the amount of data Dr Williams had claimed to have generated in some of his studies was simply humanly impossible from one person, considering there were only 24 hours a day. They published a joint statement in the prestigious medical journal Lancet challenging all of Williams's previous scientific discoveries.

The editor of *The Lancet* took a closer look at Williams's old publications and agreed with the scientists. The editorial board decided to rescind all his papers. Soon, other medical journals, which had published Williams' scientific articles, all followed suit, and discredited all of Williams's previously published papers.

Most of Williams's papers had Harold Stein's name as the collaborator.

Henry Williams lost his position with Cornell. Harold Stein stepped down as the chief of the Neuroscience Department, and hid himself in his office all day long.

Lee Jae Soong seemed to enjoy recounting Harold Stein's failures as much as Dr Victor Vasco, who went to Jason's office often, to talk about how karma had finally caught up with the evil Harold Stein.

She promised to call Jason if there was any more bad news about their old boss.

Jason became more and more active in academic circles. He published the report of Mr Tate's case in the *British Medical Journal*, with details of his technique but not the computer program. The Journal accepted the paper based on the irrefutable alibi of Mr Tate. The paper was widely cited. Every time it was, Harold Stein got a dishonourable mention.

Scientists applied to be trained in Jason's laboratory at Columbia, and he gave talks at international conventions regularly. He was a much happier man.

Harold Stein did not do himself any favour by shafting Jason. In the later part of his otherwise illustrious career, he was disgraced.

He still hadn't given up. He truly believed if only he could discover a better way to retrieve memory than Jason's, he could redeem himself.

Not being the head of the department meant he had no administrative duties and therefore all day to do research. He put aside all his other projects and worked on memory fingerprinting full time.

He firmly believed in his own ability. He thought if only he was hands-on, great things could happen. He fired all his assistants, calling them useless dimwits who were responsible for ruining his career.

He came up with the idea of building a titanium helmet instead of just a band like Jason's. But the electronic signals were so numerous, intricate, and confusing he was totally consumed by it. He forgot about the basic premise – only signals from the limbic brain mattered.

He kept on wondering how Jason did it. It was driving him crazy. He was seen pacing the floor of his spacious office like a maniac.

If only he knew how Jason did it, things would become clearer, and he could proceed in the right direction.

He still had friends in high places. He asked the Chairman of the Board of Albert Einstein College to arrange a meeting with Mr Horace Tate III.

After a few weeks of arm-twisting, Mr Tate reluctantly agreed to see him. He would grant him five minutes if he flew down to Dallas and arrived at the Tate Plaza at exactly 10:30 on a Tuesday morning. He swallowed his pride and showed up early, waited at the reception area of Tate Plaza like a schoolboy outside the headmaster's office waiting to be summoned.

Mr Tate made him wait and summoned him around eleven o'clock.

Without offering him coffee or tea, Tate bluntly asked: "What can I do you for?"

Harold Stein recited his well-rehearsed spiel, about how he finally had had a major breakthrough in the science of memory fingerprinting, something huge. The only thing he needed for it to have Nobel-prize-winning potential was to compare his technique with Dr Jason Lee's. And Mr Tate was the only one who knew how it was done. He would rather not ask Dr Jason Lee, because he was not a team player, and notorious in the scientific community as a selfish person, a loner, and a miser.

Tate kept quiet and scowled into the distance for a long while, and watched Harold Stein squirm in his chair, before he responded.

"Cut the crap. If you'd had a breakthrough, you wouldn't be in here bullshitting me," Tate said.

"I'll tell you this much. His procedure is the same as yours, without the fanfare. The big difference is in the computer program. His is smart, and yours is stupid, just like you. Now, get out of my office."

*

Harold Stein returned to the Bronx a broken man. He had left for Texas with hope and enthusiasm, and came back with nothing but humiliation and hopelessness. Driving from La Guardia Airport to his office, he thought of stopping the car by the Whitestone Bridge and jumping off it. How could he not have seen it? Even that dumb hick did. The secret was in the computer program, of course.

He was a man possessed. He knew next to nothing about computer programming. He consulted all kinds of experts in computer programming, but it was useless because none of them knew anything about neurology. He tried to work it out himself. He tried everything, but nothing he did could untangle the complicated signals he received from the titanium helmet.

He started to appreciate Jason's incredible talent, and knew in his heart he could never catch up.

He had no choice but to resort to nefarious means to achieve his goal.

He hired a private detective---the same one he and his lawyers had used years ago to find out how much Jason was worth. This time, he wanted to learn about Jason's daily routine.

That was an easy five grand for the detective. Like clockwork, on all weekdays, Jason arrived at his lab in Columbia at eight and left at six thirty, ate in a neighbourhood restaurant at seven, took a stroll in his neighbourhood after dinner and returned home around nine. Except every Monday morning he visited Rikers Island before going back to his office at noon; and every Sunday he took long walks somewhere in Manhattan.

He never carried a computer. His main computer was locked up in his lab at all times. When he visited Rikers, he used the computer he kept there and downloaded the data obtained into a memory device.

The best time to steal his main computer would be on a Sunday.

The private detective he hired to do all his dirty work was a seedy character who mingled with ex-cons and conmen. He demanded one hundred thousand dollars for the job. Half upfront, the other half when Stein had the computer in his hand.

Stein came from a wealthy Chicago family, and he came up with the cash in five days, after liquidating some of his assets.

Cash changed hands in a restaurant in Little Italy. The following Sunday the detective with his accomplice broke into Jason's office, and snatched Jason's computer from a cabinet after smashing open a lock. They triggered an alarm, but by the time the security guards arrived to check, Jason's computer was gone and the thieves had escaped in a car with an untraceable out-of-town license plate. It was a clean professional job. They left behind no fingerprints or clues of any kind.

Police came, and Jason told them who the most likely suspect was. Investigations led to nowhere. Dr Stein had a watertight alibi. He invited the police to his office, his lab, and even his home to look for the missing computer. None found. The case went cold within days.

Harold Stein rented a room in a rundown hotel in Lower Manhattan under a bogus name, and received the computer a week later, after handing over the rest of the money.

That was the easier part. How to crack the password was the real challenge.

First, he tried "marylee", not expecting to succeed; he didn't think Dr Jason Lee was a moron. He tried different catch words related to memory: fingerprint, limbic_brain, hippocampus, amygdala, and so on. None worked.

Earlier, the sleazy detective told him he knew a hacker who was a genius at this sort of thing. He could arrange for his services, for another hundred thousand dollars.

Knowing he could never find Jason's password by shooting in the dark, Stein liquidated some more of his assets and paid half of the asking price to retain the genius hacker.

The hacker arrived at Stein's hotel room ten o'clock in the morning and started work on Jason's computer while Harold Stein looked on.

He worked for twelve hours at it non-stop. He scratched his head and frowned, talked to himself and swore under his breath. Finally, he threw his arms up in the air.

"I give up," said the hacker. "There is nothing in this computer, no program of any kind, it's empty."

He thought Jason must have installed an anti-theft device featuring a self-erasing program if someone typed in the wrong password more than twice. This device was well known among hackers and IT experts, and he could detect some of its footprints in Jason's computer.

Stein had earlier tried to open Jason's program about ten times using the wrong passwords, and triggered the self-erasure a long time before the hacker started work on it.

Stein turned ashen, and sat there speechless. He almost cried.

The hacker asked for the rest of the money because he had done all he could, and it was Stein who had screwed up. Stein jumped up from his chair, cursed at the hacker, slammed Jason's computer on the floor, and left in a huff.

One could never simply walk away from these characters, though. Harold Stein didn't realize the kind of trouble he could get himself into dealing with low-lives.

The detective called the next day, to ask for more money, not only to cover the balance for the hacker, but also additional money for him and the accomplice, a career criminal with a long rap sheet. They were tired of a life of crime and they were thinking of starting a legitimate business and they wanted Stein to bankroll it. Or else.

Stein yelled at the top of his lungs over the phone, calling him the scum of the earth and worse. Finally, he screamed, "Leave me alone, or I'll call the police."

"I was thinking the same thing," said the detective.

"I'll deny everything, I paid in cash, and you have no proof that I hired you."

"We have in our possession Dr Jason Lee's computer with your fingerprints all over it," said the detective. "I have also taped all our conversations, including this one."

Stein almost collapsed at this development. He managed to mumble, "I don't have any more money, leave me alone."

"I'm a detective. I've checked you out, you are loaded," came the cold reply. "I'll call again. Have a nice day."

*

About a month after Jason's lab was broken into, on a particularly cold day, Dr Harold Stein was found dead at home.

The news of his death was widespread. The family claimed it was a heart attack.

That was when Jason knew his nightmare was finally over. For the first time in a long while, he was able to breathe easily.

He knew the value of his computer program and had taken some clever steps to safeguard it. He had triumphed over Harold Stein in the end.

He also thought it was time to apply for a patent for his new computer program.

He went to the patent lawyers again, filed all the necessary documents, and waited.

Six months later, he got a call from his lawyers, who congratulated him for the patent rights to his computer program, which the National Patent Office thought was one of a kind with no others close to its ingenuity. He immediately applied for an international patent, and obtained it within months.

*

Three months after Harold Stein's death, Jason received a package that had been sent to Columbia Medical Center. It had no return address. Jason opened it and found the old notebook he had lost in the Neuroscience Department in the Bronx seventeen years ago. He never found out who sent it. He kept it in his safe and took it out to flip through it once in a long while, to reminisce about a bittersweet chapter of his life.

*

Five years into studying memory fingerprinting of crimes, and publishing numerous articles in major medical and scientific journals, Jason was approached by a vice president of GenePharma.

The firm offered Jason three and a half million dollars to buy his patented computer program.

Jason had become worldlier; he didn't agree right away. He turned to Leroy for help. Leroy's cousin worked for a big-time agency representing professional athletes and showbiz personalities. Jason signed a contract with the agency to represent him. He didn't even have to show his face when they did all the negotiations for him.

When the offer became five million dollars one-off, and 1.75% of the gross receipts of sale of all the products based on Jason's invention, Jason was advised to take it.

Both Leroy and his cousin made a small fortune on the deal. They celebrated by spending a weekend in a high-class strip joint in Las Vegas. Jason was invited to go along, with all expenses paid.

He didn't go, of course. He celebrated by having a meal with Juanita, in an uptown French restaurant.

The next person Jason called with the good news was Jane in Hong Kong. She did the math, and concluded that Jason's investment in the lawyers protecting his intellectual rights had finally paid dividends.

37

After Harold Stein's death, Jason's life had a huge turnaround.

When Genepharma paid megabucks for his patent, most of his past misfortunes were vindicated.

GenePharma's enormous R & D Department collaborated with him in perfecting his memory fingerprinting machinery. The scientists on its payroll were all top-notch in their fields. A metal specialist was able to re-model a titanium headband, which looked and worked better than Jason's prototype. Its engineers created a more compact and yet more powerful, automated, and versatile electronic component for the system. The computer used was faster and had a much bigger capacity. Their IT experts improved overall on Jason's computer program but the algorithm component was ingenious and they left it alone. They named it Jason's algorithm.

Instead of interviewing only one inmate per week, Jason's team had been interviewing five to ten of them. A team of analysts helped him decipher the coded signal patterns in the GenePharma Laboratory. They swiftly completed the list of felonies, and included many misdemeanors and petty crimes. Memory-finger-printing's applications were far-reaching, but had the biggest impact on the judiciary system the world over. GenePharma had research centres in many countries where the legal system was under the state's control. Its biggest research focus was in China. It had become such a powerful tool there for prosecutors that just mentioning the test to a perpetrator could bring about a full confession.

In the US, there was no test case in which the defense attorney tried to use memory fingerprinting to argue for a client's innocence, because it was thrown out of court by the judge for inadmissibility before it was even attempted.

The Horace Tate's case was different. The memory fingerprinting was initiated by Mr Tate's legal team, paid for by Mr Tate, and was not approved by the court. It was done with the sole purpose of finding out what Tate did during the hours of his amnesia, and it worked out all right for him because an alibi was uncovered serendipitously.

However, judges in the US were beginning to be more conversant with the test. JUICI needed one successful test case to gain traction for memory fingerprinting to take off. Julian was counting on using Mike's case as a breakthrough.

Jason had urged Julian to use Mike as the first successful test case because he knew for certain Mike was innocent of murder. Mike would not lie to him.

After Julian reviewed Mike's case, he thought the Bronx Police Chief's informant might hold the key to the Kelly Mackenzie murder case. He wanted to interview the informant, and filed for the police chief to announce his identity under the "duty to disclose" statute.

The case dragged on, because the police chief refused to name him and used informant confidentiality as his defense. It was a legal quagmire.

While the judge was pondering over the case, Julian applied for memory fingerprinting as proof of Mike's innocence. The judge was familiar with Dr Jason Lee's invention, and realized the importance of having a landmark case. After much deliberation, she allowed the use of memory fingerprinting. But she was prudent – she decreed the result of memory fingerprinting to be classified only as circumstantial evidence in the appeal court.

JUICI wasted no time. They arranged for Mike to have the memory fingerprinting test as soon as the Judge gave them the nod.

38

Mike was brought into Jason's memory fingerprinting laboratory in shackles accompanied by two prison guards.

To avoid possible conflict of interest, Jason stayed out of the laboratory, and asked the foremost expert from the United Kingdom to conduct the test. The London neurology professor was Graham Steele, one of Jason's biggest fans who had had plenty of experience with Jason's technique, having been trained in Jason's laboratory for six months, a few years before his return to London to start his own memory fingerprinting research centre.

GenePharma was in the process of producing the prototype commercial model for memory fingerprinting, and it was the perfect occasion to trial-run it, on someone like Mike. For the first time, top-notch engineering was coupled up with Jason's computer program, which was patented and unsurpassed in its ingenuity.

Steele completed the procedure in an hour. Mike was escorted back to the medical ward in prison and stayed overnight for observation. The results would be available later in the day.

Steele worked overtime on Mike's data, checking everything twice. The incident had occurred six years ago. He quickly identified a milestone event when Mike was informed that his childhood friend Virginia had been poisoned and had lapsed into a coma. That was etched strongly in Mike's mind. Then Steele worked forward and found all the events that had preceded Kelly's death. There was on record Mike's tailing Kelly, and bludgeoning Kelly's knees, but nothing that indicated his intention to kill him, such as trying to suffocate him with a plastic bag over his head. The intention to kill or not kill could be distinguished by Jason's technique, thanks to signals from the basal ganglia.

He called Jason to report his findings, and Jason called Virginia and Juanita, and the staff at JUICI. A big relief for all. The judge was informed of the results. The onus was now on the Bronx police chief to make his next move. He was close to retirement and didn't want anything to get in the way of fly-fishing with his cousin in Florida. He decided to call the informant to discuss the situation.

His source used to work in a restaurant in Manhattan. The police chief called there, but was told the man he was looking for, the manager, had called in sick. He dug out his old phone book, and found the man's home number. Again, no one answered. But at least he knew he was still working in the same restaurant.

The police chief had met his source only once, about six years ago when he bought him dinner, to thank him in person for the tip-off which led to Mike's arrest. They dined in a restaurant in Manhattan's Little Italy. They had spaghetti and veal cutlet and shared a bottle of Chianti. He remembered him as being oddly quiet and subdued, and certainly not gushing with excitement or pride. When they parted that evening, they shook hands.

"You'd never know; we might meet again," his source had said.

His source was Sean Griffin, Virginia's father, and Juanita's old boss at Frank's Diner.

Sean had been an unhappy man for most of his adult life. After his bitter divorce, he had been assigned custody of their only daughter, much to his chagrin. But his ex-wife was in no position to raise a child, being a drug addict and a pathological liar.

In spite of his libidinous nature, he wasn't all bad. He felt for his daughter Virginia, who had always been a sweet girl. He did his best to raise her all by himself on a restaurant manager's salary. Virginia grew on him more and more, and he soon decided that his vivacious and pretty daughter was his whole life.

When Virginia was in her teens, she went through the usual rebellious stage and ran away from home a few times, staying with friends or classmates. But she always came back, and they would hug and make up.

He wasn't the perfect father. But he did his best. He would never forget the days when he got home from work and he and Virginia would do things together and that would make everything okay in spite of all the unpleasantness he had to put up with at work.

He used to take up a part time job as a cab driver on his days off, so that he could have a good reason to tell Virginia why he had to stay out overnight, leaving her on her own in the apartment. She didn't like it; but she understood that her father needed to make more money to support the household. She only insisted that he call before her bed time.

The part-time taxi driver job was a ruse. He had his needs. He spent half his night driving customers to make enough money to pay for the gas and the rental, and spent the other half of the night cruising all the singles bars in town.

He wasn't exactly a catch, and the women he brought home occasionally were usually escorted out of his apartment out of the sight of his daughter at the crack of dawn. He would be too embarrassed to let Virginia see the caliber of women he brought home.

He always had his daughter's welfare foremost in his mind. He and his daughter had a symbiotic and loving relationship, in spite of the difficulties.

His biggest rift with his daughter was when in her late teens she insisted on going to nightclubs with her friends on weekends even though her father didn't think it was a good idea. He should know, he stopped by all those clubs late at night trying to pick up young girls.

They had big fights over it. Virginia promised to tell him where she was going and that she would return home by midnight. He reluctantly relented.

Six years ago, she had left a message that she was heading towards the Stars after her prom. But she didn't come home by midnight. He stayed up and waited. At one thirty in the morning he got a call from Virginia's classmates that she was drugged and on her way to the hospital.

That incident changed everything. Virginia, his lovely daughter became quite impossible to live with. Instead of taking advantage of a scholarship offered by an Ivy League school, she forwent attending the University of Pennsylvania, and the potential path to a bright future. For the ensuing few years, she did nothing but study law books and talk to lawyers, to find a way out for Mike. Her life at home was filled with temper tantrums alternating with periods of depression when she would lock herself in her room for days on end.

After Virginia's poisoning, Sean went to the Fifth precinct police station in Queens enough times to know that Kelly was the most likely suspect. He thought of talking to some of his friends on the other side of the law, but decided against it because that would be like selling his soul to the devil.

He was able to track down where Kelly lived and had followed Kelly a few times, but Kelly was too slick to be caught doing anything illegal.

On one occasion, he saw Mike talking to one of the detectives and Kelly's name came up.

He knew Mike well enough. He watched Mike grow up. He was also well aware of Mike's reputation as a thug and enforcer. No one dared to mess with him. He would love to see Mike do something to Kelly. He followed Mike. When Mike broke into Kelly's van, he was across the street in his car doing his own surveillance. After Mike left, he, too, checked on the van and immediately knew what that was about. He saw Mike put a device under the van the following day. He returned later to install his own GPS device. He decided it was best to wait and see what Mike was up to.

He was there that night. It was his taxi night and he was following Mike in his taxi when Mike was following Kelly, first to the bar, then to the truckers' depot. He turned off the lights of his taxi before he turned into the road leading to the parking lot. He parked his cab behind a truck as soon as he entered the lot so as not to alarm anyone. He tiptoed towards the inside and spotted first Mike's car and then the van. He slid under the truck next to the van, lay on the ground and waited.

When Kelly hit the ground with a thump, he knew something was up. He counted the number of blows to Kelly's knees. As soon as Mike drove off, he reached down to the underside of the van to retrieve his GPS device. On the ground nearby there was an empty plastic bag. An idea hit him. He thought Kelly should die for what he did to his precious Virginia. He wrapped Kelly's head with the plastic bag and tied it around his neck.

He hurried to catch up with Mike's car which was quite easy to spot. He wanted to follow Mike's car to find out what he was up to next. He also took down its license plate number.

When he saw Mike throw the handle of the broken bat into the garbage dump, he stayed there to make sure no one would tamper with it. He waited until he heard from the radio the news of the homicide a few hours later, before he called the Bronx police chief, and reported a suspicious male throwing away a bloodstained broken baseball bat in Chinatown. He told the chief he was dropping a fare of in his taxi when he saw what happened. He directed the chief to the garbage dump. He also gave him the license plate of the suspect's car.

*

It had been a difficult six years. He was trying his best to hold on to his crummy job, to provide for himself and his unemployable daughter. He started to have bouts of depression himself whenever his daughter was in the dumps. Virginia had recently started to talk about suicide.

On some of his moodier days, he thought of confessing to the murder. Why should so many people in the city praise and worship Mike O'Malley for killing that scumbag when he was the real hero?

When the police chief tried calling that morning to explain to him his legal position, he had just had another big fight with Virginia, and she had packed up and gone out. She said she couldn't stand living with him anymore, and wanted to kill herself and this time she meant it. He thought if she had known he killed Kelly for her, she would know how much he cared for and loved her, and maybe her attitude towards him would change. He was in no condition to work so he called in sick. He also contemplated suicide. He was toying with his handgun when his phone rang repeatedly. From the caller ID, he knew it wasn't Virginia, and he didn't want to be bothered with any other phone call.

The police Chief got tired of calling, and went to the restaurant, flashed his badge, and asked for the manager's home address. He decided to pay him a visit instead.

When the chief was ringing the bell of the apartment in Washington Heights, Sean was staring at his phone and holding his handgun to his right temple. If Virginia called and talked again of suicide, he might just end it all there and then by pulling the trigger and letting her hear the explosion over the phone.

The doorbell continued to ring. Virginia that morning had thrown her house keys at him before she slammed the door, could it be her at the door? He put down his gun and dragged his tired feet to the door. He opened the door and there stood in front of him a blast from the past, the sublime savior of his soul and the imminent captor of his body. He broke down and sobbed uncontrollably.

He spilled his guts to the Police Chief and was in custody a few hours later.

Sean Griffin finally had the redemption of his soul, in exchange for his freedom.

Mike appeared in court three weeks later. The judge considered his time served adequate for his crime, and he was set free immediately. After the verdict was announced, Juanita wept, Jason cheered, and Virginia rushed over to hug Mike. She pressed his car key into his hand.

"Sorry it took so long to return your car."

"Sorry about your dad," Mike said. "You may need this to visit him." He gave his car key back to Virginia.

Mike got his freedom back; and Juanita got her son back. There was justice after all, thanks to JUICI and memory fingerprinting.

Good things come in pairs – another Chinese saying. Not only did Juanita get her son back. Soon, something else good happened to her, and Jason had something to do with it.

39

It happened on a Saturday morning. Jason normally went up to his study early in the morning, but that day he slept in because he had come down with the flu. He had taken some medicines the night before and was quite groggy. He was in bed sweating buckets when Juanita walked in to change the bed sheets and clean the bathroom. Seeing him sweating like that, she suggested he take a hot shower, otherwise he might end up catching pneumonia. He was groggy and feverish to the point of being delirious, and could no way make it to the bathroom. She decided to wipe his body with a hot towel for him.

Ordinarily, Jason would never let anyone, man or woman, touch his naked body. While he was too weak and drowsy that morning to resist being caressed all over by a woman, Mary Lee was realizing Mother Nature's gift of wishes for the second time in her bardo.

In a state of delirium, Jason dreamed of being a small boy again with his mother pampering him. When he was seven years old, he had some kind of childhood viral disease and suffered from high fever. The high temperature had rendered him semi-comatose. Mary took his clothes off and used a hot towel to wipe his body. All the while, he was barely conscious as he heard her soothing voice: "Jason dear, roll to the side, and let mommy do your back. You will feel better tomorrow, I promise. Tonight you drink lots of water and sleep well. I'll make you some chicken congee in the morning."

He was undergoing the same experience again. He was hearing his mother's soothing voice while Juanita took his pajama top off and wiped his torso with a hot towel.

Something strange happened to his body beyond his control – he had an erection that just would not quit.

The human male can have an erection without feeling randy. That's why even little boys can have it, usually while they are half asleep with a full bladder.

While Juanita was working on his chest and abdomen, she couldn't help but notice the bulge in Jason's crotch. She thought: You are a man after all.

As if hypnotized, she slowly took off all her clothes. She had a body she was proud of, and she wished Jason would open his eyes to look at her, but he was half asleep and confused. He didn't even notice anything different in his bed – such as a naked woman.

She pulled down his pajama bottom, and slowly eased herself onto him. She could do more if he was enjoying that. She did not have to do much after all, because it didn't take him long to reach the final stage.

Jason wasn't in the mood for sex; he never was, but the human male could ejaculate if his penis received the right kind of physical stimulation.

It happened so fast Juanita didn't even realize it was all over until Jason tried to roll to one side to continue with his slumber. Juanita woke up from the trance, and was wondering why both Jason and she were naked in bed. She then realized they actually had sex, albeit a real quick quickie. She thought she might as well take advantage of the situation to experience intimacy with Jason a little longer. She hugged Jason from behind, lying next to him in his bed and sharing his pillow, both naked.

"I love you, Jason," she whispered.

"Love you, too," Jason slurred.

*

No one would ever know whether those words Jason uttered were directed at Juanita, or at his mother Mary in his delirium. But they were the sweetest words Juanita had ever heard. She couldn't help tears from rolling down her cheek, wetting the pillow. She hugged Jason tighter.

When it was time for her to leave, she kissed him hard on the lips. By then, Jason was fast asleep, and snoring.

*

For the second time in Jason's life, he had had sex. Like the first time, it was forced upon him.

And for the second time in Juanita's life, she became pregnant. She was not protected because she had no reason to be, with a boyfriend like Jason.

*

When she used the home test kit for pregnancy and found out why she was late, she had strong mixed emotions. Among many issues facing her, she was forty-one years old, a little old to have babies. Would the baby be normal? How would Jason react to the news? Would it freak him out enough for him to run away? Did he even remember they had sex? He did blush and purse his lips whenever she went to his house to bring food or clean up. That was just for a little sex imposed on him. Having a child as a result would be a much bigger deal.

There was only one way to tackle the issue – to broach it head-on. She sat Jason down and told him the news.

Jason was shocked and speechless. He turned pale and almost passed out. Juanita propped him up and told him it was not the end of the world. She promised to bear all the responsibilities in the rearing of the child. It was going to be a beautiful child, and she intended to keep it, no matter what. Jason would like the child too, trust her.

She instinctively grabbed Jason's hand, and he let her. Holding hands was a major step forward for Jason, considering he was not delirious anymore.

After holding Jason's hand for a good half hour, and repeatedly asking whether he was all right, Juanita sort of apologized, before she said softly, "I love you, that's why I did it." Actually Juanita didn't know why she did it, but love is always the best excuse for a girl to get pregnant.

Jason turned and looked at her warmly. Weird he was, heartless he was not.

He felt ambivalent about a woman carrying his child. On the one hand, parenthood was not on his life's agenda; on the other hand, he was not someone to dodge responsibility, even though he was not responsible for the situation. He had never thought about the problem before because that was never supposed to happen. He was determined to avoid sex for the rest of his life and had been successful until then.

When Jason was a teenager, Mary asked him whether he wanted any children when he became an adult. He said he didn't want to get married. She said that one day he might regret not having a descendant, and Jason's response was that there were always alternative ways of having children.

What had happened was an exceptional way of having a child. It was like artificial insemination with a surrogate mother – except that it had been performed naturally and without test tubes.

And the child was biologically his.

Jason wondered how his mother would have reacted to having a grandchild. He thought Mary probably would have been thrilled. And he was right.

It was definitely on Mary's wish-list in her bardo.

Putting things into perspective and being pragmatic had always been in Jason's nature. When he got used to the idea he was going to be a father, he focused on how to deal with it and stopped fretting.

When an ultrasound determined it was going to be a baby girl, he asked that the girl's last name be his and her middle name be Mary. The first name would be for Juanita to pick.

Juanita named her Mira.

Juanita thought of bringing up the subject of marriage, but decided to give Jason time to recover first from the shock of being a father. She knew she would get her way with him, eventually.

40

Jason was forty-eight years of age when Mira was born.

He was making up for all the years lost in his prime because of his legal wrangle with Dr Harold Stein, and was working like a fiend. After working for six years at Columbia, he was promoted to the rank of Associate Professor around the same time his daughter was born. Most academics at that age would have made full professor; Stein had done his career a lot of damage.

GenePharma was able to market a system consisting of a headband, a compact electronic component, and a computer loaded with a program featuring Jason's algorithm and a comprehensive memory fingerprinting menu for all felonies and minor crimes. They first used the product on Mike O'Malley, with success, and had decided to name the system Sherlock Holmes.

GenePharma gave Sherlock Holmes to the judiciary departments of governments all over the world for trial. All found it impeccable in retrieving memories of suspected criminals.

The first country to legitimize its use was China. In most other countries, the test required consent from the individuals, but in China, judges would simply order the test when necessary and the defendants had no choice but to either plead guilty or agree to taking the test.

Genepharma sold thousands of Sherlock Holmes models in China alone. Venerable scientific institutions from all over the world replicated and confirmed Jason's invention, and that was how it was validated beyond reproach.

Since he became famous because of Mr Horace Tate III, many renowned academic institutions had offered him a more prestigious and lucrative position, but he turned down all of them. He was comfortable where he was, and money and fame were not part of his equation for happiness. He had all the resources he needed for his continuing research project on Alzheimer's disease. His work on the prevention of amyloid build-up in the brains, a hallmark of the disease, had led to a major discovery. He was a happy man.

After Marvin Green sold his chain of fried chicken and barbecued ribs restaurants to a giant food conglomerate owned by none other than Horace Tate III, he invested in an internet venture. Apart from being one of the cornerstone investors, he was also a key player who had developed the company into one of the most successful of its kind. The internet start-up www.iluvfood.com was an instant hit, and had been earning millions of dollars in advertising revenue annually. As Marvin repeatedly told anyone who would listen, he had spotted the potential of such a company years ago, because – any brother will tell you, one can do without news, social interaction, books and entertainment, and many other things, but no one can do without food.

He made so much money he didn't know what to do with it. So he bought himself a plaything – the New Jersey Parrots, a new major league professional baseball team in the National League.

He gave Mike a job as an assistant to the general manager as soon as he took over. From that day on, Mike could talk baseball, sleep baseball, eat baseball, and live baseball 24/7. He was the happiest man in the world.

Mike and Virginia were engaged. Virginia re-enrolled in the University of Pennsylvania. She planned to study law, and hoped to get her father out of jail as soon as possible.

JUICI was well funded, thanks to the Marvin Green Enterprise. It had a backlog of more than three hundred cases, but Julian had eight full-time lawyers helping him.

Marvin Green hosted an annual Labor Day barbecue at his sprawling New Jersey estate. Barbecued ribs and chicken wings were the main attraction, garnering kudos from all the guests, including his baseball team members, and his best friends Julian and Jason.

Jason sold the diner after Mira was born, and helped Juanita set up a dance studio in Lower Manhattan. The hours would be more flexible for her so that she could have all the time to take good care of little Mira. She trained with the pros, and taught young aspiring dancers in her studio. She also entered into dance competitions the world over, living out her dreams.

When Andrew died, Judy sold Dragon Inn and moved back to Hong Kong to join Jane in retirement. Jane had sold her bars earlier and for years tried to talk Judy into retiring back in Hong Kong. In her words: "We are too fucking old for this shit." Neither of them had to worry about money for the rest of their lives. They spent their time practicing Cantonese opera singing and volunteering for the Po Leung Kuk.

Jason could return to Hong Kong to visit more regularly, now that he had sorted out his career. They gathered for a picnic in front of Mary's grave, and had meals at Spring Deer Peking Restaurant where they would sit at their regular table and reminisce about the bad old days. Colin and Rachel joined them occasionally.

Colin had graduated from the London School of Economics, and had returned to Hong Kong to become a math teacher at King George Secondary School, his alma mater.

After three divorces, Rachel had found God, and had been ordained as a priest.

As for Mary, she was about to start a new chapter. She wanted to continue to take care of Jason, and in her new role, she could.

Mary had had many regrets in life, and her only consolation in her bardo was that her son had become one of the truly happy individuals in the world. He didn't indulge in any of the mundane worldly pleasures such as good food, good sex, or any of the decadent hobbies and habits that money can buy. His happiness was of the highest order because it came from noble and altruistic fulfillments, such as his academic achievements, contribution to science, and most of all, helping people.

Being all by himself in his old age – a big worry for Mary, was resolved by the birth of Mira.

Mira was a healthy and pretty baby. Juanita told Jason that as soon as the baby could walk, it would be her turn to have walks with daddy Jason on Sundays.

Mary just couldn't wait. She used to walk the trails around the Lion Rock with Jason in the halcyon days of her previous life. Soon they would walk the streets of Manhattan together.

Mary had cashed in on her third and final wish in her bardo. She had reincarnated as Mira.

CHARACTERS IN ALPHABETICAL ORDER

Andrew (Chu)   Orphan, friend of Mary Lee.
Colin (McBride)   Jason's classmate at St George's.
Cunningham (Mrs)   Jason's teacher at St George's, the nice one.
Frank   Owner of 'Frank's Diner'.
Gonzales (Mrs)   Owner of diner in the Bronx where Juanita once worked.
Graham Steele (Dr)   Neurologist whom Jason invited from the U.K. to test Mike.
Horace (Tate III)   Texas billionaire accused of killing his wife.
Jane (Chan)   Mary Lee's best friend.
Jason (Lee, Dr)   The protagonist, Mary's son.
John (MacFadzean)   Mary Lee's lover, father of Jason.
Juanita (Mertz)   Jason's girl friend, the waitress.
Judy (Fung)   Orphan, friend of Mary Lee.
Julian (Cromwell)   Lawyer for Horace Tate III.
Katz (Leroy)   Lawyer, Jason's roommate at Yeshiva.
Kelly (Mckenzie)   The psycho.
Koch (Leona,   Psychologist at Yeshiva College,
Professor)   Jason's mentor.
Kyle (Sanders)   (Wife Elizabeth) he deflowered Mary Lee.
Lange (Dr)   The anesthetist attending to Horace Tate III.
Lau Sifu   The Kungfu master.
Lee Jae Soong   Fellow researcher of Jason at Albert Einstein.
Levy & Associates   Lawyers for Jason.
Lewinski (Gene Dr)   The dean, Albert Einstein College of Medicine.
Lyons (Dr)   ER doctor at Columbia Hospital.
Malcolm   Lawyer who helped Mary Lee.
Marvin (Green)   Co-founder of JUICI, owner of food chain.
Mary (Lee)   The protagonist, mother of Jason.
Michael (O'Malley)   Juanita's first boyfriend, Mike's father.

Mike (O'Malley)	Juanita's son.
Michelle (Meade)	assistant lawyer to Julian Cromwell.
Rachel (O'Reilly)	Classmate of Jason at St. George's, She gave Jason a blow job.
Sean (Griffin)	Manager at 'Frank's Diner'.
Shapiro (Saul, Professor)	Senile mentor at Albert Einstein.
Stein (Harold Professor, Dr)	Jason's boss and nemesis at Albert Einstein.
Stewart (Mrs)	Teacher at St. George's, the nasty one.
Vasco (Victor, Dr)	Pathologist at Columbia Medical College.
Virginia (Griffin)	Sean's daughter, Kelly's victim.
Williams (Henry, Dr)	Researcher at Neuroscience Department at Albert Einstein.

ADVANCE RESPONSES

This exploration of a Eurasian boy's early life in Hong Kong, and his later troubled career as a neuroscientist in America, contains elements of realism and detective mystery along with Buddhist fable and modern fairy tale – an unconventional mixture that makes for a diverting read. And, in spite of moments of sadness and darkness, it is a story ultimately suffused with good karma.

—David Diskin, Winner of the Proverse Prize 2011

***

A thoroughly enjoyable and wide-ranging journey through Jason's eventful life.

Chi's engrossing saga of the trials, tribulations and ultimate fulfillment of this strange, lonely, asexual man and his dead mother appeals on all fronts: from Hong Kong to California, New York, Texas and back. He captures the essence of drama: challenges are faced; and loyalty, kindness, tenacity and determination are demonstrated at every turn.

Human qualities and malice are powerfully confronted with the Bardo backdrop an important subtext and guiding light.

Chi's description of the complexities of Memory Fingerprinting is masterly and clear – not easy qualities to achieve!

An emotional, entertaining and educational tale very well written.

Strongly recommended.

—Dr Paul Murray

***

"Momma's boy" should not on the face of it be pejorative. Its power as a taunt rests on the presumption that a boy attached too closely and too long to his mother's apron strings will have difficulty without her in adult life. So it proves in Three Wishes in Bardo, except that the momma's boy who is the book's protagonist has an extra edge – even after her death, mommy can intervene to help him from the afterlife (the bardo of the title).

The tale unfolds in two very distinct stages. The first describes growing up in Hong Kong after the war with nostalgic references to the colonial life and culture of the period. Many Hong Kong readers will find these reminiscences very appealing. Mommy dies just as the boy is leaving for university in the US, and the rest of the tale is set in New York. Momma's boy lives a solitary life with no close friends, few acquaintances, devoid of sex.

The plot owes a lot to Horatio Alger as the straight arrow struggles ceaselessly for success and finally achieves it when his good deeds attract support from a rich patron. The other men in the tale (even the tycoon, indeed) are all scoundrels driven in most cases primarily by their need for sex. The few women attracted to the hero are attracted in large part by his disinterest in sex. It's not very realistic, but this is a fantasy, after all.

With a little supernatural assistance all that hard work eventually pays off and the hero becomes a renowned neurologist. But the story concludes with a nice surprise ending.

Three Wishes in Bardo is a simple, clever story that will appeal particularly to those who remember post-war English Hong Kong.

—Bill Purves

THE INTERNATIONAL PROVERSE PRIZE

The Proverse Prize, an annual international competition for an unpublished single-author book-length work of fiction, non-fiction, or poetry, the original work of the entrant, submitted in English (translations are welcome) was established in January 2008. It is open to all who are at least eighteen on the date they sign the entry form and without restriction of nationality, residence or citizenship.

The objectives of the prize are: to encourage excellence and / or excellence and usefulness in publishable written work in the English Language, which can, in varying degrees, "delight and instruct". Entries are invited from anywhere in the world.

Entry forms available each year from	No later than 14 April
Closing date for entry forms, fees and entered work	30 June
Judging	July-September
Semi-finalists announced	No later than November

THE INTERNATIONAL PROVERSE POETRY PRIZE (SINGLE POEMS)

Entry forms, entry fees, and entered work received from	7 May
Closing date for entry forms, fees and entered work	30 June
Judging	July-September
Winners announced	No later than November

More information, updated from time to time, is available on the Proverse Hong Kong website: proversepublishing.com

FIND OUT MORE ABOUT PROVERSE AUTHORS BOOKS AND EVENTS

Visit our website:
http://www.proversepublishing.com
Visit our distributor's website: www.chineseupress.com

Follow us on Twitter
Follow news and conversation:
<twitter.com/Proversebooks>
OR
Copy and paste the following to your browser window and follow the instructions:
https://twitter.com/#!/ProverseBooks

"Like" us on www.facebook.com/ProversePress
Request our free E-Newsletter
Send your request to info@proversepublishing.com.

Availability

Most books are available in Hong Kong and world-wide
from our Hong Kong based Distributor,
The Chinese University Press of Hong Kong,
The Chinese University of Hong Kong, Shatin, NT,
Hong Kong SAR, China.
Email: cup-bus@cuhk.edu.hk
Website: www.chineseupress.com

All titles are available from Proverse Hong Kong
http://www.proversepublishing.com
and the Proverse Hong Kong UK-based Distributor.

We have stock-holding retailers in Hong Kong,
Canada (Elizabeth Campbell Books),
Andorra (Llibreria La Puça, La Llibreria).
Orders can be made from bookshops
in the UK and elsewhere.

Ebooks

Most of our titles are available also as Ebooks.

PREVIOUS WINNERS OF THE PROVERSE PRIZE

Rebecca Tomasis, *Mishpacha – Family*
Laura Solomon, *Instant Messages*
Gillian Jones, *A Misted Mirror*
David Diskin, *The Village in the Mountains*
Peter Gregoire, *Article 109*
Sophronia Liu, *A Shimmering Sea*
Birgit Linder, *Shadows in Deferment*
James McCarthy, *The Diplomat of Kashgar*
Philip Chatting, *The Snow Bridge and Other Stories*
Celia Claase, *The Layers Between*
Lawrence Gray, *Adam's Franchise*
Gustav Preller, *Curveball: Life never comes at you straight*
Ivy Ngeow, *Cry of the Flying Rhino*

www.ingramcontent.com/pod-product-compliance
Lightning Source LLC
Chambersburg PA
CBHW051341020726
47501CB00007B/2210